FULL CIRCLE

Dillon Watson

2015

Bella Books, Inc.
P.O. Box 10543
Tallahassee, FL 32302

This is a work of fiction. Names, characters, businesses, places, events and incidents are either the products of the author's imagination or used in a fictitious manner. Any resemblance to actual persons, living or dead, or actual events is purely coincidental. The publisher does not have any control over and does not assume any responsibility for author or third-party websites or their content.

Printed in the United States of America on acid-free paper.

First Bella Books Edition 2015

Editor: Medora MacDougall
Cover Designer: Linda Callaghan

ISBN: 978-1-59493-436-0

Other Books by Dillon Watson

Keile's Chance
Back to Blue

Acknowledgments

I'd like to thank my mother and sister for their continued support and encouragement, D Little for her fashion sense, the readers for asking "what's next?", my editor for making the process painless and my family at Bella for always being entertaining.

CHAPTER ONE

Sara Elaine Gordon slapped her hand over her mouth to muffle a giggle. She and her dad were playing hide and seek, and she just knew he wasn't going to find her today. How could he when she was in the greatest hiding place ever? She'd found it by accident while checking for hidden birthday presents. In one week she was going to be seven, and she just knew even if she couldn't find it, she was going to get something good.

She was hoping for a new bike 'cause she'd gotten too big for hers. Her mom had explained it wouldn't be a brand-new bike with the baby due soon. But that was okay with Sara. A baby brother was better than a new bike. As her dad said, the bike would be new to her. And please, God, don't let it have a sissy basket and pink handle bars like her friend Elaine's, she prayed.

Sara thought she'd talked her mom into getting her a boy's bike. Especially after her dad said the geometry was better with the third bar—whatever that meant. To Sara they were better 'cause they had ones with Batman stuff and she could ride up and down her street in her old Halloween costume and be matching.

She yawned and wondered what was taking her dad so long. He probably got distracted by her mom—again. They were probably in the kitchen kissing and hugging. They did that a lot. She didn't really mind, and it was a whole lot better than Danny's parents, who screamed bad words at each other all the time. Real loud where you could hear it outside the house and had to pretend to Danny that you couldn't. Yeah, she thought, covering another yawn, it was good that her parents liked to kiss and hug instead of yell.

Her stomach rumbled, and she covered it with her hands, afraid the noise would give her away. But maybe she should give up. Her mom would be calling her to come set the table soon anyway. She could keep this hiding space a secret and use it next time. And she could tease her dad about not being able to find her 'cause she had the bestest hiding place ever.

Convinced she'd won the game, she pushed on the knob and slowly eased out the piece of wood covering the opening to her hiding place. The wood barely made a sound as she lowered it to the thick carpet covering the floor of her parents' huge closet. Once she put the wood back, she made her way through her parents' room. She couldn't help giving the bed a look. It was high off the ground and fun to jump up and down on, but she was only allowed to do that if her mother or father was in the room.

Holding on to the rail, she hopped down the stairs two at a time. The downstairs was quiet, without the sound of the news or her father talking back to the TV. She didn't even hear her mom moving around in the kitchen as she fixed dinner. Sara wondered if her parents were playing a trick on her and hiding.

She crept into the kitchen as quietly as she could so they wouldn't know she was coming. Sometimes her dad liked to hide behind the pantry door, then make scary sounds and flash the lights. But she wasn't sure her mom could fit behind there now that her stomach was so big.

The lights stayed off when she entered the kitchen. She

looked real hard, but she couldn't find either of her parents in the pantry or anywhere else in the kitchen. She hurried through the empty dining room, which didn't have any hiding places, to the family room. It was empty as well, as was the office room and the small bathroom.

"I give up," she announced loudly, standing in the foyer by the front door. "You can come out now. Dad?"

Silence. All she could hear was the sound of her own breathing. This wasn't right. Her mom and dad never left her alone in the house. Never. She wondered what she was supposed to do, what would happen if she never found them. When her chest got so tight she could hardly breathe, she felt a scream in her belly. A scream that was trying really hard to fight its way out…

* * *

"Shit!" Sara sat up and took deep breaths to calm her racing heart. Lucky for her, she'd had enough control to pull out of the dream before the screaming began—her own. Swinging her legs over the side of the bed, she cleared the sleep out of her eyes.

"You okay?"

Double shit. She suppressed a groan. She couldn't remember the last time she'd had this dream. Couldn't remember the last time it had seemed so real. Fixing a smile on her face, she turned to look at her bed partner. "Sorry. Gotta go."

"But it's only three thirty." Vonnie Lewis peered at her owlishly.

The expanse of milky white skin brought back memories. *Limber* and *enthusiastic* were two words that came to Sara's mind. No wonder she'd been too tired afterward to do her usual hit and run. "I…I forgot. Need to be ready early. New job. Make a good impression, you know." It wasn't all a lie, but what she mainly wanted was to get home, where she could exhaust herself on the treadmill and rid herself of the last vestiges of the dream.

"Okay. Call me?"

"Sure," she said, knowing she wouldn't. Vonnie was enjoyable, but all Sara had been looking for was a few hours of company. Someone to occupy her thoughts and keep her in the moment. The sex had been a bonus.

In less than ten minutes, she was on the road. The highway stretched out before her, all but empty. Sara enjoyed driving in the early morning hours when Atlanta's notoriously bad traffic was nonexistent. Her Hyundai sedan ate up the miles, taking her from the northern suburbs of Fulton County to south of downtown Atlanta and her tiny basement apartment within walking distance of the Atlanta Zoo.

She got off at Boulevard Avenue, made a right, then drove past a mix of businesses and large older homes. A left onto Berne and up the hill and she was at one of the larger older houses, where she lived. She was lucky to have off-street parking right at her door. A door her landlords, for reasons known only to them, had painted turquoise. If she ever invited anyone over, it would serve as a great landmark.

A loud meow greeted her entrance, and she had to step carefully to avoid tripping over the fat, purring tabby threading through her legs. "No. It's not time to eat," she told Tabitha firmly as she picked her up and rubbed under her chin until purrs filled the room. It didn't matter to Tab if the person she allowed to keep her had only gone out for ten minutes or for hours; she always expected to be fed.

Feeling more awake than she had a right to, Sara changed into workout clothes and headed to the tiny second bedroom, which served as both gym and storage. The treadmill had come with the apartment and now was a good time to put it to use. In deference to her mood, she ran with heavy metal blasting on her MP3 player. Once she got her stride, she worked really hard not to think back to that day her life changed. Really hard.

New job, she told herself. Think of the new job. On paper it was better than her previous one. The hours were better and there'd be no more drama with Jill, the boss she'd made the terrible mistake of having sex with. The boss who in the end wanted more than Sara had to give. But she'd learned a valuable lesson, hadn't she? Getting falling down drunk around the boss was a no-no. Especially if the boss was drop-dead gorgeous, had shapely legs that went on for days and made no secret of her willingness to play.

"Look, yes. Touch, no." That was going to be her motto from now on. Not that she had to worry about that with her new boss. Word was he was an older male and her interest in them had died in the car wreck along with her father. Tears burned the back of her eyes at the thought of her father and she quickened her pace.

She wasn't going to think about that now. She just wasn't. But it was hard not to remember a father who'd picked her up and twirled her around until she was dizzy when he came home from work. If he was really quick, he would do the same to her mother, then laugh when she swatted his arm. He hadn't been able to do that once the pregnancy advanced.

Despite her best efforts, tears streaked down Sara's face. Maybe it was okay to cry for what she'd lost almost twenty-seven years ago, she thought, not bothering to wipe them away. She was alone. There was no need for the tough-girl front she'd perfected over the years. No need to pretend she didn't miss her parents, didn't miss her previous life every damn day. It was always harder to take this time of year with the anniversary of that day looming. That's the way it was for her. The way it would probably always be.

Being back in the city where it happened did seem to make it more difficult to keep the loss off her mind. She hadn't expected that. Hadn't expected the memories to be clearer here, more bittersweet.

At the five-mile mark, Sara decreased the speed until she was walking. Her tears had long since dried, but the ache was still there, close to the surface. Maybe she'd made a mistake returning to the city of her birth. It had been an impulse, a place on the map she hadn't seen as an adult.

But if it got to be too much there was nothing holding her down, she told herself and reached for a towel. No commitments she had to keep. She was free to go where she wanted, to do what she wanted. Finding a job to meet her meager needs hadn't ever been much of a problem, and she had stashed money away with the idea of maybe going to college one day, but there was nothing written down about not using some of it to get out of her lease and leave Atlanta behind.

* * *

"Well? How did it go last night?"

Mikaela Vanessa Small made a big show out of turning her head to look at her treacherous roommate and supposed friend. Casey Atoms was leaning against the door jamb, looking as if she hadn't set up Mikaela on the worst date in human history. To add to the insult, Casey had won their unspoken contest and was already dressed in a steel gray pantsuit, her black hair pulled back in her trademark French plait. She looked ready to kick some lawyer butt. "Last night was your lucky night," Mikaela finally deigned to say.

"That good, huh?"

"No, no, no," she said rapidly, shaking her head. "Your luck was that I was so grateful to be away from that woman I let you live. If you ever have occasion to *think* about setting me up with a friend of a friend of a friend, your life will cease to exist." It was small of her, but she took great pleasure in the death of Casey's grin. "That woman should have come with a hazardous material sticker. Bright orange. No. DayGlo orange that can be seen from outer space, giving innocent bystanders the chance to plan an escape route or, failing that, the chance to end it all."

"She couldn't have—"

She pinned Casey to the wall with a glare. "Gratitude is melting like the Wicked Witch. You too can die."

"I owe you big, don't I?"

Her lips twitched at the look of shamed resignation on Casey's face. "*Big* being the operative word. I'll throw out a couple more: *bitter* and *vindictive*. She spent the entire evening trashing her ex. I didn't have to say a word. She never shut up. *Never*. Not ever." Mikaela blew out a breath and dug through the top bathroom drawers. "Have you seen my red hairclip? Didn't you borrow it last?" Mikaela's hair was thick and fell below her shoulder blades, so she always felt the need to confine it during work hours. Made her feel more professional.

"Tried to. You never found it, remember?"

Frowning, she pulled out the black one. It wasn't as fancy, but it would do. "So then she had the nerve to ask when she could see me again. My jaw hit the ground. I mean, really? The pained expression on my face wasn't a big fucking clue? Seriously, I was having fantasies about strangling her with her own tongue and she has the nerve to want to know when she can see me again. As if. Can you believe it?"

"Uh, 'takes all kinds'?"

Mikaela's pointed finger stopped Casey's retreat. "You don't get to talk. You should be afraid. Your friend of a friend of a friend should be afraid." Satisfied that Casey was frozen in place, she pulled back her hair and fastened the clip. "Lucky for you I'm running behind and don't want to spend any money on parking."

"Should I draw up papers promising to never set you up again, even if the woman in question thinks you're the most beautiful woman in the world? Or should I loan you the money for parking so you can punish me to the fullest extent of the law?"

"Don't try your lawyer sweet talk with me. I refuse to be amused or flattered. And I already owe you twenty. Which I absolutely promise to pay back Friday." She took one last look in the mirror and decided the red blouse that she shouldn't have bought because it blew her budget looked good against her olive complexion. Very good.

"What's with the nice suit?" Casey asked as Mikaela shrugged on a jacket to match her skirt. "Oh, wait. Headquarters guy, right?"

"Yeah, so I'd better run." She rushed into the living room, drew on her heavy winter coat, grabbed her industrial-sized pocketbook, then hoofed it down the long hill to the bus stop. She arrived at the same time as the bus. Breathing heavily, she dug out her monthly transit card and climbed aboard. After greeting the bus driver and the regulars, Mikaela found an empty seat near the back door, removed her coat, slipped in her earbuds and listened to a mix of slow songs on her phone.

As usual, the sounds of her favorite tunes took her away from the overheated bus. They failed to totally clear her thoughts of last night's disaster however. Going out with "that" woman, as Mikaela had decided to think of her, had to be an all-time low on the Mikaela Small dating scale. What made her situation more depressing was that it was in keeping with the last six months. Well, the last year if she was honest and counted from when she'd come up with the crazy notion that Nina Carson was the best she could do.

Mikaela looked at her ringless pinky finger with disgust. Dumped. She'd been dumped like trash and after six months it still stung. Stung more because she hadn't been the one to do the dumping than because of any hint of heartache. Everybody and their blind grandma had known the relationship was spiraling down the drain. She, in her infinite stupidity, had ultimately decided not to decide. After all, she had been busy working full time, taking courses at Georgia State University and foolishly thinking of putting more effort into her relationship with Nina. With all that, it wasn't any wonder she didn't have time to come up with a great "this isn't working" speech. And you couldn't end a relationship without one.

Too bad Nina hadn't known that bit of breakup etiquette. She'd announced they were through without a good spiel and without having the decency to let Mikaela recover from the beating she'd received from the late afternoon August sun as she'd trudged the five blocks from the train station. Hell, Nina hadn't given her a chance to do much of anything. And to Mikaela's continued shame, she'd stood there sweating like a pig, her mouth hanging open as she was given her "cease and desist" order.

Mikaela remembered having one clear thought once the haze brought on by Nina's pronouncement dissipated—it wasn't love, had never been love. All she and Nina had was lust twisted into like, which she'd convinced herself to parade as love. Somewhere along the way they'd lost the like. And on her part the lust too, she admitted with a melancholy sigh. Losing the lust had been the hardest thing to deal with. Even harder than having to clear out of Nina's townhouse with a few days' notice. It was a good thing she prided herself on accumulating only as many possessions as she could stuff into her old, beat-up station wagon. It had been an even better thing that Casey's guest room was available and fully furnished.

She looked out the window, noting absently the expert way the bus driver threaded onto the packed highway heading into downtown Atlanta. She wished she could maneuver her way through life half as well. At thirty-two she had a fairly decent job and, thanks to Casey's generosity, she was working on paying down her credit card debts and student loans. Eventually she'd get back on track to saving for a house.

And probably sooner than later she'd get over last night's trauma and give dating another shot. She liked being in a relationship, liked going through the mating rituals. While she didn't have Casey's beauty, she was by no means on the bottom of the Good Looks Chart. Thanks to the genes she'd inherited from her white mother and secrets in her black father's gene closet, she looked, according to her grandmother anyway, like the epitome of the melting pot. With her long, curly, dark brown hair, gray-blue eyes, flat nose, bottom-heavy lips and skin more golden than brown, she'd been quizzed by more than one person about her ethnic background. Having been raised by her father's mother, she mostly replied "black." But after a few drinks, she had been known to say anything from "Native American" to "Middle Eastern."

The bus passed the Fulton County Courthouse, which meant they were almost at Five Points, the end of the line. Time to put away negative thoughts, she decided as she slipped back into her coat. Maybe she should start by not counting the thing with Nina as technically getting dumped. After all, Nina had called *her* a couple of weeks ago, begging for another chance. Admittedly—Nina had been drunk, but still...Mikaela was ashamed to admit it but for a hot second she had fantasized about taking Nina back, staying long enough to toy with her affections, then calling it quits, making herself the dumper. Luckily that stupid bubble had burst, and despite not having a speech prepared, she had managed to decline Nina's offer, though in terms that were none too gentle.

"I'm an idiot," she muttered. She'd obviously been looking at things the wrong way for months. Surely the dump didn't count if the dumper tried to get back together with the dumpee within a certain time. She shook her head. All those hours wasted brooding over nothing.

Mikaela joined the throng exiting the bus. Most crossed the street to transfer to the train. The rest were like her and worked downtown. Her office building was located three blocks from the stop. The brisk wind, funneled by the tall buildings on Peachtree Street, tore through her puffy winter coat and had her speeding to her destination.

Her office was located in a fifteen-story white brick building. Two of the three retail spaces facing the street on ground level were occupied. One was a high-priced deli that probably wouldn't last, the other a small but packed convenience store. In the past week, the third had shown signs of future occupancy. Mikaela was hoping for something different, with a fresh and natural bent. She hadn't gotten her hopes up though. There had been signs of occupancy before. And even if such a restaurant opened, with the current retail climate downtown, it was likely to have a short life.

She barely had time to stow away her belongings before being surprised by a summons from her boss. Mikaela had worked as Talya Buttons' administrative assistant for three years, and thanks to Talya's openness to staff training, had been able to improve her technical skills in each of those years. While she loved her boss to death, when she entered Talya's office she was thinking longingly of the cup of coffee or two she was usually able to enjoy before her boss arrived.

"Sorry to bug you first thing," Talya said, waving at the two chairs in front of her desk. "It's important and I promise to be quick, given that you haven't had time to grab coffee." Her thin, red-painted lips pulled into a sly smile.

"Are you trying to suggest I'm an addict?"

Talya shrugged her thin shoulders as if that said it all. "I rode the elevator down with Bill Friday evening. It's official this time. Jolene turned in her retirement papers. As much as it pained me, I strongly urged him to consider you for the position, and let me tell you, he was not averse to the idea."

"Wait! What?" Mikaela jerked upright as thoughts of coffee dissipated. "Me? I thought you liked working with me?"

Talya tucked her shoulder-length brown hair behind her ears and leaned forward, her deep blue eyes intense. "As your boss and friend, I think—no, I know—this is a good next step up in your career. You can do all the stuff I throw at you with your hands tied behind your back. Moving to executive assistant would require you to stretch a little. In a good way. And despite being the head honcho, Bill would be a great guy for you to work with. Ask Jolene."

"Stretch a little? That's more like a leap." She blew out a breath and her shoulders slumped. "I don't know about this, Talya."

"I wouldn't have mentioned your name if I didn't think you were capable. I have my reputation to think about as well. It's not like you have to do anything about it right away. Go grab coffee and let it sink in. We'll talk more after you're caffeinated and can see reason."

"Funny. But wait, why should I worry?" Mikaela stood and dismissed the notion of her getting the job with a wave of her hand. "I can think of three admins who'd be ahead of me in that line. They've been here longer and have more experience. There's nothing for me to think about." Mikaela was referring to the Righteous Three, as she liked to call them. They were a group of older admins who thought they ran the company and could dictate the behavior of the other admins. The "righteous" came in because they held Bible study every Wednesday during lunch, where, according to a former disciple, they spent more time trashing staff than discussing the word of God. No doubt they would have plenty to say about her if they knew she was a lesbian. Only the people she worked closely with knew and she wanted to keep it that way. Not because she was ashamed, but because it wasn't anyone else's business.

"Before you get all smug, you should know Bill immediately asked me to pull together a summary of your accomplishments. And somehow I can't help thinking a letter of reference from your boss detailing your willingness to go the extra mile, your ability to work well with others and your thirst for knowledge will weigh heavily with Bill. More so than years with the company alone. But that's just me. Now go." Talya made shooing motions. "I have to pimp your résumé."

Mikaela smiled despite the tightness in her chest. "How many times do I have to tell you to quit watching those reality shows? They give you the false sense of being hip." Her smile vanished as she made her way past her desk, then down the hall to the break room. If Talya had been any kind of boss, she would have had the decency to wait for Mikaela to down her second or third cup of coffee before dropping a bomb of this proportion.

Back at her desk, she sipped her coffee, not with her usual pleasure but absently, as she considered the implications. Was she ready for what the next level entailed? More importantly, was she ready to give up the comfortable working relationship with Talya? They were at a point where she could speak her mind knowing she would be heard and without worry of retribution. Plus she'd miss working with Gerri and Pat, who rounded out the foursome in their small section.

She sighed and stared at the company logo zipping across her monitor. The job of Bill's assistant did come with a hefty increase in salary. It also came with a hefty increase in office politics, local and from headquarters. She'd heard plenty of complaints from Jolene over the past few years. Okay, so maybe not as many since Bill had taken over, but still it was something to put in the con column if she were inclined to make a list of pros and cons. Which she was not, right?

Her phone buzzed, and she quickly thrust the possibility of a new job to the back of her mind. She would focus on the job she had. A job she knew inside and out. A job she knew wouldn't make a fool of her.

* * *

At twelve twenty-five p.m. Mikaela made her way down to the lobby. She'd convinced her friend, Marianna Kirkland, who worked two floors down on five, to join her for lunch. They were going to the newly opened noodle house in what was known as the Fairlie-Poplar district, a narrow two blocks lined with restaurants. She absently waved at the older, half-asleep security guard sitting at the front desk as she crossed the lobby and leaned against the wall near the glass front doors. Marianna was usually late, so Mikaela liked to spend the time people watching. Pedestrian traffic was light, no doubt due to the unrelenting cold wind sweeping down Peachtree Street.

"Hey, why are you all bundled up? We're just going down the block," Marianna pointed out as she joined Mikaela.

"Winter, wind," she replied, shaking her head at the thigh-length white cardigan sweater Marianna had draped around her curvy body. "What is it you white people have against coats? Come on, even if the sun is sort of shining, it's January and cold as hell."

"Racist," Marianna said. She pulled the hood of her sweater over her long wavy hair, then pushed open the door. "You're jealous because you inherited thin black blood. I mean, shouldn't you black people have adapted to America's climate by now? The way you're dressed you'd think we were going on an Arctic expedition."

"When that wind blows up your cootie and gives you a cold, don't even think of asking me to run to the drugstore and pick up medicine. Now come on before the wind gets to me."

The House of Noodles was only a two-block walk from their building. But it was a cold two-block walk. Mikaela smirked but didn't say anything when Marianna shivered once they were inside the warmth of the restaurant.

"God, did everybody decide to come here today?" Mikaela asked, taking in the line that stretched the length of a long wall and almost to the door.

"One word." Marianna pulled a piece of paper from her slacks. "Coupon. I think everyone in downtown but you received one *and* decided to use it today. So, what's up with you?"

"First, Talya tells me she wants me to apply for another job—"

"Is that the new way to say you're fired?"

She almost laughed at the shocked look on Marianna's face. "Not even close. It's another job. A promotion. Problem is, I'm not sure I'm qualified. Seems Jolene's actually retiring and Talya tells me first thing this morning that she thinks I should go for the job. And not only that. She's already told Bill he should hire me for the job. Me! Then later on in the copy room, when my head's still all messed up, Jolene's making conversation. She's leaving, blah, blah, blah. I'm all like sorry, blah, blah, blah, thinking it's nothing until she tells me the job will be posted soon and that *I* should apply for it. How *I* would be perfect for it and Bill." Mikaela shook her head. "Come on, she's got to know the Righteous Three would have strokes and then make everyone's life miserable. I don't get it. Why pick me? Jolene, that is, not Talya. Talya has to say something nice. I do her work."

"Why not you?" Marianna countered. "You work hard and you're always going to some new training thing or another. As for the Righteous Three, how many times have you complained about them being stuck in the last century when it comes to technology and ideology?"

"That's not strictly relevant."

"Please. But say I disallow it for the sake of argument. How many times have you complained about them not wanting to do their jobs?" Marianna held up her hand when Mikaela opened her mouth. "Not finished. How many times have you bitched about them *jokingly* saying you're trying to make them look bad by working so hard? And how many of them will have a college degree in May? Point, set and match." She dusted her hands, then turned her attention to the menu hanging on the wall.

"Winning makes me hungry. Oh yeah, Drunken Noodle Soup. I see what I'm having."

"Let me get this right. I'm having a crisis of major proportions and all you can worry about is what you're going to eat?"

"First, *you* asked me to lunch. Lunch means food," Marianna added slowly as if talking to a half-wit. "And second, I already shattered your little crisis. Now quit worrying about unimportant things and tell me what you think of the new woman in security. Is she smoking or what?"

"Huh? I didn't see anyone new."

"You must have been brain-dead when you walked in this morning not to notice her." Marianna let out a sharp breath. "She's tall, blondish-brown hair, amazing blue eyes, athletic build with shoulders wide enough to lay your head on. I hear she's Dickhead's replacement."

"Dickhead?" She stopped pouting over missing the new guard long enough to really pay attention. "Oh, you mean creepy guy who thought he was all that. Thank God he left. The words *not interested* must have been missing from his vocabulary because he sure didn't understand them."

Marianna laughed and wiggled her eyebrows. "Hopefully those words are missing from Sara's vocabulary as well."

"Hey, you're a married spud. No checking out the ladies."

"Erin doesn't mind if I look. And I was thinking of you. It's not like your last date was all that," Marianna said with a smirk. "You know, the one you texted me about *before* it was even over?"

"That's low. True, but low. And because it's true I'm forced to ask if you know what Sara's ex was like. I can't spend another evening hearing one get so thoroughly trashed. Especially from a woman with the vocabulary of a preteen who's just learned to curse. You can't imagine how painful it was. Not to mention embarrassing. The worst part is that she was oblivious to the fact that she still loves her ex."

"Painful, embarrassing *and* boring. Can't get much worse. Does Casey understand how much trouble she's in?"

"Gave her a little taste this morning. Planning to lay out the full-course meal tonight."

CHAPTER TWO

Tuesday morning, Sara again arrived ten minutes before the start of her shift at the basement-level office of Anderson and Company. Today would be a little different because she was finally going to meet, Jackson Davis, her boss at the building management company, who had been at training the day before. She was ready to get the meeting, the assessing, out of the way.

The office consisted of a large room with lockers on the back wall, along with the time clock and two smaller areas portioned off for the shift supervisors. Jackson Davis was seated at a photo-laden desk in the first cubicle.

"Good morning," she said to get his attention.

"Morning. You must be Sara Gordon." He held out a hand. As the day supervisor, he was responsible for the maintenance workers, the smaller day-time cleaning crew and the five first-shift guards. "Welcome aboard."

"Thanks." Jackson Davis was tall and lean. She judged him to be in his mid-fifties based on the lines on his face and the liberal sprinkling of gray in his hair. She'd heard he'd been working for the company for over thirty years and was a good boss.

"Okay if I look at last shift's report?" she asked. She liked to have time to check over the report from the evening shift before clocking in. It was a habit she'd gotten into on her last job and it had saved her from running into trouble on a couple of occasions.

"Always. Things have been quiet since the holidays. Hope it stays that way."

"Then yesterday was normal?"

"The biggest issue we run into is keeping the bums from wandering in off the street, trying to panhandle or steal. That happens, makes us look bad to our clients. Other than that, we might get a disgruntled former employee looking to cause trouble. Doesn't happen often. Mostly it's about getting to know the people and making sure they feel safe. In addition, we welcome the visitors and help them get to where they need to go. But you probably heard all this yesterday."

Sara hadn't, but she replied, "Reinforcement never hurts." She replaced the report, then neatly arranged her belongings in her locker.

"Couldn't help notice you move around a lot."

"Nothing weighing me down," she replied since he seemed to expect an answer. "I like the change in scenery, seeing new cities."

He nodded. "Today's duty roster's up on the board by the door."

As Sara clocked in, the rest of the first shift began arriving. Her first duty was to check floors two through eight and make sure no homeless person had decided to set up camp for the night. She'd been warned that sometimes the crafty ones managed to sneak in and avoid the evening security check. They usually preferred the top floors because those were cleaned and secured first.

So far, the new job had been a piece of cake. She worked six thirty to three thirty, which meant traffic wasn't an issue coming or going. And that she could get to the gym afterward and have a good workout with the weights or exercise equipment before the nine-to-fivers showed up.

After a clean sweep, she made her way to the lobby. Her next duty was to stand by the back doors, used by employees coming from the parking deck, and ensure the morning rush went smoothly. She smiled and nodded as the majority of the workers began to pour in, keeping an eye out for anyone who looked like they didn't belong.

"Excuse me. Can I get a hand?"

Sara moved quickly to relieve a petite brunette of the large package she was carrying.

"Thanks. Can I leave that with you for a moment while I run upstairs to get a cart?"

"I'd be happy to take this upstairs for you, ma'am."

"Oh, you're a godsend," the woman said with a sigh of relief. "I almost got a hernia carrying it from the car. I'm on the seventh floor. Baker International. Talya Buttons, if anyone needs to know." She led the way to the bank of four elevators.

Sara signaled the guard at the desk. She assumed it was okay to leave her post to offer assistance. The situation had not been specifically spelled out in training or the handbook. But she was being courteous and that came after safety on the company's list of principles to follow.

"It's quicker to go this way," Talya said, making a right after getting off the elevator. Sara stood patiently while Talya unlocked the unmarked door on the north side of the building. They wound through a maze of cubes and ended up at one of the smaller window offices. "I really appreciate the help…" She peered at the badge attached to Sara's jacket. "Sara. I'll be sure to let Jackson know how helpful you were."

"It was no trouble, ma'am. I'd better get back downstairs." She turned and almost bowled over someone who was trying to enter the office. Quick reflexes had her reaching out to halt the woman's backward fall. It took longer than it should have for Sara's brain to realize she had her hands on the waist of the other woman. An attractive, curvy woman with bright, grayish eyes that seemed to see right through her. "Sorry, ma'am." Red with embarrassment, Sara dropped her hands. "Are you okay?"

"I think so," the woman replied slowly and smiled. "On the upside, I'm wide awake now."

Sara managed to tear her gaze away from those arresting eyes. “Glad I could be of assistance.” She all but ran from not one, but two very attractive women. Who knew doing a good deed could be dangerous? Definitely need to stay away from Bright Eyes, she told herself as she stepped into the empty elevator. She shouldn’t even think about her glossy lips. And she really wouldn’t think about how the conservative suit had done little to hide generous curves. Curves she had felt with her own hands. That one should come with a danger warning, flashing yellow lights at least.

As she stepped off the elevator, Sara told herself not to think about the quick appraisal from Bright Eyes that seemed to find her satisfactory. No, she needed to get back to her post and concentrate on keeping the lobby safe and not on the fact that Bright Eyes had felt good in her hands.

* * *

“Marianna Kirkland. How may I direct your call?”

“You were right on,” Mikaela said with no preamble.

“I usually am. What was I right about this time?”

“The new security guard. I got a chance to see her up close and personal. In fact, she couldn’t keep her hands off of me.”

“What?”

“Okay, so I was about to fall down at the time. Didn’t lessen the jolt that zinged through my body like a double shot of caffeine.”

“Have you been drinking already?”

Mikaela laughed. “Feels like it after getting the once-over from those amazingly blue eyes.” She exhaled. “I thought I was going to self-combust.”

“You need to rewind to the beginning.”

“I literally ran into her as she was coming out of Talya’s office. Lucky for me, she caught me before I dented the floor with my ass.”

“And what was she doing in Talya’s office?”

“Gutter brain. She was nice enough to carry up a box. Wish I could have seen her muscles bulging.”

"Kind of hard to see through the jackets they're required to wear."

"Don't go toying with my fantasies."

"Did you get a number? A woman needs to act on her fantasies."

"Get real. Like I'm going to try to pick up a woman with my boss standing right there. Unlike you, I am a professional. But..." She sighed. "That is one gorgeous woman—who's bound to have not only a girlfriend, but a million women throwing themselves at her feet. Definitely 'Look, but don't touch' material, and looking is just fine. Mighty fine."

"How selfish of you. What fun is it for me to live through you vicariously if you can't make the big move? Dang. Another call's coming in. We'll talk more later."

Just as well they got interrupted, Mikaela thought and hung up the phone. She hadn't been thinking right, calling Marianna and opening her big mouth. Now she'd be dodging ridiculous suggestions on how to get Sara to go out with her. Hell, she wouldn't put it past her fool of a friend to try and set them up. Not like she hadn't done it before. Mikaela cringed as she recalled the date with the cute woman who hadn't been up on basic things like industrial-strength deodorant.

"I've been summoned upstairs." Talya stopped in front of Mikaela's desk. "The big shot from the main office finally made it in. I might not get back until lunchtime."

"Gotcha. I'll go ahead and take a final pass at the brochure for the summit meeting while you're gone. And don't forget you're supposed to be working on the handouts that go with the brochure. We have to get those packets out by Friday, meaning everything has to go to the printer by noon Thursday."

"Too late. I forgot." Talya pursed her lips, her expression thoughtful. "Why don't you start working on the handouts based on what I've already given you. Then when I get back, I'll take over. Yeah, that would be a good task for you."

"Good for what?" She eyed Talya with suspicion. Knowing her boss, and she did, this had something to do with Jolene's position.

"Your future marketability, of course." Talya gave her a finger wave as she left.

"Marketability, my ass."

* * *

By the time Mikaela made it home, almost two hours later than usual, she was ready to veg out in front of the TV and give her brain the evening off. Talya had ended up spending most of the day holed up with Bill and the big wig, Mr. Trenton, leaving Mikaela responsible for finishing the job of turning Talya's meager notes into handouts. She'd done enough today that by the end of the day tomorrow the materials should be ready for Talya's approval.

As she trudged up the steep hill to the gated condos, which had formerly been an all-girls school, she felt a good measure of satisfaction. She had to admit it had been stimulating to use something she'd learned in her business classes. But now she was ready to un-stimulate, maybe with a glass of wine. A big glass of wine.

Her cell rang as she was punching in her code on the keypad for entry. "Un-fucking-believable," she said, seeing Nina's name on the screen. Had she brought this call upon herself with yesterday's thoughts? she wondered. If so, she took it all back. The technical dump was now back to an official dump. "Hear that, phone? You can stop ringing now. I, Mikaela Vanessa Small, do solemnly declare I got dumped." Grumbling under her breath, she stuffed the ringing phone back into her coat pocket and trudged across the parking lot to Casey's four-bedroom condo.

After hanging up her coat, she was drawn by the scents of garlic twined with onions and tomatoes into the kitchen. Casey, dressed in old sweats, her hair pulled back into a casual ponytail, stirred a pot of heaven.

"Spaghetti sauce?" Mikaela guessed. She took a deep breath and her stomach rumbled.

"With turkey meatballs."

Mikaela, who'd been considering having canned soup for dinner, almost melted. "I love you."

Casey laughed. "Enough to throw a salad together?"

"So much more. Back in a sec." Motivated by food, she quickly shed her work clothes and rejoined Casey. "You should know I met a goddess today. Five-nine, handsome, gorgeous blue eyes." She sighed as she washed her hands. "Eye candy for days. The yummy kind with caramel in the middle."

"Does the goddess have a name?"

"Sara Gordon, according to her name tag. She's new in security. Oh, and quick reflexes," she added, removing the salad ingredients from the fridge. "Her saving me from falling was the highlight of my day. I swear I could spend all day looking at her and be satisfied. That is as long as I had someone on the side for the occasional booty call." Mikaela wiggled her eyebrows.

"Speaking of someone on the side, Nina called me looking for you."

"She can look all she wants. She will not find." Mikaela took great pleasure in ripping the lettuce to pieces. "She called me about five minutes ago. I was smart enough not to answer. You should start screening your calls."

"Yeah, yeah." Casey grabbed a knife from the block and sliced a baguette, then slathered it with butter. "Why is she calling you anyway?"

"My fault. Yesterday I was thinking about the lame date, then getting dumped. Hey!" Mikaela turned to Casey, her eyes narrowed. "That means it's your fault, not mine. Without the date from hell, I wouldn't have awakened Nina from the dead by thinking of her."

"Uh, turkey meatballs, my famous spaghetti sauce and garlic bread. Come on, Mike, that has to balance the scales some. The yang to your yin." Casey moved her hands like she was practicing martial arts. "And there will be wine."

"Wine?"

"Got it breathing." Casey pointed to the bottle of red, sitting on the counter.

"I guess you get another lucky day."

Casey bowed her head. "The future love of my life thanks you."

"What future love? You're never going to find her pulling all those billable hours of yours. When was the last time you did anything on the weekend but work? Are you expecting her to come waltzing up to the door?"

"Waltzing, no. Maybe on horseback using her long curly locks to cover her nakedness."

Mikaela snorted as she chopped an orange bell pepper. "Pour us some wine, so you can say you have alcohol to blame for your foolishness."

"It could happen."

"Not likely. You could even your odds by going to places Lady Godiva might hang out. I'm thinking she might want to get to know you *before* she comes over naked. But that could just be my way of thinking."

"Okay."

To Mikaela, Casey sounded entirely too agreeable. "Okay, what?"

"You're right. I need to get out more." Casey turned off the beeping oven timer and reached for a pot holder. "I was thinking of checking out this place near work tomorrow. It's called Pool. I hear a lot of lesbians have started showing up on Wednesdays for the drink specials."

Mikaela studied her friend carefully and not only because Casey was removing mouth-watering meatballs from the oven. Something was going on here. Was Casey trying to set her up without seeming to set her up? Surely not after Sunday night's fiasco. Still…"Look, if this is some way to introduce me to another friend of a—"

"No." Casey shook her head vehemently. "Believe me, I want to live. I want to find Lady Godiva. I heard it was a cool place and thought I would check it out. Seems like it would be more fun with a friend along."

It did sound like fun. Mikaela weighed the pros and cons as she sliced a cucumber. A little conversation, maybe some flirting, would go a long way to erase the taste of defeat lingering at the back of her throat. "No funny stuff, right?"

"Come on, cool place, lesbians, remember? Bound to be some funny stuff, but not from me. But the drinks will be. On me, that is."

"I'm there." She scraped thinly sliced cucumbers into the salad bowl and moved to halving cherry tomatoes. "What time? I shouldn't have to work late tomorrow."

"I could pick you up after work, go from there." Casey slid the pan with the bread into the oven and set the timer.

"That doesn't make sense if it's near your office. I'll catch the train and meet you there. Five forty-five?" That would give her more than enough time to redo her makeup and take the train to Midtown. She could wear the red dress to work. It pushed against the borders of professionalism but didn't cross them. She would have to take an extra pair of shoes—the black ones with the red stripes, which were more suited for showing off her legs than being practical for work. And she should probably take that little bottle of perfume.

It took Mikaela a minute to realize Casey was trying to get her attention. "What?"

"Wine. Where did you go?"

"Planning my outfit." She accepted the glass of wine, then took a sip, enjoying the smooth, the tang. "Definitely your lucky day."

CHAPTER THREE

Sara sat quietly in the dark, dirty corner. She had her legs clamped together, but it didn't really help. She had to pee bad. Real bad, but she was too scared to leave the hiding place though she didn't exactly know why.

Grabbing her crotch, she wondered if maybe she could sneak out real quiet like and use her parents' bathroom, then come back. That would be better than peeing on herself like a baby. She took off her shoes, crawled over to the opening, leaned her ear against the wall and listened for any sound before she eased out the cover to her hideaway.

Her heartbeat was loud in her head as she waited for something bad to happen. When it didn't, she dared to ease through the opening. On all fours, she crawled through the closet and into her parents' room. Once again she paused, listened carefully. Once again nothing happened. She pushed herself to her feet and tiptoed to the bathroom.

Holding herself, she bit her lip as she stood in the doorway, unsure if she should close the door or not. If she closed the door, someone might notice, but if she left it open someone might hear her peeing. Gently closing the door most of the way, she rushed to the toilet and peed. Although it would get her in trouble with her mom, she didn't flush or wash her hands after she finished.

Her stomach rumbled loudly before she made it back to the closet, reminding her she hadn't had dinner. The alarm clock by the bed showed seven. Her mom should have called her by now, or her dad should have come looking for her. He never let the game go this long. She crept to the door of her parents' bedroom and listened carefully. The downstairs TV wasn't even on and her dad always watched the news and fussed at what the people said. Something was wrong. Something was very wrong.

With a longing look at the closet, Sara went down the first four stairs, then stooped down. The area by the front door was clear. Beating back fear, she slowly made her way down the rest of the stairs, making sure to miss stepping on the creaky parts. The floor felt cold under her bare feet and she shivered. "Mom, Dad," she called softly. And again silence was her only reply.

* * *

"No!" Sara had to force the word past the scream stuck in her throat. Panting, she put a trembling hand over her heart and felt its rapid beating. She'd been sure a heavy workout before she went to bed would keep her knocked out and dreamless until morning. She'd been wrong.

If anything, the dream had been stronger. And different, she reminded herself, taking deep breaths. In the numerous years since her parents' deaths, she'd had the dream numerous times, but this was the first time she dreamt about having to pee. Always before she'd left the hiding spot to give up and never with any sense of danger lurking. Usually the only time she'd felt scared was after discovering she was alone in the house.

"It's the city," she told herself and hugged her arms. Being back in Atlanta, where the accident had occurred, had to be the reason for the change, the high-definition quality of the dream. Maybe it was time she tracked down the accident report, visited the location where the drunk driver had plowed into their car. Maybe if she met the demon head on, she could put it to rest. Then she might be able to sleep through the night the week leading up to the anniversary of the accident. Then the dream might go away for good.

But not tonight. Sara threw back the covers, swung her legs over the side of the bed and rested her head in her hands. The cat blinked at her from the foot of the bed as if chastising Sara for disturbing her sleep.

"Sorry, Tab. It's been that kind of week." She crossed to the dresser and picked up the lone photo. It was a picture of what her family used to be, taken not long before that terrible day. Her mom looked so beautiful with her strawberry blond hair, hazel eyes and big grin. Her dad looked so handsome and tall with his dark brown hair falling into the blue eyes he'd gifted to her and the dimple in his right cheek. God, she didn't remember being that happy, but there she was grinning from ear to ear with an arm around each parent. Her hair was pulled back into a messy ponytail and her two front teeth only halfway in.

Sara smiled. She'd been six and two months when the first tooth fell out. She remembered because of the two shiny quarters under her pillow that had replaced the tooth. God, she wished she could go back to those days when the Tooth Fairy was real. When she'd believe dreams could come true.

"I miss you. I miss us." She replaced the photo and glanced at the bedside alarm. Too early to get up, but she didn't want to risk going back to sleep. Sometimes a change of scenery helped quiet the thoughts.

She moved to the tiny living room and settled on the futon. Channel surfing, she stumbled across the classic cartoon station and was instantly transported back to the times she and her dad had gotten up early on Saturday mornings. They'd down huge bowls of cereal while sitting on the floor, watching cartoons. He had been playful that way. Her mother used to complain he was a kid trapped in a man's body, but she always said it with a smile and never protested when she received a loud, smacking kiss in response.

Sara drifted off without being aware and dreamed of happier times. Times when her mom and dad were part of her life. When the alarm went off in the bedroom, she wanted to cry, not ready to let the good times go. With a sigh, she pushed off the futon and got ready for another long day.

* * *

Mikaela darted into the lobby of her office building at eight twenty Wednesday morning and immediately removed her coat. She quickly discovered the effort was wasted. Sara was nowhere to be seen and thus couldn't be amazed by how good she looked in the red dress.

"Mikaela, wait up."

Forcing a smile, she turned and waited for Christine Newsome to join her. Christine was the ringleader of the Righteous Three and in terms of admins had the most seniority. Mikaela didn't know how old she was but assumed it was somewhere in the range of the Stone Age. Christine had been with the firm for well over twenty years and made sure everyone knew it. To Mikaela's knowledge she had not done much of anything work-related in the past few years. That wasn't really her fault though, her boss hadn't done much either according to rumors. She was, as usual, impeccably dressed.

"Morning."

"Good morning to you." Christine loosened her scarf and added it to the coat arranged over her arm. "I think it was a little bit warmer this morning."

Mikaela nodded politely and resisted demanding that Christine get to the point as they made their way to the elevators. They might nod at each other in the hall, but they weren't "stop and chat" buddies.

"Have you heard Jolene's actually retiring this time?" Christine asked. "My sources say her job will be posted any day," she continued without giving Mikaela a chance to reply. "Of course, given my experience with the firm, I have a good chance at getting it. But don't let that keep you from applying. I imagine they want to give some appearance of fairness."

Keep telling yourself that, Mikaela thought, wanting to wipe that condescending smile off Christine's face. "Jolene did mention she's ready to spend more time with the grandkids. And she wants to help out now that her youngest daughter has one on the way. I think that's admirable." For once she was grateful for a full elevator. She did not want to have this discussion with Christine, and she blamed Talya for putting her in such an uncomfortable situation.

"Are you thinking of applying?" Christine pressed, seemingly unconcerned about the lack of privacy.

"I enjoy working with Talya."

"Then maybe you should stay there. But I would think a young girl like you would want to move up. Didn't I hear you're going to school?"

She kept her gaze fixed on the numbers above the doors and prayed seven would soon light up. "Finishing my B.A. in business." She'd started working on it fifteen years ago and got sidetracked. One of her grandmother's last wishes had been for her granddaughter to finish her degree. So Mikaela had gotten back on the degree track, at first because she hadn't wanted to disappoint the woman who'd raised her, then for herself. She enjoyed taking classes and hadn't ruled out the possibility of returning for a master's degree at a later date. They reached the seventh floor before she could be grilled further. "See you." She jumped off, giving thanks that Christine had one more floor to go.

She barely had a chance to grab coffee to go with her bagel before Ilene Jacobs dropped by her desk. In terms of power, she ranked number two in the Righteous Three cult. Among other things, Ilene prided herself on being able to wear clothes meant for a younger woman. Today it was a tight sweater, which barely hit the top of her mid-thigh-length skirt. Her figure was nice and trim, but the stamp of age on her face made a mockery of her wardrobe choices. Mikaela often wondered how she had time to do her job as much as she flittered around, flirting with every male in sight.

"Christine says you're not going to apply for Jolene's job. Do you think that's wise?"

Mikaela didn't bother hiding the sigh. Ilene spread gossip as effectively as bees spread pollen. "That's not what I said." She took a sip of coffee and wondered if Ilene would be satisfied with that. "Why the interest? The job hasn't even been posted. They might decide to bring in someone from another office like they did with Bill." It was mean, but she got a kick out of the look of shock on Ilene's face.

"Is that what you heard?"

"No," she said, waving her hand airily. "I was speculating. I don't know anything about the job, okay?"

"Oh. I thought Talya might have the inside scoop. She and Bill have been awfully chummy lately."

"If she has, as you say, the *inside scoop*, she hasn't shared it with me."

Ilene seemed to take that as an invitation to talk and plopped her flat butt on the desk. "Who do you think will get the job if they don't bring anyone from the outside? Christine seems to think she has it sewn up." She looked around and then lowered her voice. "Did you know they skipped over her when Jolene got the job ten years ago? Why would they hire her this time? I ask you. Everyone knows she doesn't do anything. I think I have a good shot." She fluffed her store-bought blond hair. "Bill likes me."

"Isn't that special. Was there anything else you needed to talk to me about? Anything, say, work-related?"

Ilene looked insulted. "I heard you talked to Jolene the other day. I thought she might have mentioned something. Some of us do care about advancing around here."

"I talk to Jolene most days. We work for the same company and, news flash, some of us actually talk about work matters."

"If you're going to be that way, I'm leaving."

Torn between amusement and exasperation, Mikaela watched her stalk off, no doubt on her way to report part of their conversation to Christine and Debbie Larson, who was the third member of the triad. They would probably spend a good hour trashing her name, then spread out to grill the other admins.

She took a bite of her bagel and wondered if poor Bill had any idea that a wasps' nest was about to fall on his head. He wouldn't hear it from her, but surely Jolene would warn him a perfect storm was brewing. If he was half the manager she thought he was, he would bring someone in from the outside.

Maybe she should suggest that. It might save the Righteous Three from feeding on each other in a bid for the job. Not that it wouldn't be entertaining to see how far they would go to elbow one another out of the way. It could turn out to be as fun as the melee that had broken out at one of her cousins' wedding. Mikaela had been the one to upload the video to YouTube of the single women battling to near death over the bouquet. The title "Weave Fight Fest" had seemed most appropriate as all the bridesmaids had gotten long, flowing weave for the occasion.

"Good times." She polished off her bagel and began working on the handouts from where she'd stopped the day before.

By the time Talya arrived at close to noon, Mikaela had a good handle on the handouts and thought she'd be ready for comments in another couple of hours. "You still work here?"

"If by here you mean my office, I'd have to say maybe. Between meetings. Anything happen?"

"Let's see. I was accosted by Christine *and* Ilene. Seems both of them think they'll get Jolene's job."

"Hope still springs eternal, I see. What about Debbie? What does she have to say for herself?"

"Hasn't reported in yet. I did stoke the fire by suggesting Bill might hire someone from the outside. Being an outsider himself, you know."

"Evil, but genius." Talya gave her a thumbs up. "I need someone to help me understand why they would want the job. It's a lot of work, especially since Bill's taken over."

"So you *do* realize that?"

"No more than you do now," Talya said quickly. "I meant it's a lot of work for people who aren't used to being productive. You would never fit in that category."

"Good save. I think the idea of having Jolene's job and not so much the reality of doing it is driving their want."

"Sounds right. Might be interesting to see how long either one of them would last."

Mikaela snorted. "I thought you liked Bill."

"I do. I said interesting, not funny."

"Well, then, that makes all the difference. By the way, I should be able to send you the materials for markup by the time you get back from your last meeting. Need them back early tomorrow at the latest if they need to be run by Bill."

"I'll take care of it, boss." Talya dug a pad out of her briefcase. "Can you type up my notes from this morning's meeting? I need them for the briefing with Bill. Also, I finally reviewed the annual report and have a few comments. Finished version needs to get to Jolene before you leave today. Oh, and any chance I can bribe you to grab lunch for us? Your choice. I'd like to sit down with you and discuss a few things while we eat."

"No problem." Her leftovers would be okay in the fridge for one more day, and she'd have to push lunch with Marianna to tomorrow. That actually worked out better. She might get lucky tonight and have something worth sharing.

* * *

Because someone on her shift had called in late, Sara had spent a good deal of the morning stuck at the front desk. After her restless night she would have preferred to be on her feet, moving around. As it was, she was struggling to stay alert. Her lunch break couldn't come too soon. She could grab one of the chairs near the back door and pretend to read with her eyes closed. Ten, fifteen minutes of shut-eye and she'd be as good as new.

"What floor is Baker International on?"

The question caught her in mid yawn. Baker International. Home to the brunette with the big box and bright eyes. "Seventh floor…ma'am," she added, despite the realization the powerfully built butch standing in front of her was anything but a ma'am. Sara thought the grin on the other woman's face said that she too realized the dilemma.

"Thanks."

Sara mentally shook herself awake as she watched the woman enter the elevator. With her gaze fixed in that direction, she had no problem seeing Bright Eyes exit a neighboring elevator moments later. The smile from the other woman had Sara feeling like a deer caught in headlights. Her only option was to freeze and wait for impact.

"Hi. Sara, right? Mikaela. We sort of met the other day."

"Uh, yeah. I remember." More like she couldn't forget.

The smile got brighter. "Thanks again for the save. See you around." She gave a little finger wave.

It took a minute for Sara's pulse to return to normal. How could she have forgotten how lethal that smile was? At least she hadn't forgotten the "no touching, no looking too closely and definitely no thinking about having her hands on Mikaela's womanly curves" rule. Not entirely anyway. Her eyes had not gotten the memo, it seemed, remaining firmly fixed on Mikaela as she glided across the floor, her hips swinging from side to side. Sara supposed she was lucky Mikaela was wearing a coat.

She sighed. There was some serious fatal attraction going on. Well, probably not fatal in the true sense. Maybe dangerous was a better word. Whatever the word, she no longer needed a power nap to jump-start her system.

"Mikaela," she said, testing out the name. A little bit exotic like its owner, she decided, wondering how it was spelled. She did not get the chance to embarrass herself by writing the name on her pad because the phone rang. It took her ten minutes to give directions to some geographically challenged soul who'd gotten off at the wrong side of the transit station and then headed north instead of south. By the time she finished the call, her relief was waiting.

"Sounds like you went above and beyond."

She shrugged. At five-eight and two-hundred-plus pounds, Roger Caruthers considered most things above and beyond the call of duty. He was less than a year away from retirement and counting every second. "Is Alexander going to make it in?"

"At one. But she's still kind of iffy, so you could be outside the rest of shift." He made it sound like punishment.

"Good. You can keep desk duty."

After collecting her coat from downstairs, Sara headed out for some food. Standing in front of the building, she fastened her coat against the dreary chill. The wind had died down, so as long as she kept moving this afternoon, being outside would work.

"And how is that your business?"

Recognizing the voice, Sara looked to the right. Mikaela was talking to the butch who'd asked for the floor number earlier. Neither one looked happy, making Sara wonder what she should do. True, it wasn't her concern if they chose to argue in public, and yet she couldn't just walk away. Her stomach clenched when the butch grabbed Mikaela's arm and squeezed. The decision had been made for her.

"Excuse me," she said pleasantly. "Is there a problem?"

Mikaela pulled her arm free. "Not now."

"Mind your own," the butch said at the same time, without taking her gaze off Mikaela. "Personal business."

"Kind of hard to do when I'm supposed to be security."

"Give it up, Nina. We have nothing to talk about." Mikaela slid around Sara and entered the building.

Sara tensed as Nina's anger was directed her way. Nina was three inches shorter at five-six, but her body looked solid with muscle, not fat. "Just doing my job. I'm not looking for trouble."

"Then stay out of my business and remember it's still a free country. I can talk to whoever I want."

"As long as the other person wants you to talk to them, I got no problem. But from my perspective it didn't read that way."

"Didn't ask you to read. Next time stay back."

She waited for Nina to walk away, then headed in the opposite direction. She was probably on shaky ground policing outside the building, but what could she do? Mikaela had obviously needed assistance extricating herself from a possibly dangerous situation, and the handbook clearly stated it was her duty to help. A few feet didn't matter. That was her story and she was sticking to it. The fact that she was attracted to the person needing assistance had nothing to do with her response.

But as she made her way to the Korean place a block over, Sara couldn't help feeling a tiny bit of satisfaction at discovering that Mikaela batted for her team. Not that it should matter considering her new rule, but it did. After checking for oncoming traffic, she crossed the street, all but chanting, "Nothing is going to happen with that."

CHAPTER FOUR

Mikaela drilled her finger into the elevator button with the same force she would have liked to use to drill into Nina's chest. The nerve to get all up in *her* face about being out with another woman when Nina had been the one to find someone else. She drilled the button again, mad at herself for not realizing sooner that Nina had a crazy side. Crazy was the only explanation for why Nina would come to her job spouting bull about having made a mistake while at the same time questioning her for being out with another woman.

She blew out a hot breath, but it did nothing for the anger burning bright. Who the hell did Nina think she was, claiming she made a mistake? She drilled the elevator button again. That was bull of the highest order, beaten only by Nina's claim that she was human. "'And humans make mistakes,'" Mikaela parroted. "Right."

"That doesn't sound very forgiving," Marianna said, coming to stand next to Mikaela.

"Wasn't meant to be." She looked around to make sure no one from her office was within hearing distance. "Nina took a trip on the crazy train and decided to come see me here since I wasn't returning her calls. Wanted to take me to lunch, see if we could talk things out. Can you believe that?" She followed Marianna onto the elevator.

"I'm guessing the answer was a big 'hell no.'" Marianna pushed the buttons for their respective floors.

"I started with the polite 'You know, we've already said everything six months ago.' How devastated I was when she threw me over. But how I had to be strong and get on with my life." She sniffed, then laughed. "I laid it on thick and damn if she didn't buy every word. So now that stupid bitch's convinced we need to get back together to let her make up for what she did. I lost polite at that point. You can't be polite to crazy. Told her there was no need to drag out yesterday's garbage. I'll tell you the rest later," Mikaela said when they reached Marianna's floor.

"We'll trash her good over lunch tomorrow."

"I need to eat the leftovers I brought today. Meet you in your break room at twelve thirty." She waited until the doors were closing to say, "Maybe I'll have something interesting about my outing tonight to tell you."

Mikaela was pleased to note the two Diet Cokes on Talya's desk when she entered the room. "Got you the chicken salad sub with extra avocados, everything else but onions and an extra pickle." She placed the sandwich on the desk, then added a bag of plain potato chips.

Talya turned away from her computer and rubbed her hands. "Brochure looks great. I'll plan on looking over the other materials tonight." She unwrapped her sub. "Not that I think there will be any changes, judging by the job you did on the brochure. I can't tell you how much I appreciate you taking this over."

"Not like you haven't been busy with extra stuff yourself."

"You don't know the half of it. Close the door," Talya said and waited till Mikaela returned to continue. "You'll hear soon enough, but Brannon is retiring. Officially, at the end of the month." She bit into her sub.

"His choice?"

Talya shook her head and swallowed. "It's better than getting fired, which was a close thing. This is what happens when you don't have a good system of checks and balances. His staff was producing most of the necessary what some might call 'reports,' but he never bothered to check them, and let me tell you, they're a mess. Even I was shocked at how bad things are. All that to say I'm temporarily taking on a lot of that mess, so don't be surprised when I shift other things your way."

"What about Christine's job?"

"She still has one. But she should be too busy in the near future to quiz you about Jolene's job or anything else. I'm happy to say her days of running the 411 hotline will be curtailed."

Mikaela popped the top on her drink and took a deep sip. "Couldn't happen to a better person."

"The other managers and I will be discussing the best way to get that department turned around this afternoon. Whatever happens, it'll mean extra duties for Pat and Gerri as well."

"We can handle it. Any chance you'll move up the ladder and take over Brannon's position?"

"At this point, I don't know if there will be a position to move up to. I do know changes are in the works. All I can do, is do what's asked of me, knowing my efforts are finally being appreciated."

"Good, on the changes." Mikaela had long thought the company structure lacked efficiency.

"Between you and me, that's one of the reasons Bill was brought in. He's spent the last six months learning the ins and outs."

"And now it's time to act." She polished off her sandwich. "I sort of have plans tonight. Should I reschedule?"

"You mean you didn't wear that red dress for me?"

"Funny. Casey talked me into going out for happy hour. There's this place near her office called Pool. Supposed to be a hot spot for lesbians on Wednesday nights."

"Go, enjoy. Not too much. There'll be plenty of work waiting for you in the morning."

Mikaela ripped open her bag of chips. "I don't expect to have that good a time. Maybe a couple of drinks, a little flirting, some pool. Not necessarily in that order."

"I think I remember those days. Long ago, before I laid eyes on Harry and knew he was the one."

"Do you miss those days?"

"God, no. Harry and Jason are enough for me." Talya picked up a photo of her husband and ten-year-old son. He looked like her with his father's warm brown eyes. "You can have your happy hour. I'll take my boys."

"There's a lot to be said for that." Mikaela didn't see kids in her future, but having someone to still be in love with twelve years down the road sounded good.

* * *

"Thanks for this." Mikaela closed the back door of Casey's SUV. She'd decided it was smarter to store her extra belongings in Casey's car rather than lug them around for the evening. The garage where Casey parked her car was an easy block from Pool.

"Makes sense," Casey said as they entered the elevator. Mikaela had refused to walk down three flights of stairs in her heels. "Now you only have to worry about that miniscule thing you call a purse."

"And don't I know it." She fluffed her hair and exited the elevator. "I hope this place is worth my efforts."

"We'll know soon enough."

Judging by the steady throng of women entering the place, Mikaela thought Pool was going to live up to its reputation.

"This is a good sign," Casey said of the noise spilling out into the street from the opened door.

"Of good taste in music." Mikaela swung her hips from side to side in tune with the heavy beat. Once inside, she removed her coat and blinked, adjusting her eyes to the darkness. They bypassed the empty hostess stand and wove their way past the mostly empty tables at the front of a large room to a long, busy bar at the back. The crowd mingling near the bar was mostly female, ranging in age from twenties to sixties, by Mikaela's guess.

"Was I right?" Casey asked softly.

"Oh, yeah," she replied, letting her gaze linger on a particularly attractive butch, her back against the bar, muscular arms crossed. Mikaela smiled and flipped her hair over her shoulder before looking away. "Midori sour," she said in response to Casey's gesture toward the bar. She was in the mood for something light and sweet to match her mood.

"Couldn't stay away from me, huh?"

Mikaela didn't curse, but she wanted to. She turned and for the second time today found herself faced with her ex. It was petty, but she was pleased her heels gave her an advantage of a couple of inches. If she hadn't been caught in a haze of irritation she might have admitted that Nina looked good. She had smooth brown skin and big brown eyes that used to make Mikaela feel like she was everything. Then there were the cut muscles, shown off by a tight white T-shirt. The whole package used to work on her, but no more.

"My luck is gold for running into you like this." Nina smiled. "You look good."

The cocky attitude was such a turnoff now that she wondered why she'd thought it cute. "I'm here, you're here, but we are not here together. So go find somebody else to bug," she said with a wave of dismissal.

"You can't even talk to me now?"

"Did you not hear me earlier today?" She held up a hand to stop Nina's response. "Let me clarify it for you then. We have nothing to talk about. Not now, not ever! Bye-bye." Once again, Nina grabbed her arm as she tried to walk away. The situation with Nina was getting old and stupid.

"I can admit I was wrong. Hear me out, I'm only human."

Mikaela rolled her eyes at the "human" part. It was a phrase Nina threw out when she didn't want to accept responsibility for her actions. She could have debated with Nina about the being human part and won that match. In the month after their breakup, she'd done so ad nauseam. But the outcome had always been a resounding "not human." Bitches from hell would never be classified as human in her world.

Being no dummy, she kept those thoughts to herself, saying, "Listen, I haven't wanted to say this, but you weren't wrong. We were done. We're still done, so take your hand off my arm and we'll call it even."

"Why are you here exactly?" Casey handed Mikaela her drink and gave Nina a decidedly cool look.

"Fuck off!"

"That was fun." Mikaela downed half of her drink after watching Nina stalk off—toward the exit, thank God. From now on she was going to do a better job of picking women. Maybe dig a little deeper past the yummy butchly exterior to the soul.

"I hear the pool room is the place to be tonight," Casey said.

"Then why are we here?"

They had to go through a dark narrow hallway and down a flight of stairs to get there. Mikaela quickly discovered that "pool room" was a misnomer. In addition to eight pool tables, there were three booths big enough for large groups, an assortment of plate-sized tables and another bar. The music didn't attempt to drown out the conversations and laughter coming from the room's many occupants.

"I vote we hang at the bar after I put money down for a game."

"Where? Do you see the number of people down here? And I thought the other bar was crowded."

Casey scanned the bar area and her eyes widened.

Mikaela scanned the women mingling around the bar, but she didn't see who might have drawn Casey's obvious interest. "What?"

"What 'what'?"

"Don't play me." She gave Casey a light elbow jab. "Who were you looking at?"

Casey pulled some bills from the pocket of her tight-fitting jeans. "Nobody."

"Fine, don't—" Mikaela sucked in a breath and all thoughts of looking past yummy exteriors to the soul flew from her head.

"What?" Casey demanded.

"Oh God, she's here." The words sounded like a sigh.

"Nina?" Casey asked, frowning.

"No! Sara. Sara Gordon." At Casey's blank look she added, "The goddess of a security guard from work that I told you about. Second stool from the left. Short blondish hair, black leather jacket, broad shoulders. You probably can't see her now." She exhaled. "I wonder if she's here with anyone. Of course she is. Look at her."

"Can't."

"You'll have to take my word. She's gorgeous and gorgeous women are never alone."

"Could be. Can't hurt to say 'hey' and get us another round while you're over there." Casey thrust some money at Mikaela, her attention on one of the pool tables. "I think they're wrapping up," she said, moving toward the table. "Munchies wouldn't hurt."

"Take my coat and grab a table."

"Will do." Casey retraced her steps, grabbed the coat, then strode off, clearly on a mission.

Mikaela's steps faltered as she got close enough to the bar to see Sara shake off a stunning blonde who was thin in a way she would never be. That could only mean she was here with somebody, she thought. But she wouldn't let that bother her. She was only after a friendly hello, and she'd be rude if she didn't give Sara the chance to check her out in the red dress. It was her civic duty, and her grandmother would come back to haunt her if she shirked her civic duty.

She pushed through until she was standing next to Sara's stool and decided to go for casual but not surprised. "Hey. Thought that was you." Okay, so maybe she preened a little when Sara's eyes widened in obvious admiration. Okay, so maybe it was a lot.

"Hi. Haven't seen you here before."

"First time. Nice place." Lame, lame, lame. Her vocabulary would pick this time to desert her. "You come here regularly?"

Sara picked at the paper label on her beer. "I wouldn't say a lot. I do like the Wednesday prices and the chance to play pool."

"Oh? My friend Casey and I are trying to get a game in. You could join us later. That is, if you want to." A nervous laugh escaped. "No pressure."

"You a pool shark?"

For a second Mikaela let herself believe she was being flirted with. That Sara's warm smile was more than friendliness. "Me? I haven't played regularly in a long time."

"Meaning you *had* skills," Sara pointed out quickly.

"Okay, got me there. Friend had a table when I was growing up. We spent our high school afternoons playing while waiting for Prince Charming to show up. Wasn't till college that we realized we should have been out looking for Princess Charming." She shrugged. "Live and learn, right? Think about my offer." Thinking she'd said more than enough, Mikaela edged closer to the bar and caught the attention of one of the bartenders.

* * *

Sara forced herself not to watch Mikaela walk away. Instead, she argued the wisdom of even considering the offer thrown her way—an offer that to her way of thinking had little to do with the game of pool. The look in Mikaela's eyes had been all about interest. She'd be a fool to act on that interest, no matter how much of a pleasant distraction it might prove to be. Would be, she corrected. The sparks flying between them would see to that.

She took a sip of beer and tried not to think of how good Mikaela looked in the red dress, her hair loose and hanging about her shoulders, just begging to be touched. Sara looked around. There were other women equally bed worthy and without the surety she'd have to see them five days a week. That she'd have to be polite to even if they cursed her name or, worse, begged for more than she had to give. It might sound conceited to some, but it had happened too many times for her not to consider it.

"Buy you a drink?"

Sara took in the woman's thickly-lashed bold brown eyes, the sculpted cheek bones, patrician nose and the red lips and didn't feel even half the pull she'd felt earlier with Mikaela. Beddable, yes, and at the same time, somehow not. She shook her head. "I'm good."

The woman flicked back her streaky brown tresses and shrugged good-naturedly. "Oh well. Gotta try."

Realizing she'd been fooling herself, Sara left the bar. It was easy to spot Mikaela, seated at one of the tall tables, taking in the action at a nearby pool table. She was chewing on her bottom lip, her brow furrowed, then for some reason she looked Sara's way and smiled. Sara felt that smile to the tips of her toes, squashing the warning signal screaming *danger*!

"Hey, you found me," Mikaela said.

"I would have brought a refill, but I don't know what you're drinking."

Mikaela laughed. "The hard stuff. I switched to Diet Coke with a shot of cherry. With the way Casey plays, I need all my faculties." She pointed to a nearby table.

Sara followed the direction Mikaela was pointing and took a moment to admire the stylized playing motions of the lanky redhead, who, from the look on her opponent's face, was cleaning up. "I can give you pointers along with the Diet Coke." Sara took a sip of her beer and considered switching to Coke. She too needed all of her faculties, because Mikaela was like a siren's call—impossible to resist. "What about your friend?"

"Miller Lite. She's a heavyweight too. But you don't have to buy us drinks."

"I know. Want is a different thing."

"Is it ever. I accept your gracious offer." Mikaela ran her fingers through her hair, fanning it across her shoulders.

Sara had a hard time looking away. She wanted to be the one running her fingers through Mikaela's silky-looking curls. She downed the rest of her beer. It didn't slow the burn in her stomach, and maybe she didn't want it to. Tension wasn't always a bad thing. "Be right back."

"Trust me, I'm not going anywhere without getting my pointers. I'm thinking maybe they could help me win."

"Why do I get the feeling she likes to win?" Sara muttered as she crossed the room. "And better yet, why do I think that's sexy?" She shook her head, needing to clear it of doubts. She wasn't being forced and she wasn't doing any forcing. They were adults and if they hooked up for a night, so be it. As long as both sides understood the rules, it was all good.

She was ready to accept whatever happened by the time she made it back with the drinks.

"Just in time." Mikaela was standing by the pool table, watching Casey rack the balls. "I should warn you she's in the zone. The one where she has no mercy, even for her good friend."

"I've been known to go there myself." Sara deposited the drinks on the table and wiped her hands on her jeans.

"Then maybe you should take the first game. I hate to lose." Mikaela pouted playfully.

"I'm not falling for your tricks," Casey warned. "Hi. Casey Atoms."

"Sara Gordon." She shook Casey's hand. "You've got some moves."

"I try."

Mikaela snorted. "Try? Really? For that I am going first."

"Be my guest."

It soon became clear to Sara that Mikaela did not need any help. But that didn't stop her from providing assistance. She took the opportunity to sidle next to Mikaela under the pretense of helping her line up a shot and got a whiff of perfume, making her head spin just a little with want. When the ball went into the pocket, it was almost anticlimactic.

"Thanks." Mikaela turned her head and their cheeks almost touched. "You have a nice touch. Can't help wondering if it applies to…other matters."

Mikaela's breath felt warm against Sara's cheek. "It does. Or so I've been told."

The remainder of the game—and Sara thought "game" was a good word for what they were doing—passed in a series of lingering touches and heated gazes. They made a good showing but were no match for Casey's skills.

"Anybody else hot?" Mikaela asked, lifting her hair off her neck.

"With the show the two of you put on, who wouldn't be?" Casey fanned her face.

Hearing the murmured assents, Sara became aware of the outside world, blocked out by the duet they'd been performing. She met knowing glances without embarrassment.

"I'd pay to watch another game." A short brunette pulled a wallet from baggy jeans. She wasn't fast enough to duck the swat to the head from the woman standing next to her.

"Sorry. One's my limit," Mikaela declared, letting her hair settle about her shoulders. She shot Sara a glance out of the corner of her eye. "And I'm hoping to have something better to do."

Sara's heart raced along with the catcalls. Hadn't she known this was what they'd been playing toward? "Your place or mine?" she whispered against Mikaela's ear.

"Mine. Probably closer." Mikaela nipped at Sara's neck, then laughed at the resultant shiver. "We'll get there faster."

Sara didn't have to be sold. She couldn't get out of the place soon enough. The gentle tug of Mikaela's teeth on sensitive skin had loosened a ball of heat that was now firmly lodged between her thighs. A tremor passed through her as she unlocked her car and opened the passenger door.

"One thing first." Mikaela stepped up to Sara and slid her arms around her waist. "I've been dying to do this." She brushed her lips against Sara's, once, then twice. "So soft, unlike the rest of you," she murmured.

Sara cupped the back of Mikaela's head and brought their lips back together. When she parted Mikaela's lips with her tongue, the ball of fire inside her erupted into an inferno. The kiss led to more kisses that were like the sweetest of drugs, heightening the senses and blanking out everything else except need. She slid her hands down Mikaela's back and pulled her closer until she ran out of air. Her breathing was ragged as she rested her head against the top of Mikaela's head.

"Unless you want to be arrested, we should leave."

It took a moment for Mikaela's breathy words to compute. "Yeah" was all Sara could manage. She blew out a sharp breath and waited for the haze of desire to back off. Heat didn't begin to describe what they had, and she wasn't sure what would. As she walked around the car, she decided words weren't necessary in this situation, only feelings.

Even as she followed Mikaela's directions, Sara focused her attention on the warm hand drawing lazy circles on her thigh. Circles that kept the flame burning high and her foot heavy on the accelerator. When she took the exit ramp to Boulevard, that wonderful hand moved up her thigh. She held her breath as her clit throbbed, waiting for contact.

The sound of a horn pushed at the edges of the fog surrounding Sara's brain. Some part of her realized the light was green and green meant go. Go, when all she wanted was to come.

"You should probably make that right," Mikaela said, her voice husky.

Sara nodded. But when she made a right and then the next left by the drugstore, she wasn't so frazzled she didn't notice how close to her apartment they were. She touched her brakes as they came to a stop sign and wondered if this was the smart thing to do.

"Almost there," Mikaela said and moved her hand to Sara's inner thigh and squeezed. "I for one can hardly wait."

Doubt flew out of her head so fast, Sara was surprised she didn't get whiplash. She coasted through the next stop sign and soon they were through the gate and pulling into a parking space across from Mikaela's place. She remembered to turn off the ignition before she reached for Mikaela. Kissing her slowly, deeply, erased all thoughts from Sara's mind but the taste, the softness, the need.

Kiss after kiss they shared until Sara was sure she was drowning. She pulled back, took a breath, then found Mikaela's soft, tender neck with her lips. The moan that resulted was like music to her ears. "I owe you this for the thigh rub."

Mikaela let out a shuddering breath. "Aren't I the lucky one? But I want you naked. Want to feel your skin rubbing against mine." She tugged at Sara's bottom lip with her teeth. "You want?"

"Oh yeah."

Once inside, they tugged and pulled at clothes. Before Sara could do more than wonder at the beauty of Mikaela's body sans dress, hot lips were on hers and Mikaela's fingers were inside her boxers, then inside her. A couple of thrusts, a little pressure, and she came with a hard cry.

Not sure her legs would hold her, Sara rested her forehead against Mikaela's and hung on. "No fair. I was supposed to ambush you. This was not in the script."

Mikaela gave her a quick kiss, then a sultry smile. "Me, I always like to flip the script. But if you insist, I'll be happy to do it your way next time."

CHAPTER FIVE

"Mom?" Sara called softly as she made her way to the kitchen. That's where her mom would be. And her dad. She'd be safe if she was with them.

The silence was a little scary. She rubbed her arms and shivered, then quickly looked back over her shoulder to make sure nobody was there. The kitchen was a real mess. Her mother was going to be so mad that somebody had spilled paint all over the place. Madder even than about the mess in the bedroom. Sara was glad she didn't have anything to do with making either mess. Not this close to her birthday.

She entered the room on her tiptoes, trying not to get her feet dirty. "Dad?" A scream left her mouth at the sight of him. He was lying on the floor by the open refrigerator door, covered in red.

Getting her feet dirty was forgotten as she slipped and slid across the floor to get to his side. "Dad? Wake up." She shook him as hard as she could, but he didn't respond.

The phone. She had to get to the phone and call for help. Sara pushed to standing and hurried to the phone, the one on the wall that her mother used when she was cooking. She tripped over something, ending up on the floor with red painting her hands. When she looked back she saw that the something was her mom.

"Mom? Mom, wake up. Please, Mom, I'm scared." She crawled to her mother's body, sobbing. Something was wrong. When she dropped down next to her mother's still body, the scream started in her belly and worked its way up and out. Once she started, she couldn't stop.

* * *

"Sara? Sara, are you okay?"

The rough shaking more than the loud voice helped Sara break away. Shit, she thought. Not again. She rubbed her eyes and slowly let the nightmare go. What she couldn't let go was the sorrow and hopelessness the child she used to be had felt. It was close to being debilitating.

"Hey, what's wrong?"

"Fine. I'm fine," she said brusquely, looking away from the concern in Mikaela's eyes. God, why did they have to be so expressive? She glanced at the bedside clock and groaned. It was almost five o'clock. She hadn't meant to stay, hadn't meant to fall asleep. But then she couldn't seem to help herself these days. "I gotta run."

"Okay." Mikaela grabbed at the sheet and watched as Sara hunted for her clothes. "Might be some in the living room."

Sara couldn't stop the memory of how efficiently Mikaela had removed her shirt, pushed down her pants. "Uh, yeah." Dressed only in boxers and bra, she retrieved the rest of her belongings, then returned to the bedroom. Mikaela had gotten up and thrown on a robe. As she finished getting dressed, Sara hoped there wouldn't be any pressure to see her again. She'd never quite gotten around to sharing with Mikaela that she was strictly a one-night woman, and although admittedly their one night had blown her mind, she wasn't about to change a hard and fast rule. "I'll see you around at work," she said casually and pulled on her leather jacket.

"Sure. Thanks for the pool tips," Mikaela replied, her tone as casual as Sara's as they walked to the front door. "Safe trip home," she added, making no move to kiss Sara goodbye.

Sara nodded, feeling an irrational tinge of disappointment. Irrational because she wanted it to be like this. "Yeah." She shivered as the crispness of the predawn air seeped through her unbuttoned jacket. She had to stop doing this. Had to stop falling asleep in another woman's bed. It only made her feel more vulnerable when she awakened from a…nightmare. Tonight it had been a nightmare.

Sara wondered if she'd cried out like a baby. How humiliating. That was the only word she could think of to describe going from stud to frightened child in a scream. No wonder Mikaela hadn't been sorry to see her go.

She turned the radio up full blast for company on the quick trip home. But despite the music, she realized it was past time for her to find some discipline. Rolling around naked with a woman was okay. Not getting her satisfied ass up after the last orgasm was not. No more getting caught off guard for her. No more waking up scared out of her mind. "Discipline." That's what she so desperately needed until her birthday passed.

Gripping the wheel as she coasted to yet another stop sign, she wondered if she'd screwed things up at work. Or at home, she reminded herself. Mikaela didn't know where she lived, though, didn't know her number. So maybe it would be okay that two single women hadn't attached any strings. Mikaela had acted cool when she left, so there was no reason to think she wouldn't be later today, tomorrow.

"A-okay," she said and made a right into the driveway.

But as she scooped up Tabitha to go inside, Sara knew worry about Mikaela and any future reaction wasn't her real problem. Wasn't the reason for the dread at the base of her spine. The dream…no, she thought she'd had it right before. It had been a nightmare tonight. So vivid, so colorful, so real that she didn't have to close her eyes to see it again. The child she'd been might not have known the substance covering her parents was blood, but the adult she was did. If she took a breath, she'd swear she could smell the coppery overtones talked about in the mysteries she loved to read. She could definitely see her father, splayed out on the floor, his sightless eyes wide open.

"Why would I dream that?" she whispered against Tabitha's thick neck. "Why the hell would I?" Tabitha's response was to butt her head against Sara's cheek. "So we're agreed—it's the location messing with my head." She took a shuddering breath and wanted so much to believe.

Tomorrow after work she'd head to the main Fulton County library, which was located practically across the street from the office building. They'd have free Internet access. A major pileup like the one her parents had died in had to be newsworthy. Once she read the accounts of the accident, visited the site, the nightmares would stop. They had to or…They had to.

She shivered, remembering the silence in her mother's stomach. Giving the cat one last scratch, she set her down. A run around the park was what she needed. If she pushed hard enough she would clear her mind, erase, at least temporarily, images of the blood bath.

* * *

When Mikaela's alarm clock sounded she groaned. "Ten more minutes." She hit the snooze button and flopped back down. What had she been thinking? And on a Wednesday night when she still had Thursday and Friday to get through. She knew she was tired when a weak chuckle escaped. Obviously, she had been thinking. Thinking about Sara's hands, her mouth, her taut body. She was alive, after all, and there could be no better way to celebrate Hump Day than to enjoy an exceptional hump or two.

She stretched, feeling a slight tenderness in muscles that hadn't had that kind of workout in a while. Throwing an arm across her eyes, she smiled as scenes from the night before flashed behind her eyelids. There might be worse reasons to wake up feeling tired and thoroughly used. But even if she thought about it really hard, she didn't believe she could come up with many better reasons than what she'd experienced—fantastic sex.

TWI. Totally worth it, she thought and gave another laugh. Lord knows, she'd do it again in a heartbeat, despite the fact that her bed partner had all but run off screaming. Mikaela thought that probably said something about her, and maybe she'd think on it later. Much later.

When her alarm sounded ten minutes later, she shuffled to the bathroom, a smile still fixed on her face. As the warm water soothed tired muscles, she poured shampoo into her hands. You only live once, and last night she'd been living. She wasn't stupid enough to have any expectations of a repeat. Sara struck her as a player, and nothing good ever came from getting stuck on players. She should know. She'd been there and done that—more than once. This time she was going to be smart and accept that last night had been about sex. Really good sex, but only sex.

She would not embarrass herself by waiting for a call or, worse, make the call herself. Which, lucky for her, she couldn't do because they had never gotten around to exchanging numbers. She must have been thinking somewhat clearly despite being caught in the throes of desire. A big fat point for her.

Mikaela was feeling pleased with herself until it occurred to her that not calling wasn't the hardest part. No, that would be keeping herself from loitering around the lobby, hoping for a glimpse or a chance to start conversation. Sure, they'd had fun playing pool before the sex, and yes, she'd taken flirtation to another level, but that was then and this was…

"Not me thinking about seeing her again." She was simply reminiscing about a good time. She deserved that. Had earned it considering how awful that last date had been.

Later, fortified by her first cup of coffee, she figured she'd burnt enough calories the night before to have one of the sausage and French toast sandwiches she only allowed herself on special occasions. She hummed as she watched the time count down on the microwave.

"Somebody's cheerful this morning." Casey entered the kitchen and headed directly to the coffee maker. She made her selection and pushed the start button before glancing at Mikaela. "Could it have something to do with the clothing I had to step over to get to my room last night? No, wait. Maybe it's related to the noises coming from your bedroom. Pun intended."

"We weren't that loud. Were we?"

Casey nodded and removed creamer from the fridge. "Sounded like wild animals attacking each other."

"Get out! No way," she added dismissively. Casey's bedroom was on the other end of the condo. "Must be jealousy talking."

"I'm willing to let you think that," Casey said with a broad smile. "While I did not have your immediate success, I did set up a date for Saturday. And of course I got her number. Can you say the same?"

"Don't need it." She removed her sandwich from the microwave and wrapped it in paper towel. "One-shot deal. Yummy, maybe even scrumptious, but a one-shot deal nonetheless."

"How can you say that? You looked hot and heavy to me and everyone else in a fifty-mile radius."

"Realist over here." She raised her upper lip at Casey's pointed look. "I can be a realist. Women with that level of hotness don't settle for one. And why should they?" She glanced at the microwave clock. "Damn. Gotta run. We can argue this later, even though you're wrong."

Mikaela caught the bus with seconds to spare. Ignoring the sign forbidding eating or drinking on the bus, she knocked off her breakfast sandwich, then thought longingly of the to-go cup she'd filled with coffee that was still gracing the kitchen counter. She drifted off to sleep, berating herself. It was only the shoulder tap from a fellow rider that had her getting off at her stop. Yawning, she trudged up the street, fighting the cold head wind all the way.

As luck, or un-luck, would have it, Sara was at the front door when she walked in. She managed a polite smile even as her heartbeat quickened and certain parts tingled in remembrance. Mikaela sighed and thought maybe she wasn't going to be smart this time either. But really, she reasoned, no woman who had spent a night with Sara Gordon would fault her. And if they did, they were obviously delusional.

Upstairs, her un-luck continued in the form of Jolene, who was in front of her desk scribbling something. Mikaela cursed under her breath. After the night she'd had, it shouldn't be too much to expect to be left alone until she had the chance to down two or three cups of coffee. Suppressing a sigh, she hung up her coat. "Morning."

Jolene was wearing a dark blue tailored pant suit that worked well with her tall, thin frame. Her hair was pulled back from her face, and she liked to say she'd earned every one of her numerous gray hairs. She was extremely competent, and every inch the professional, unlike some Mikaela could name. "Sorry to bother you before you've had a chance to settle."

"That's okay. What can I help you with?"

"According to Talya, you did the majority of the work for the summit meeting packet."

Mikaela felt her back stiffen. "Yes, but that's because she's been busy with other duties. I hope there are not a lot of changes. They need to go to the printer's before noon."

"That's not why I'm here," Jolene replied quickly. "Far from it. You did such a wonderful job that Bill wants you to do something similar for the regional meeting. He heard yesterday that it's going to be his baby, and as you can imagine, he's a little anxious to get it done. I have a lot of loose ends to tie up before I get out of here, but even if I didn't, let's be frank, I couldn't even come close to what you pulled together so quickly."

"Uh…sure," she replied, caught off guard by the request and the praise. "As long as Talya clears it."

Jolene smiled. "I'll have Bill send her a memo when he gets in. Probably wouldn't hurt to leave this background information for you to look over in the meantime. The meeting's over a month away. However, the sooner we can get something in place, the better. This is a first for Bill and Big Brother is watching."

"Understood." She tried to sound nonchalant but was intrigued enough to peruse the folder as soon as Jolene left. Writing was something she enjoyed doing and it had always come easily to her. It wasn't in her job description, but she'd been doing more of it over the past few months as Talya's workload increased.

Ideas were floating around in her head when she went to grab a much-needed cup of coffee. She could use what she'd already done as the base, then make changes so it was different. A big thing for Bill, she thought as she added cream and sweetener. That meant added flash was needed. But first she had to finalize the materials for Talya's meeting. She slurped down coffee on her way back to her desk, welcoming the zing as more caffeine entered her system.

She found that all she needed to finish was to send the materials to the printer. Talya had already gotten Bill's approval, which explained her newest assignment. And now that she thought about it, Mikaela wouldn't put it past Talya to have put a suggestion in Bill's ear. No doubt it was the next step in Talya's nefarious plot to get her Jolene's job.

Her first task done, Mikaela gave the meeting notes another look. She was soon pulled into the world of possibilities and barely had time to register the footsteps before Ilene appeared at her desk. "Yes?"

"I hear Jolene came to see you first thing," Ilene said. "The two of you seem to talk more now that she's retiring."

Mikaela told herself that as soon as she got rid of Ilene she was going to find the camera they'd planted and smash it to bits. She probably should be grateful they hadn't splurged for sound. "I'm kind of busy, so is there something specific to work that you need?"

"Seems curious, that's all." She angled her head to peer at the material in front of Mikaela. "Have you heard any more talk about them bringing in a replacement for Jolene from headquarters?"

Mikaela closed the folder. "I haven't heard anything about anything. Go to the source if you're that worried about it."

"Worried about what?" Talya asked, looking from Mikaela to Ilene as she came to stand in front of Mikaela's desk.

"Oh, nothing," Ilene replied quickly. "I'd better get back."

Mikaela rubbed her eyes and wondered what she'd done to deserve this roller coaster of a morning. She hoped it was not a sign of things to come.

"Worried about what?" Talya repeated once Ilene was out of earshot.

"Apparently I can't talk to Jolene without it warranting an interrogation." She blew out a sharp breath. "Make them stop."

"Aren't we a little grumpy? Told you not to stay out too late."

"Wasn't that late." Mikaela switched to rubbing her temples, fighting a burgeoning bout of bitchiness. "I need more coffee in my system if I'm going to have to deal with these things."

"Things as in getting asked about Jolene's job?"

Talya's amusement was duly noted. "Among other *things*."

"Ah, so any more thoughts about it?"

"How can I not when my boss keeps bringing it up? You do realize that if by some chance I decided to apply and then actually got the job, heads would have to be knocked together, right? Is that really what you want for me, your loyal assistant?"

Talya laughed. "Only if I can watch. I've wanted to slap Christine around for...well, let's just say for the past few years." Closer in age to forty than thirty, Talya had made it known she didn't like to admit how long she'd worked at Baker.

"Could happen. She'll be the most upset and the loudest about expressing her displeasure."

"Only because she mistakenly believes the job is hers. Do *not* let them keep you from going after this." Talya dropped into the chair by Mikaela's desk. "Bill's no dummy. He knows enough of what goes on around here to realize some feathers will get ruffled. He also knows who is and who isn't qualified for the job, so don't think my recommendation is the reason you would get the job. Clear?"

"Loud and." She waited until Talya entered her office to add, "Bill's awareness of what's going on won't be any comfort when I have to pull a knife out of my back." It seemed she was going to be forced to deal with that damn job, sooner rather than later. Talya wouldn't keep bringing it up if she didn't think there was a good chance Mikaela could get it. Pushing back from her desk, she went for more caffeine.

Back at her desk, the issues of Jolene's job hung around like low-hanging rain clouds, waiting to dump on her head. She knew there wasn't a choice. Not applying would make Talya look bad with Bill, and she liked and respected her boss too much to let that happen. It all came down to loyalty. In Mikaela's book if your boss went to bat for you, the least you could do was run the bases, then hope someone would tag you out. Though for her ego, she'd prefer if that someone was from the outside.

She frowned and wondered if she sounded as defeatist as she thought she did. Yeah, last night had been a short one, but that was no excuse for a piss-poor attitude. Since she *was* going to apply, then she'd damn well give it her all. That was what she'd done her entire work career, no reason to change now. If that wasn't enough, then so be it. She couldn't see how trying hard and failing would impact her negatively. Not if she continued to do the job well.

And speaking of the job, she went back to reviewing the information Jolene had left. She knew Bill's request was a formality.

"Do it."

"What?" Mikaela looked up at Talya. Once again, she'd been caught in possibilities and visions of grandeur. "Apply? Have they posted already?"

"Not that. I'm talking about the materials for the quarterly meeting," Talya explained. "Make it happen. Coordinate with Jolene directly, but keep me in the loop. If you run into any problems with overscheduling, I need to be the first to know."

"At this point I don't foresee any problems. Based on the information I've read so far, I can start with the templates I created for your meeting. Of course I'll change the color scheme, the layout, so it looks fresh. I've also got some ideas of how to make the brochure look even better."

"Consider this your number one priority."

"This wouldn't be a test, would it?"

Talya shrugged. "I don't know what you're talking about. But isn't it a good thing you've decided to apply for the job?"

She nodded, getting the message loud and clear. "I won't let you down. I realize you stuck your neck out for me despite what you said earlier. And you're right. I shouldn't let worry about what the Righteous Three may or may not do stop me. But I'd be lying if I didn't say I'm concerned about measuring up. Jolene's set that bar high."

"I'd be lying if I didn't say I would have been disappointed if you'd let those three hold you back. As for Jolene, you're right. But think about how much you've grown into this job. Don't sell yourself short, kiddo."

"I'll try to remember, but no promises."

CHAPTER SIX

"What?" Marianna cupped her hands over her mouth, then quickly looked around. They were seated in one of the two alcoves in the break room of Marianna's company. When she and Mikaela ate in, they liked to come here. It was bigger than the one Mikaela had access to, had two microwaves and a better selection of soft drinks and snacks in the vending machines. "Sorry. Now say that again."

"You heard me." Mikaela enjoyed seeing the comical expression on Marianna's face.

"No," Marianna said, shaking her finger. "No way you said what I thought you said. Must be a disturbance in the air."

"I slept with Sara Gordon," she said slowly.

"Our Sara Gordon? The one who works downstairs?"

"Yeah, that one," she said dryly. "The only Sara Gordon we know."

"Oh my God! Need a minute to adjust." Marianna put her hands on either side of her head and squeezed. "You slept with Sara Gordon. I actually know someone who slept with a goddess of hotness."

"Going overboard."

"Who could blame me?" Marianna sighed. "Okay, start at the beginning. How the hell did you manage it?"

"I do know an insult if I hear one." Between bites of leftover casserole and interruptions, she talked Marianna through her evening.

"Wow. Just wow. Told you that red dress would pay off." Marianna was obviously proud; she'd been the one to talk Mikaela into the purchase. "Sounds great until morning. What was up with the nightmare?"

She shrugged, wishing she'd omitted that part. "Does it really matter in the grand 'I-had-fantastic-sex-with-Sara-Gordon' schemata? I'm telling you that is *not* the part that keeps playing in my mind."

"Good point." Marianna picked at her low-cal previously frozen entrée. "Fantastic sex, huh? Might be hard to look at her and not think of that, but I'll do my best." She took a bite, chewed, then swallowed. "So, considering you're going to be seeing her on a regular basis, you okay with not getting another shot?"

"Why wouldn't I be? No promises made, no promises broken. Win-win."

"But if you should somehow get another shot, would you take it?"

"Hello. Hot sex, hot woman."

"Got it. But what if she wants more?"

Mikaela rolled her eyes, thinking Marianna needed to dump her rose-colored glasses. "Remember the part where she couldn't get out fast enough? Message received loud and clear. Don't go wrapping some sort of fairy-tale ending around this. We had fun, we had sex, we had done. I swear you and Casey have been talking."

"Just asking for my own voyeuristic fantasies. Changing gears. Tell me again what we're doing Monday."

"Working hard. I bought this cute little pink tool belt for the occasion. Although we'll mostly be doing painting and cleaning. Talya and I went to the place and after checking out the community room, we agreed it desperately needs a facelift.

Since most of the people who use the facilities are on a fixed income and the city has cut back funding, there hasn't been enough money to do it."

"You don't have to convince me. I hope there's some kind of building involved for my sweetie's sake."

"No worries. I'll hunt up something for Erin to hammer. And don't forget the company's springing for barbecue after. Fox Brothers."

Marianna's eyes grew brighter. "Yum. Note to self. Work extra hard, then you can eat extra hard." She looked down at her lunch. "Definitely something to look forward to."

Mikaela laughed. "As much as you love barbecue, you should be black."

"Racist. But you know, I do love me some watermelon." Marianna's eyes got wide. "I'm black."

* * *

Sara rubbed her eyes, fighting against a brain shutdown. She'd come directly to the library after work. Once she'd seen the waiting list for Internet access, she switched her strategy to researching old newspapers. Since she knew the exact date, she'd figured it would actually be smarter to browse through them.

Initially, nerves got her adrenaline flowing, but after an hour of searching and coming up with nothing, she felt empty. Although she'd looked at papers two weeks before her seventh birthday and two weeks after, she hadn't been able to find an article on a massive interstate pileup.

"How's it going?"

Sara bit back a snarky reply. It wasn't the librarian's fault she couldn't find what she was looking for. He had gone out of his way to assist her. "Not so good. I checked both the *Constitution* and the *Journal* and nothing."

"How sure are you about the dates?"

"Before this I would have said one hundred percent. I don't get it."

Robert Young rubbed his clean-shaven chin. "Did you check for an obit? Find that and you can zero in on the date."

"Hadn't thought of that."

"Don't forget the obit can show up as much as two days after death."

With renewed enthusiasm, Sara returned to the search. She found her mother's obituary first. Her eyes burned as she read information that had been fed to her over the years. Even though she already knew, it was disconcerting to see her mother had been only twenty-nine when she died. Creepier yet to see her own name in the "survived by" section. No mention was made about cause of death.

She blew out a sharp breath, willing the tears away. Crying was for babies, or so she'd been told. And crying in public had brought swift punishment. She could almost feel the slap to the back of her head.

"Doesn't matter," she whispered, blinking rapidly. Her Aunt Liddy, as she'd been told to call her mother's cousin, wasn't in striking distance and hadn't been for years. She had information to collect. Information she was counting on to keep her insanity in check.

Her father's obit followed her mother's. The surge of pain took her by surprise. They'd been close, she and her dad. He'd been more like a playmate, always ready for a game.

Fumbling around in her backpack, she found a ragged pack of tissues. After wiping her eyes, she looked around. Luck was with her. She was out of sight of the nearest table and the stacks on her right were empty. That would be all she needed—to have someone catch her bawling like a baby over someone who'd been gone for most of her life. But damn, she missed him. Missed *them*, she corrected. The love between her and her mother had been strong, something she'd known she could count on. She even missed what would have been a baby brother, who would have probably driven her crazy at one time or another.

Five minutes passed before she had enough control to read her father's obit. She wasn't expecting much. Aunt Liddy always said he didn't talk much about his past. What she had known was that he and his relatives from New England were on the outs. So much so that they hadn't acknowledged his death or shown any interest in her welfare.

Sara was surprised to see he was two months younger than her mother and had an undergraduate degree from Yale. In addition to her, he was survived by a cousin and a grandfather. Both of them had been residing in Cambridge at the time of his death.

"Assholes." She didn't bother writing down their names. It was much too late to try to make a family connection with people who were too small-minded to attend a funeral or be concerned about an orphaned child.

Rubbing her eyes, Sara sat back in the chair. Time to go home and grab a nap. She must be tired if a slight from so long ago was causing her pain. She was bigger than that. At least she wanted to be bigger. Saddened, she gathered her belongings and then dropped the microfilm rolls into the wire container.

Sara was down the steep flight of stairs and on the lobby level when it hit her. Their deaths had occurred during the times she'd searched the newspapers, but she hadn't found any articles. She turned around and went back up the stairs and found the librarian behind the desk. "Excuse me."

"Found what you want, did you?"

"Not exactly. If it wasn't in the newspaper, how else can I find information on it?"

"Auto accident, right? Then you want to check police records for the accident report. Best thing to do is go to their website. Might get lucky and find they're available online. But knowing the way this city works, I doubt it. Computers are on the fourth floor if you need Internet access."

"Librarians rock." He didn't have to know she'd started her search upstairs.

He smiled. "Wish everyone thought that."

The line for Internet access was even longer than it had been earlier. Sara put her name on the list, but as she was looking for a place to sit, she noticed the express line. Five minutes was more than she needed and there was only one person in front of her.

Sara soon found out Robert had been right. The only ways to get records were in person or through a snail mail request. And since the office was not near downtown or open on weekends, it was going to have to be snail mail. If she mailed the form tomorrow, she might get it back in two weeks.

* * *

Sara jerked awake, her heart pounding. "Shit!" With a bleary-eyed glance at the TV, she wondered when this twist on her usual dream was going to go away. Ellen had been replaced by the national news. Three hours. She'd been napping for almost three hours—for all the good it had done. If anything, she felt groggier than when she had stretched out on the couch looking to be entertained. Nightmares of blood and death were not her idea of entertainment.

In the bathroom, she splashed cold water on her face and took in her washed-out complexion. "Perfect," she muttered. If anyone was casting for the role of vampire, she would get the part—no makeup needed.

She couldn't continue this way, plagued by nightmares at every turn. She was stronger than this, damn it! It was time for her to get a grip, get a handle on the situation and get her head back in the game. The dreams had been a part of her life for a long time. So what if they were more intense, more violent. She'd made it through before, she would again. But not by sitting around or napping. She had to get out, do something. Not a bar, she decided. That hadn't worked the past two times. Maybe she needed exercise. A long run on the hills around Grant Park would get her blood flowing.

As she was lacing her shoes, she remembered the voucher she'd won for a two-week membership at the new gym a quarter-mile from her place. The one with the basketball courts. She also remembered Thursday was ladies' night until nine. If she hurried, she could get in on a game. A little pushy-shovy, some trash talk, and she'd be set. If not, at least working out in a different environment should prove distracting.

The temperature had dropped, forcing her to zip her hoodie and pull on gloves before getting into her car. The gym was less than ten minutes away by car, located in a recently redeveloped strip mall. Half of the spaces were already occupied by businesses ranging from a Mexican restaurant to a funky consignment store.

Sara eased her Hyundai between two SUVs and felt a moment of vehicle envy. Inside, the gym smelled of new. The lobby was bright, with comfortable-looking seating, posters of athletes with a local connection and a shiny floor that squeaked. She was tempted to turn around and head to the older, more "gym-like" place she liked to frequent, fearing she and her old workout clothes might not fit in here. The sight of a sweaty woman in clothes more worn out than her own changed her mind.

After filling out more forms than she thought necessary, Sara was given her temporary membership card. She declined a tour, heading for the basketball courts instead. Here she felt at home—the squeal of rubber soles meeting the polished floor, the sound of dribbling accompanied by trash talking. Newness still hung in the air, but not on the women running up and down the court.

"Sara?"

"Jackie, right?" she replied, recognizing one of the trainers from her regular gym. If she remembered correctly, Jackie had played pro basketball until her knee went out. At six-two, with a powerful build and wide arm span, Jackie had undoubtedly been a dominant center. "How's it going?"

"Good. You here for some ball? We're one person short if you want to get in on the next game."

"Sure. Yeah, sure. Uh, I haven't played in a while. Hope it's okay if I'm a little rusty."

"No sweat. It's all for fun. Grab a ball and warm up." Jackie pointed to the back section of the other court where several women were shooting hoops. "I'll let you know when we're on."

Nervousness fought excitement as Sara grabbed a ball. She'd played some in high school and always tried to grab a game when she could. There had been a couple of times when she'd stayed in one place long enough to join a league and keep her hand in that way. She wasn't star material, but she was a solid player.

When Jackie called her over and introduced her to the rest of the team, she was calm, certain she wouldn't make a fool of herself. She was also certain that Carmen, the hot Latina with the flashing dark eyes and miles of hair, wouldn't mind doing something more than playing ball.

After a couple of games where she'd held her own, Sara felt pleasantly tired and agreed to meet up at the wing place on the other side of Grant Park for a couple of beers. Carmen's eyes seemed to promise more as she offered Sara a ride. Wanting the flexibility of having her own vehicle, Sara declined. Before leaving, she took a moment to wash most of the sweat from her face.

Wings and Such was located half a mile from the gym and half a mile from Sara's apartment if she cut through the park. She'd driven past it a few times but had yet to stop in. The restaurant was larger than it looked from the outside and not very crowded. The smell of fried meat and hot sauce hit her hard, stirring her appetite.

As she crossed the room, she couldn't help but smile when Carmen patted the seat next to her. The woman was persistent. In Sara's book that wasn't necessarily a bad thing. She slid into the seat and accepted the glass of beer pressed upon her.

"You play damn good for somebody who's rusty," Jackie said, raising her glass.

"You sure do," Carmen agreed. She loosened her hair from its ponytail. "You'll come back again, I hope? Sometimes we try to take over at least half a court on Wednesdays and for sure on Thursdays."

"I'll see what I can work out. I do enjoy the game."

"What else do you enjoy?" Carmen asked, putting a hand on Sara's knee. "You look like the type with a variety of tastes."

"Watch out, Sara," one of the other players called out with a touch of bitterness. "Carmen's set her sights on you. Be careful about getting caught in the crosshairs."

"Thanks, but I can take care of myself. I'm a big girl." She smiled to take any sting out of the words. "Old acquaintance?" she asked Carmen softly.

Carmen shrugged and tossed her hair over her shoulder. "She never did understand the game. What about you?"

"Me?" She took a swig of beer. "I live the game."

"Good," Carmen said with a satisfied smile. "Cheers." She touched her glass to Sara's.

CHAPTER SEVEN

A very tired Sara dragged her ass in to work the next morning. Basketball and bed aerobics with Carmen had not been enough to hold back the dreams. At least she'd been smart enough to go home after said aerobics. Only Tabitha had been witness to Sara's screams, followed by a move to the living room and the distracting noise of the TV.

As she clocked in, she gave a silent thanks for Friday. Eight hours, then she was going home and crashing. If there was an all-knowing deity, she'd be allowed to sleep through the entire weekend.

"Rough night?" Jackson asked.

Seeing the concern on his dark brown face, she found herself saying, "Well…yeah." Embarrassment had her quickly following with, "I'm okay for work though."

"Didn't say you weren't."

Not sure how to reply, Sara stowed her belongings in her locker, then checked the assignment board. Good, she was on door duty during the morning rush, then garage patrol. No way would she fall asleep while on her feet. "Anything I should worry about? I mean work-related."

"Friday's always light, and with King Holiday on Monday, it'll be even lighter."

His matter-of-fact tone had her daring to turn around. He wasn't going to press for information. "I'd forgotten we have Monday off." Another day for which she'd have to find something to chase away the nightmares. "You have plans?"

"Oh, yes indeed. I'll be doing some work at one of my grandbabies' school. Do something like that every year to pay my respects to the Man."

"That's cool."

"A group of us will be sprucing up the grounds, painting, building some reading lofts. What about you?"

She shrugged. "Don't know. Probably nothing."

"We can always use an extra hand if you're interested. For a good cause."

Sara stuck her hands in her pockets and rocked back on her heels. It would get her out of the apartment, take her mind off the nightmares. "Do I need to sign up or something?"

"Nah, just show up and find me." He dug around on his desk. "Here's a flyer. I've recruited a couple of the other guards, so there'll be someone there you know. Be sure to bring work gloves if you have them."

She nodded, folded up the flyer and stuck it in her pocket. "I'll, uh, get to it then."

As Sara took the elevator up to the fifteenth floor, she decided she must look pitiful. That's the only reason she could come up with for Jackson's invitation. But whatever the reason, she was going to show up and work her ass off. What she wasn't going to do was think about another birthday without that Batman bike, another birthday without her mother or father.

Her eyes stung. "Not here." She blinked furiously, blew out a sharp breath, forced herself into the now.

She was doing a good job of it by the time she pushed open the bathroom door on the fourteenth floor. The smell hit her nose and then her stomach. She swallowed hard and breathed through her mouth. Someone had obviously gotten past security. Someone who didn't have access to a bath tub or know how to flush a toilet.

"Security. Come on out," she said, trying to sound authoritative. It was hard when she wanted to hurl. "I said, come on out." Sara squared her shoulders and advanced on the stalls. There were five stalls, but most likely the culprit was in the handicapped one because of its larger size and location farthest away from the door.

The smell got worse with each step. Using her foot, she pushed open the door and took in the bundled up older woman sitting between the toilet and the wall. The puddle on the floor accounted for some of the smell. "Ma'am, you need to get out of here." The woman didn't stir. Sara slipped on a pair of plastic gloves. Now she understood why they were recommended. She shook the woman's shoulders, and her head lolled as if it wasn't attached. With dawning horror, Sara realized the woman wasn't just asleep. She ran into the next stall, where, to her shame, she lost her breakfast. Once she cleaned up, she let Jackson know, then stood guard outside, not wanting anyone else to go through what she had.

Jackson arrived shortly, and Sara was glad to have him take over. Shock set in and she slid down, her back to the wall, and prayed for the day the poor woman's face would be a dim memory. A dead body. She'd discovered a dead body. She rubbed her arms, taking deep breaths to get rid of the shakes.

Why me? she wondered. *Wasn't it enough she had the dreams? It wasn't fair she had to deal with the dead during waking hours as well.*

"Police'll be here soon. You just tell them what you saw. Nothing else." Jackson knelt beside her. "Looks like she's been gone less than three hours."

That made Sara feel worse, like if she'd gotten there a little bit sooner, the woman might still be alive. She exhaled and told herself to stop being stupid. Three or four minutes earlier wouldn't have changed anything. That woman's death was not on her.

By the time the first police officer arrived, Sara was no longer afraid she'd break down and make a fool of herself. He was a big, burly guy with a kind demeanor. He took her report without asking many questions, then entered the bathroom. Sara wondered if cops became desensitized to dead bodies over the years. She didn't think she ever would. She swallowed hard as a picture of the blood-spattered kitchen, along with her parents' bodies, tried to form in her mind. It could have been worse, she told herself, rocking back and forth.

"You okay?" Jackson asked, putting a hand on her arm. "You're looking mighty pale."

She nodded automatically. "I thought she was sleeping, I swear I thought she was sleeping and I ordered her to leave."

He patted her arm awkwardly. "That's okay. Why don't you take a walk? Get some air. I'll do the rest of the floors."

"I'll wait until they come get her. That seems like the right thing to do."

"You sure?"

She really wasn't. "Yes." She ran her fingers through her hair. "Yeah. I…I can do that."

"If you want, you can clock out after that and go home." He was obviously concerned.

"No, no. I'm okay. I'm okay. Just shook. I'll go outside… after. Walk around. I'll be okay."

It seemed to take hours, but finally the body was taken away. Sara said a prayer, asking for someone to bless the poor soul even as flashes of her own nightmare tried to surface.

When the cleaning crew arrived, she all but sprinted to the stairwell, a sudden need to be outside overwhelming her. She had to get away from the scene before it changed into the one from her nightmare. If she stayed near that bathroom one more second, she was afraid she'd be back in that kitchen, back to crying over the dead bodies of her parents.

As she tore down the first few flights of stairs, her head began to clear and reason returned. The dead woman in the bathroom was real. Her nightmares about her parents were not. "Simple, you idiot." Her laugh, which was close to being hysterical, made her realize she wasn't in control, wasn't close to being in control.

She slowed her pace to something less than breakneck speed and wondered if she was ever going to be able to deal with what happened years ago. Wondered if everything that happened to her went back to that loss. Wondered if she had it in her to stop letting everything that happened to her be colored by her loss. Because that's what she'd been doing for far too long. Her parents hadn't wanted to die in that car crash, and they certainly wouldn't have wanted her to die along with them. But that's sort of what she'd been doing, more and more these last few years. Maybe not dying, but she'd certainly been shutting down, pulling away from living a full life. Sara dropped down on a stair and pressed her fingers to her burning eyes. She had to find a way to deal with her parents' deaths, to finally put the senseless tragedy behind her.

A door slammed against the wall just below her, bringing her to her feet. She felt her eyes go wide as a woman entered the stairwell, put her hands over her mouth and emitted a muffled scream. Looked like her day was going about as well as Sara's.

This was intended to be a private moment, obviously. But where could she go? No matter which way she went, the woman would hear her. She settled for clearing her throat loudly. The woman dropped her hands and whirled around, her eyes wide. It was Mikaela.

"Oh! Oh God, I thought I was alone." Her eyes zeroed in on Sara's. "Sara? What are you doing here? You okay?"

"Not really. Found a dead person in the bathroom on the fourteenth floor."

"Oh. I'm sorry that was you. Homeless, I assume."

"Looks that way. She...She had a couple of bags with her."

"Probably only wanted a warm, safe place to spend the night. What a shame. For both of you, for humankind."

Sara nodded and walked down the remaining stairs that separated them. "So, what's up with you? Don't tell me you found a dead homeless woman too."

"In retrospect, my problem's not that bad. Death does a great job of putting things in perspective. Again, I'm sorry you had to find her like that."

"I'm sorry she had to die alone and on a public bathroom floor. Shouldn't happen."

"Sometimes this world sucks. The family I do have may be on the minus scale of normal, but I know I can depend on every one of them to be there if need be."

Lucky you, Sara thought. After graduation, Sara had been quickly introduced to self-sufficiency. The one cousin she sort of kept in touch with could not be termed supporting. "Listen, I need to get back, uh, to it. See you later." She ran down the next flight of stairs before Mikaela could make another comment. She wasn't looking to talk about family or the lack thereof. Not now when she was still off balance, when the past and the present seemed too closely intertwined.

It would be different one day, she vowed. Maybe even next year. By then she will have seen the police report of the accident. She will have visited the site where her parents died and finally made her peace. Next year she would actually celebrate her birthday, do something big. At least that's what she told herself over and over again while circling the block to clear her head.

* * *

Sara glanced at the stairs. She wanted to go to her parents' room, crawl into their bed and pull the covers over her head. That's what she did when she got scared during the middle of the night. But it wasn't the middle of the night, and even if it was, that wouldn't work now. She couldn't be safe if her mom and dad wouldn't wake up. Couldn't be safe if her mom and dad had gone to heaven like their dog, Zippy. So she would sit on the sofa and wait for the police like the lady on the phone said to do.

Her heart galloped when the doorbell rang. What if it wasn't the police? What if it was the bad guys coming back to get her? She wanted to return to her hiding place real bad. Maybe if she did that things would be different. Maybe if she went back up there and then came back down, her parents would be in the kitchen kissing or dancing.

The door opening had her diving behind the couch. She covered her mouth to hold back a scream.

"Sara? Sara Gordon, it's the police. You can come out now, we're here to help."

She peered around the sofa and saw two officers standing by the front door. They looked official to her. "I'm Sara," she said quietly and stood so they could see her.

"Hi, Sara. I'm Officer Rick," the one with the blond hair said. "And this is my partner, Officer Meeks. Can you come to the car with me? We can talk about what happened."

"My mom and dad won't wake up. The kitchen's all messy and they won't move." Tears welled up in her eyes and her bottom lip trembled. "My mom doesn't like a messy kitchen."

"My partner will look after your mom and your dad while you and I talk." He smiled and held out a hand. "I have a girl about your age. Her name is Wendy."

"Like in *Peter Pan*?" she asked and slipped her hand in his. It was big like her dad's.

"She keeps waiting for him to come fly her away to Neverland."

Sara thought that was silly. People couldn't fly. Even her dad said people couldn't fly. But her dad couldn't say that anymore. "I'm scared," she whispered. "I don't wanna be all by myself."

Officer Rick picked her up and patted her back. "You should let me worry about that for now."

Sara blinked back tears and rested her cheek against his shoulder. It was hard, just like her dad's. Only she didn't have a dad anymore. Or a mom. "The baby stopped moving. I put my head against Mom's stomach, but he didn't kick me like he does sometimes. Is he dead too? I don't want them to be dead."

* * *

"No!" Sara forced her eyes open, forced herself to look around the darkened room and realized where she was. "Thank God." She sat up, happy to be in the apartment, in her bed. "Okay. I'm okay. Only a dream." Drawing her legs up against her chest, she wrapped her arms around her knees. The dream had seemed so real. She would swear she could still feel the hardness of the policeman's shoulder under her cheek, the feel of his big hand as he patted her back, the smell of his cologne, so different from her dad's. She could swear she remembered staring at the blue light flashing on top of the black and white car as it sat haphazardly parked, partly on the driveway and partly on the grass her dad was so proud of.

When she rubbed her arms, she could feel the goose bumps brought on by the sight of the black body bags being loaded into the long car, could remember how hard she had cried, sitting on Officer Rick's lap in the back of the cruiser.

She shook her head, needing to distance herself from a dream so vivid it felt like a memory. Her parents had died in a car wreck. That's what she'd been told, what she'd grown up knowing. Her Aunt Liddy had no reason to lie about that.

Sara slid from the bed, hanging onto her sanity by a thread, and turned on the light. Even as bright light flooded the room, the memories kept coming. Memories of talking to Officer Rick about the hiding space, about hearing the loud noises and about going downstairs to the kitchen. Later, after she'd talked and talked, a short round woman came and took her away. Left alone in the strange bed with the scratchy pink sheets, Sara had cried herself to sleep, then awakened later, screaming for her parents.

"Oh God, not a nightmare." It was a memory.

She pressed her fingers against her eyes, surprised when they came away wet, surprised when she broke down and cried, much like her younger self had in that room where nothing was familiar.

There was a dull throbbing behind her eyes when the tears finally dried up. She held her head and tried to make sense of what was happening, of what had happened. Maybe the events had been too traumatic for her to think about? So she'd just crawled inside her mind and blocked everything out? She couldn't remember waking up the next morning. Couldn't remember meeting Aunt Liddy or traveling to Oklahoma City. But she had lived through that and more.

"Either that or I'm crazy." The idea of being crazy wasn't as scary as she'd thought it would be. And perhaps being crazy was more palatable than her parents being shot to death.

With a sigh, she worked a pillow under her head and remembered the police report. It was now more important than ever. Jackson would have to let her take a couple of hours on Tuesday. She'd go to the Records Department and get the report in person. Then she'd know for sure. Then she could… What? Be sane?

"You trying to help?" Sara looked down at Tab, who was butting her arm. "I guess you think if I'm awake I should pet you." She hefted the tabby onto her lap, stroked her soft, shiny fur and was rewarded with a deep purr. "If only my problems were so easily solved. Problem," she corrected. There was only one problem, and come Tuesday, she'd have a handle on it. Other than that, her life was fine. She was happy being the carefree single, able to pick up and move when the mood hit. Hadn't she been proving that since she was eighteen?

"Damn straight," she told Tab around a yawn. "I do fine by myself." But as she drifted back to sleep, thoughts of the homeless woman crowded her mind. Would that be her—dying alone with nobody to care she was gone? Sleep was a long time coming.

* * *

Mikaela got up with the daylight Sunday morning. She'd made the horrible mistake of getting on her sadistic roommate's new scale the day before. After the shock of seeing how much she weighed had faded, she'd resolved to start exercising regularly. Of course she'd made that resolution before, but this time she meant it.

She put on her workout clothes and grabbed her cell. Next stop, Grant Park. It should take her less than thirty minutes to circle the park, longer if she did it twice. During the week, she *would* get up early and jump on Casey's fancy treadmill with all the bells and whistles. Maybe eventually get to a slow jog. The running she did all too regularly to catch the bus in the morning would not count, even if it did get her heart pumping.

Once outside and inspired by a throbbing beat coming from her ear buds, she set a fast pace up the car-lined street. At Boulevard she hooked a left, deciding the steep hill on Atlanta Avenue was best tackled going downhill today. The temperature, which had seemed cold when she started out, turned invigorating as she warmed up. There were a few others out running or walking their dogs, but mostly she had the sidewalk to herself as she huffed and puffed her way to weight loss. The experience was unexpectedly pleasant.

After twenty minutes, she was ready to upgrade the experience from pleasant to enjoyable. Her heartbeat was strong, sweat was beading on her forehead and she felt like she was accomplishing something. This exercising was almost fun. Almost something that could become a habit as long as that damn scale didn't continue to taunt her.

She looked at her watch as she rounded the corner onto Park Street, realized she was making good time and decided to prolong her walk by doing a lap inside the park. The path that ran through the park meandered and the scenery was better. She smiled as two adorable black puppies wrestled each other under the watchful eye of their owner. One day she'd have her own place and a dog. One day.

"Cute, aren't they?"

"Hey, you!" Mikaela mentally cringed at her overly enthusiastic greeting. It wasn't as if Sara needed to know how glad she was to see her. How much she'd been thinking of her, both with clothes and without.

Seeing Sara's rosy face, her form-hugging, long-sleeved T-shirt damp with sweat, Mikaela was taken back to their night together. Sara had been rosy with sweat then too.

Don't go there, she told herself sternly. Going there led to danger.

"What is with you catching me off guard? You stalking me?" she demanded playfully, her hands on her hips.

Sara raised her right eyebrow. "How do I know you aren't stalking me? Lying in wait until you know I have to acknowledge your presence."

"No way to know, is there?" Before she could help herself, her hand was on Sara's arm. Mortified, she quickly dropped her hand. "I'm flattered you stopped your run to say hi. How far you going?"

"I was, uh, almost finished with my five-mile loop. What about you?"

"I was doing a loop around the park. Walking, not running. You usually run at this time? Not that I would know, because hey, usually lolling in bed at this hour. And maybe I should let you answer, huh?" She flashed a smile, her best—she hoped.

"I'm more of a treadmill runner. Today I was up early and… well, I needed to get out, get away." Sara pushed a wispy strand of hair off her forehead.

She took a closer look at Sara's face and thought she saw more than tiredness about her eyes. It made Sara seem vulnerable and her heart gave a little pang. "Great morning for a run. You live around here?"

"A couple of blocks east on Ormewood."

"That is close. So, uh, good that you didn't have far to go the other night."

Sara nodded.

Not a talker, Mikaela thought. Great. "Well, I'll let you get back to it."

"Wait." Sara held out her arm. "Are you…" She paused, breathed in. "Do you like the zoo by any chance?"

"Zoo? Can't say I've ever been. Which is kind of shameful, considering it's so close. You?"

"Yeah. I enjoy watching the animals." Sara once again swiped at her hair. "Any chance you wanna go? Later, I mean."

Who was this delightfully shy woman? "Sure. I should warn you that I love taking pictures." She didn't have to admit that the majority of them would be of Sara. "I'm talking a lot."

"That's cool." Sara's smile made it to her eyes. "I do a little sketching, so I know what you mean. We can take our time."

"Works for me. When?"

"Eleven? Maybe grab some wings across the street after?"

The scale—along with the word *diet*—was instantly forgotten. Time with Sara plus hot wings—there must be a heaven, she decided. But to be on the safe side, she'd skip the fries, make do with celery sticks. "Why don't I meet you near the entrance?"

"I'll, uh, I'll see you then."

"Then." Mikaela walked away, floating on air. This had to be a reward for getting up early, for exercising. If only she had known this before.

Casey was spread out on the sofa in her PJs when she arrived home. "Hey, you. Didn't realize you were up already."

"Your fault, Atoms. You had to get that fancy new scale." She put her hands on her hips and peered at her roommate suspiciously. "Were you trying to tell me something? Leaving a message in the bottle?"

Casey covered her face. "Casey's not here right now. Leave a message at the beep and she'll get back to you the first of never."

"Ha-ha. Whatever your Machiavellian plan, it worked, damn you. I got on the damn thing and let me tell you, I screamed. I'm surprised you didn't hear me. Are you laughing? I think I hear laughter. Put down your hands," she demanded, stomping her foot.

"Hell yes, I'm laughing. Laughing at the crazy woman I live with."

"My grandma always said skinny bitches are mean." She sat on the side of the recliner and pouted for half a second. "Lucky for you I ran into Sara when I was out on my walk. The walk *you* forced me to take because of that damn shiny scale. Why does a skinny bitch like you need a scale anyway? I mean, come on, look at you. You don't need to worry about your weight."

"Hey, back up." Casey sat up. "What's this about Sara?"

"I ran into her. More like she ran into me 'cause she was the one doing the actual running. But that's not important." She put a hand to her heart. "She asked me out. Well, sort of. We're going to the zoo and then maybe grab wings after. So it's not really a date. More a thing than anything else, you know?"

"Maybe. But somebody swore up and down you guys were a one-time deal. What happened to that?"

Mikaela tsked. "This is not about sex. Truth? I think she's having a rough time and needs company."

"And you, being the kind person that you are, agreed," Casey said dryly.

"Okay, so yeah, she looked yummy. Even in her ratty and sweaty running gear. But this is no biggie. Just something to do. Like I said, a thing."

"Can I remind you of that later?"

"Hell no! And Casey? A true friend wouldn't have to ask."

CHAPTER EIGHT

At ten to eleven Sara was stationed near the entrance to Zoo Atlanta, searching the faces in the crowd for Mikaela. After changing several times, she'd settled on a long-sleeved T-shirt and jeans. This wasn't a date, and she wanted to make sure Mikaela understood that. They were simply going to take in the animals, have some lunch and help her forget about…She firmed her lips. She would *not* think about that now. She was here to have fun, spend some time with another human being, then later have a cold one. Boom, boom, boom. The end.

She blinked and refocused her thoughts on the people entering the zoo. The sun, defying the weatherman's prediction, was bright and had warmed the day to a pleasant sixty degrees, no doubt contributing to the size of the crowd in the park. Many of those entering the zoo were families with young children who were spazzing to get at the animals. Sara couldn't blame them. Zoos had always held a fascination for her. Although Aunt Liddy had never been the type to visit a place like this, Sara spent plenty of time at the Oklahoma City Zoo courtesy of school outings.

All thoughts of zoos flew from her head when she spotted her "un-date." Mikaela was wearing hip-hugging jeans and a long-sleeved red shirt that showed off a chest her hands and mouth remembered. Her hair flowed around her shoulders, making Sara's fingers itch to run through it. An unbidden memory of their night together surfaced and she stuffed her hands into her front pockets.

Mikaela stopped a few feet away and raised her camera. "Say 'cheeseburger.'"

"Bacon cheeseburger." Sara smiled and let Mikaela get in four or five shots. "You weren't kidding about the camera."

"Nope. The camera loves you, by the way. Not a bad side anywhere. Not that I expected there to be. I mean, I have…" She stopped and cleared her throat. "I'm not late, am I?"

Wouldn't have mattered to Sara. As she was discovering, Mikaela was worth the wait. "No. I got here early. It's a fault."

"Better than me. I'm always running behind. Then I have to rush, go out not fully put together. Like for example my hair."

To Sara's regret Mikaela pulled out a hair band and tamed her glorious mane.

"You ready to rumble?"

"Does my hair look okay? Wouldn't want the animals to mistake me for one of them."

"Looked great before," Sara said before she could censor herself. "Uh, yeah, it's good."

"Thanks. Maybe I'll take it down later."

She shrugged as if she hadn't been hoping for just that and removed her membership card along with an extra ticket from her wallet.

"You have a membership?"

"I like the animals and it's, you know, close." Sara held out the extra ticket. "To me that makes membership a must."

"God, I hope you don't think I'm belittling you. I mean, I think it's great that you're a zoo supporter and all. Shutting up now. Sorry. I talk a lot when I'm nervous," Mikaela admitted as they passed through the turnstiles. "You're the expert. Where to first?"

"I like to start with the flamingoes and work my way around clockwise."

"Sounds good." Mikaela held up her camera and took more shots. "Let me know if I get too obnoxious with this thing. It was a surprise—I mean *huge* surprise—Christmas present from, well, I'll call him Father for clarity's sake. We're still in the honeymoon phase. The camera and I, that is."

"Shoot away."

Sara soon found that watching the animals with Mikaela was a new experience. Mikaela wasn't afraid to let out her inner child and voice her enthusiasm for the warthog babies or her displeasure at the smell and size of elephant dung. She made Sara laugh by sharing her opinion of what the animals were thinking. And to Sara's relief, she was able to set aside her problems and join Mikaela's game.

"My camera and I had the best time," Mikaela said as they exited the zoo. "Thanks for the invite."

"Anytime. You up for wings?" Sara wasn't ready for their outing to finish, and it wasn't only because she didn't want to be alone with her thoughts.

"Lead the way. All that walking has given me plenty of room."

Sara started up the road leading to Cherokee Avenue, truth to be told, a little dazzled by Mikaela's smile.

"So what was your favorite exhibit?" Mikaela asked.

"I've always been partial to chimpanzees, but I like gorillas too."

"I have to go with the pandas. But I also like the warthogs. They're so ugly they're cute."

"And like you said, they reminded you of *The Lion King*. Or should I say, like you sang?"

"So I'm loud. You would be too if you'd grown up around my extended family where, I'll have you know, I'm known as the quiet one."

Sara's eyebrows shot up. "You're the quiet one? Does anyone wear earplugs to family reunions?"

"If I ever had someone I wanted to take, I'd be sure to have a pair available." Mikaela scrunched up her nose. "We generally talk over and around each other. Jumping from this conversation to that conversation without missing a beat. Somehow it works for us. As a courtesy, we tone it down for company. That's without alcohol, of course."

"Sounds...interesting. How often do you go back?"

"Twice a year now that my grandmother's gone. Just enough to keep my play mom happy. Out of all the kids—and let me tell you there are many—only two of us have moved away, and she and the rest of the family never let me forget it."

"Play mom? What's that?"

"Not really a mom, but sort of acts like one. I think it's something we black people made up 'cause I don't think I've heard of a white person having one. Tell me you don't have a play mom by another name."

"I don't."

"Good. I won't have to change my thinking there. Anyway, in my case my play mom is my father's ex-wife. The one he was technically married to when I was born." Mikaela laughed. "If you could see your face. Yeah. Weird, I know. He's never been much of a father to any of his kids, so I don't usually use that word to describe him."

"She must be a really nice person." Sara was thinking *saint*. As for fathers, she hadn't had hers for long, but the time they did have had been great. Maybe she got the better part of the deal.

"She's a step above that. I owe her a lot for never holding his actions against me, going so far as to make sure I got to know my brothers. Everyone in the neighborhood knows they can count on Miss Janey." Her affection for her play mom came through loud and clear.

"Why did you move away? From your family."

"To go to Spellman College. I dropped out after two years when my money ran out and I started working full time. The plan was to save money, then go back. But a year turned into another and..." She shrugged.

"I know how that is. You never quite get back to what you meant to do."

"Exactly. But I started back part time a few years ago, and I'll get a degree in business this spring. Not the first kid in my family to get one like I intended, but still…"

"At least you'll finish. Will you look for another job?"

"Hoping to use the degree to give me a boost where I am."

"You must like it there."

"I do. I really like my boss, and I like the way management is going about changing the way we work. Plus it looks like there's a chance for a promotion soon. What about you? You like your job?"

"It pays the bills."

"So, uh, any plans for tomorrow?" Mikaela asked after a moment's silence.

"I let my boss talk me into helping out at his grandkid's school. You?"

"Along with a bunch of my coworkers, I'll be sprucing up the activity room at a community center. I'm psyched because it's the first time we've done it as a company."

"They make you do it?" Sara asked.

"No, not at all. We're owned by a new company and they're into this kind of thing. I think it's great. They even put up money for food and drinks afterward."

"You do a lot of that? Volunteering, I mean."

"Not as much as I'd like between work and school, so tomorrow's a win-win."

"Cool." Sara pushed the walk button as Cherokee Avenue was a steady stream of cars. "I uh, want to thank you for doing this at the last minute. You, well, you're helping me get through a tough time."

"No prob. I got a day at the zoo and a chance to talk your ear off. Another win-win for me."

Mikaela's smile seemed forced to Sara, and she wondered how much to say. "Thanks anyway. This…this time of year is… around the time my parents died, so it's kind of, you know."

Mikaela put a hand on Sara's arm. "I'm so sorry. How old were you?"

"Seven."

"That must be hard losing your parents so young."

More than you know, she thought, and nodded around the lump in her throat. "Uh, we should, you know, cross while we got the light."

The rest of the trip was completed in silence.

Wings and Such was packed. They had a forty-minute wait for a table and decided to grab a couple of seats at the bar in the back.

"Looks like we can order most everything right here," Mikaela said, looking through the menu the bartender had passed their way.

"Sounds better than waiting. I recommend the wings and beer."

"I'm leaning toward the extra hot with extra sauce."

"Brave."

"That's me."

They gave their orders to a thin bartender with a bushy beard that was wider than him.

"I hope I didn't upset you earlier," Mikaela said, "asking questions about your parents."

"No." Sara shook her head. "You were right about it being hard. This year seems worse because, well, it happened here in Atlanta and this is the first time I've been back." She picked up the glass of beer as soon as the bartender placed it in front of her and took a long pull. "After, I moved in with my mom's cousin and her kids in Oklahoma City."

"That had to be a shock, coming on top of the other."

"To tell you the truth, I didn't remember much about that time." She wished she could say that was still true. "And the subject never came up. I guess that was a good thing."

"That would never happen in my family," Mikaela said, then winced. "Sorry. I probably shouldn't be talking about family to you. I tend to suffer from 'foot-in-mouth' disease."

"It's okay. You talking about your family doesn't keep me from mine."

"Okay. Question, then. Why chimpanzees?"

"That's easy. I was always drawing animals all over my notebooks, so my sixth-grade teacher made me read a book about chimpanzees in the wild as punishment." Sara smiled at the memory. "Best punishment I ever received."

"Was it by the woman who's lived with them for like forever?"

"Jane Goodall."

"Yeah, her. I used her as a reference for a report I did for a biology class."

"Reports. I don't miss those days at all. If I have pen and paper, I'd rather draw."

"You'll have to show me your etchings sometime."

Before she could formulate a response, the bartender dropped off their meals.

"Ah, food." Mikaela snagged a fry. "You know, I should probably confess that one of my great uncles kind of looks like a chimpanzee. Really," she added when Sara looked at her. "Of course, he doesn't act like one. More's the pity. Uncle Willy's my grandmother's oldest brother and may be the oldest person to appear on one of those reality shows about cops. He was walking drunk and decided he could outrun the police. They caught him when he stopped to *chat* with a hooker."

"No way!"

Mikaela threw back her head and laughed. "Way. Like I said, we don't keep things to ourselves in my family and he loves to tell that story. How he got off when he convinced the cops he stopped because he thought she was lost. Of course he was younger then. Seventy, I think. Maybe older."

"You have such interesting…characters in your family."

"Characters. I like that." Mikaela grinned. "My neighborhood was full of *characters*. Stereotypes get started for a reason. Not that everyone likes that, mind you, but…" She shrugged, then spent the rest of the meal entertaining Sara with stories about neighborhood characters.

"You up for dessert?" Sara pushed away her empty plate and reached for her second beer. Maybe she'd finally done something right. Mikaela was keeping her from drowning in sorrow, and she couldn't ask for more.

Had even convinced herself one night would cure any itch. She didn't usually delude herself like that. Well, now she had, so she was stuck lying around mooning by the phone like some damn sap.

"What are you moping about?"

She looked up at Casey in irritation. "I'm not moping. I'm trying to catch up with all the shows I foolishly recorded last week."

"Now that's a hopeless task." Casey moved Mikaela's feet aside and sat. "No wonder you're moping."

"Did you not just hear me say I wasn't?"

"Then what has you in such a bright and cheerful mood?"

Mikaela bit her lip to keep from smiling. "Go to hell."

Casey looked around the living room, then back at Mikaela. "And here I thought I was already there. Come on, you know you want to tell me. Bad day at the senior center?"

She shook her head. Did she really want to admit her stupidity? Oh yeah, this was Casey, and over the years she'd admitted more stupid things to her than this. "Okay, I was kind of hoping Sara would call. Dumb, I know." She sat up and clutched a throw pillow to her body. "It's just…I thought we'd connected enough for her to call and tell me how her volunteering went. Thought she'd want to call and talk, you know, friend to friend. Obviously I was wrong." She punched the pillow. "Damn if I didn't jump into the deep end. Again."

"Will you hit me if I say I told you so?"

She shook a fist at Casey. "Right in the kisser, baby."

"Okay," Casey said, drawing out the word. "Will you hit me if I tell you I had a little bit of fun today?"

"I'm giving it serious consideration." She pursed her lips and pretended to think. "Tell me who she is so I can make up my mind."

"Suzette."

"Wait. I heard wrong. I know you did *not* say Suzette." But looking at the smile on Casey's face, Mikaela knew Suzette had somehow found her way back into Casey's life. "I thought she and her *partner* moved up north someplace."

"They broke up eight months ago and she's back down here with her old firm. I ran into her, we got to talking and—"

"Is that who you spotted at Pool? Tell me the truth."

"I thought I did, but she didn't show up until after you left. I kind of knew she might be there and that's why I wanted to go."

Mikaela gave her a pinch. "You could have told me. I wouldn't have said anything. Okay, I wouldn't have said much. So, are you pretending to be *friends* like you did before or are you actually dating this time?"

"Dating," Casey admitted with a little smile. "There's no need for me to pretend I'm not interested in her that way this time."

"I'm happy for you, Casey. I always knew she was it for you, so it's good she has another chance to realize what a Princess Charming you are. 'Course you know I thought she knew that before."

"Let's not go there again."

"Fine, but I still think if you had pushed a little harder she would have left her cheating skank of a girlfriend and fallen into your arms."

"You really need to back away from the Disney movies."

"Never!" she said, putting her hand to her heart. "So where did you go?"

"Lunch, then did the Botanical Garden. I can't remember the last time I went, but it's really nice. After that we went to this little wine bar in Midtown not far from my office and talked. And talked."

"Judging by that goofy look on your face, you had a crazy good time. If you weren't my landlady, I'd punch you."

Casey shivered. "I'm so scared."

"Shut up." She pulled her arm back, then dropped it onto her lap. "You're saved. I don't much like the thought of sleeping on the street or lowering my hygiene standards."

"You could always call Nina. I bet she'd come running to the rescue."

"You didn't *even* have to go there. Aren't I suffering enough?"

"Oh, but I did have to go there. She called me. *Again*. Left a message for me to tell you to call her, seeing as she couldn't get through to you."

"Told you to block her number. And what is it with her anyway? She didn't put this much effort into our relationship." Mikaela frowned. "I don't get it. She's the one who found someone else, so why call me?"

"Maybe she's the type who loves you more after it's over."

"Too bad. I'm the type that when it's done, it's done. And the way she did it, it's dead and done. Let her go find another little coed and leave me the hell alone. And please for the love of God, block her number."

"She's blocked. But I don't trust her. You need to watch your back, make sure she doesn't go all stalker-chick on you."

"She's all talk, but if it makes you feel better, consider it done. Now, enough about crazy." She waved her hand, dismissing Nina from her universe. "I talked to Bill today. Well, he talked to me."

"What? When?"

"He surprised us by actually showing up to work. Stayed the whole time, pulled his weight. Then later at Talya's house, he took me aside." She recounted the conversation almost word for word. "Doesn't that sound like he wants *me* for the job? Can you believe it?"

"Yes. Sometimes I think the only one who undervalues you is you. The Mikaela I know will throw herself into the job from day one. Why wouldn't he want you? Shows what a good manager he is to not only recognize your worth, but also to recognize that the Righteous Three are totally wrong for where he wants the firm to go. If I were them, I'd be more worried about my job than hassling you."

"Shame you're not them. A big part of the job, if I get it, will be finding a way to work with them."

Casey waved a finger. "You got that reversed. Remember, as Bill's assistant you'll be top dog. They have to find a way to work with *you*."

"Don't have the job yet and The Three, as I intend to call them from now on, will probably, no, they will *definitely* work my last nerve between now and the time the job is filled."

"Aren't we the executive?" Casey laughed. "Seriously, I'm glad you decided to go for it. The extra pay won't hurt that spreadsheet of yours."

"I guess I should think about moving out if I get the job. I imagine you're ready to have the place to yourself again," she added, playing with the ruffle around the pillow. "Having a roommate thrust upon you with little notice was hard, I'm sure."

"Actually having you around is like freshman year, only better. Don't rush to move out on my account. I mean, who would I race, and beat, in the mornings?"

"Suzette?"

"We're a *long* way from that. Truthfully, the thought hasn't crossed my mind."

"Which one? Me moving out or her moving in?"

"Either. There will be no moving truck involved in the second date."

Mikaela lightly tapped Casey's thigh with her fist. "Anytime you change your mind let me know. A week's notice would be nice."

"For you, I can do seven days."

CHAPTER NINE

"Happy birthday to me," Sara whispered as she finished off another beer. Looking at the bottom of the glass, she wasn't sure if it was her fifth or sixth. Maybe she should have gone with shots, she thought. They seemed more festive, more in keeping with turning a year older, going another year without that Batman bike.

"Can't go there." She rubbed the back of her neck and looked into her glass again. When she wondered again if this was her fifth or sixth, she knew she was well on her way to being drunk. It didn't really matter if she was. She had already done her MLK volunteer work, she wasn't driving, and crawling home was still an option. It was her birthday and she could celebrate it any damn way she wanted. "So there," she said and lifted her glass so the solidly built bartender could see she was ready for another beer.

And if maybe she was drinking to keep away thoughts of what she'd find out tomorrow morning, that wasn't so bad, she told herself. It wasn't so bad if she forgot for a while that she'd soon know for sure her parents hadn't died in a car accident like she'd grown up believing. If she forgot, that she'd know for sure they'd been murdered in their own home, shot down while she was hiding. Her breathing hitched and she realized she'd gotten sucked back into the rabbit hole she was desperately trying to get out of.

Beer. She would think about drinking more beer, she told herself, accepting another cold draft. Taking a sip, she leaned back in the high-backed chair and tried to focus on how much she enjoyed drinking beer. It shouldn't have surprised her when instead Mikaela popped into her mind. It was hard to believe that only yesterday they had been in this same place, talking and laughing and having a good time. Now that she was here alone and close to being drunk, she could admit she wanted to be with Mikaela again. Admit she'd spent a good part of the afternoon fighting against the urge to pull out that scrap of paper and make the call.

Hell, she was fighting urges right now. She gripped the glass tightly, knowing she couldn't, wouldn't call. To do so would make her dependent on another person, and she'd sworn that would never happen to her. She didn't want to be someone who felt better at the sound of another's voice. Those days had been gone for a long time and she wasn't going to let them come back. She wasn't going to let Mikaela slowly inch into her life until she was a necessity and then have her turn around and leave. No. She was the one who left first. That's the way it had to be.

"You doing okay?" the bartender asked.

"I'm fine," she replied, managing to sound steady. "But this should probably be my last one. Got things to do tomorrow."

The bartender nodded. "Let me know when you need a taxi."

"I'm walking. Only live a few blocks over." She peered at the clock on the opposite wall. "What time is it anyway?"

"Almost ten."

Sara reared back and wobbled on the stool, surprised she'd been at it for over four hours. How many beers had she had? "Maybe could use an order of fries to soak up some of this beer."

"Coming right up."

She rubbed her temples, thinking about how much she would really regret this indulgence in the morning. At least she didn't have to get up as early. Jackson had agreed to give her the time off, and the Records Department didn't open till eight-thirty. Still, she wanted to be first in line, first one finished and out of the door.

"Damn!" She wasn't supposed to be thinking about that. She wasn't supposed to be thinking about anything.

The sound of loud voices drew her attention to the front of the restaurant. A group of women were laughing and jive talking about the basketball game they'd won. Wishing she could have been playing in that game, Sara took another sip of beer. Thursday. She'd go Thursday.

"Hey. Don't I know you?"

Sara didn't bother to look up. She didn't know anyone but Mikaela. But she wasn't supposed to be thinking about her either.

"Yo, white girl at the bar. Don't I know you?"

She blinked, looked right, then left. She was the only woman sitting at the bar, white or black. Curiosity piqued, she managed to swivel around and narrowed in on the speaker. It took a moment for recognition to get through her beer-soaked brain and she sat up straighter. "Know? I wouldn't call it that." That sounded better to Sara than the truth, and technically it was true. Stopping the other woman from hassling Mikaela did not constitute knowing.

The woman walked over to the bar. "I've seen you before. Oh yeah." Her lips twisted into an ugly snarl. "I remember now. You're the bitch who got in my business the other day."

"Technically it was also my business," Sara felt compelled to point out. "You were bothering a tenant in front of the building where I work. Doing my job, that's all."

"Bothering? I was talking to her, bitch."

"It's not so much talking when the other person does *not* want to participate in the conversation. If I remember correctly, Mikaela said she was done with you." And later that night she took me home with her, she thought. Imagining what the would-be bully would think of that made her grin.

"What the hell you smiling about?"

"Nothing. Absolutely nothing."

"Ooh, Nina, I think she just dissed you," the shortest in the group said. "You gonna let her get away with that?"

Sara's mind cleared enough to realize she might be in trouble. There was one of her and four of them. And the one of her was none too steady. "No dissing. Hold on." She blew out a breath, fished her cell phone out of her pocket and dialed the number from memory. "It's Sara."

"Hey! I can't believe you called. How's it going?"

"Could be better. There's this, uh, situation here and I need you to clear things up."

"Are you drunk?"

"I…yeah, probably."

"You need a ride?"

"Walking. I'm at the wings place and there's someone here who claims I got in her business the other day. Someone you know."

"And did you?"

The amusement in Mikaela's voice came through loud and clear. "See, no. Gotta make sure the tenants are safe or I'll get fired. Your fault," she added, after taking another look at Nina and her gang.

"Mine? I drove you to drink?"

"You had your part. Hold on." She handed the phone to Nina, hoping that would clear things up. "Tell her."

Nina gave her a hard look but took the phone. "Who the hell is this?"

Sara smiled her thanks when the bartender delivered fries and a glass of water along with a beady-eyed look at Nina and her posse. As Sara shook malt vinegar over the fries, she listened with enjoyment to Nina's struggle to get a word in against Mikaela's loud rant. Nina was still trying—and failing—when Mikaela's voice cut out. Sara wisely kept her smile to herself.

"What you think that proves, white girl? I got her number too."

She wiped her mouth and would have stood, but she wasn't sure she could so without stumbling. "Nothing to prove, black girl. Thought you'd appreciate talking to the source."

"This ain't no game, bitch. Whatever you *think* you have with Mikaela is done."

Laughter bubbled up as Sara was drinking water and she choked. "What is this, high school?" she rasped out, then cleared her throat. "Grow up. Mikaela's old enough to make her own decisions."

"I should kick your ass right now."

"No ass-kicking allowed." The bartender crossed her powerful arms, looking like she could bench-press a small car. "I suggest you find a table and order or find the door."

"You'd better be glad you ain't worth my time." Nina's lips curled in a sneer. "Let's roll up outta here."

"What was that about?" the bartender asked once Nina and her friends were gone.

"I wish I knew." Sara blew out a breath. "I could use another glass of water, and I'll probably need a cab as well." Her hand shook as she picked up a fry and tried to figure out what the hell she'd gotten herself into. Calling Mikaela when she was drunk had to be the height of stupidity. Lucky for her, she'd given the phone to Nina before she said anything she'd later regret. Maybe next time she'd thank Nina for distracting Mikaela by pissing her off before she planted a fist in her face. But probably not.

Sara had downed another glass of water by the time Mikaela arrived seven minutes later with Casey in tow. Her brain was still fuzzy, but it was clearer than it'd been when she made the call. Clear enough to appreciate how the purple sweater hugged Mikaela's chest and the silky strands falling on Mikaela's shoulders begged to be touched.

"Where is she?" Mikaela demanded even as she scanned the restaurant.

Sara was glad that fury wasn't directed at her. "She left shortly after you quit screaming at her."

"Did I not tell her to wait here for me?" Mikaela demanded and stomped her foot. "Did I not tell her that if she wanted to talk I was ready?" She fisted her hips.

Clichéd as it was, Sara thought Mikaela looked damn hot in a rage. "She sort of had to leave." Those mesmerizing eyes zeroed in on her and she swallowed hard. Not from fear, but from something entirely different.

"Explain."

"She wanted to kick my ass because I told her she didn't get to decide your life. Thankful to say, the big bartender over there stepped in and they decided to leave."

Mikaela gave a strangled scream. "I can't believe her! She ditched *me* six months ago and now she decides to act like some territorial idiot. Unbelievable. You okay?"

"Ah, yeah. Look, I swear I don't normally get drunk and call people."

"I know exactly where the blame lies. Why don't we give you a ride home for your trouble. You remember Casey, right?"

Sara smiled a hello. "I'll take you up on that. Let me settle up and I'll be ready to go." Sara left a generous tip along with her thanks. When she got off the stool, to her relief, the floor didn't try to buck her off.

"I'm sorry," Mikaela said as they exited the restaurant. "I never expected Nina to act like this. I…" She shook her head. "I don't know what to say except to tell you again I'm sorry you had to put up with that."

"Does she have reason to believe you're her girlfriend?"

"Hell no! She's acting the fool and I honestly don't know why. But you'd better believe I plan to have a conversation with her and soon." Mikaela smoothed a palm across her forehead. "Wish I could guarantee it'll do some good, but I can't. So please, please, please call me if she pulls any more stupid shit."

Sara put a hand on Mikaela's arm. "Better yet, no more getting drunk and stupid for me, okay?"

"Yeah, 'cause sober you could have taken all of them, right?"

She gave an easy grin. "Damn right! All jokes aside, I can and will take care of myself. Been doing it for most of my life."

* * *

Mikaela's bad mood swirled around her like an invisibility cloak when she got out of bed the next morning. She had no trouble getting on the treadmill, her energy fueled by thoughts of what she'd like to do to Nina, who'd been sneaky enough to dodge her calls last night. So the bitch can't be too crazy, she thought as she increased her pace to a mild jog. The rest of the workout was spent fantasizing about the moves she'd use to cut Nina down to size for blowing her chance with Sara, posse or no posse. The chance might have been smaller than a molecule, but it had been a chance. Mikaela was panting at the forty-minute mark, having dispatched the lot of them two or three times. During the cool-down walk she got real and thought about what she could actually do to get Nina off her back.

She arrived at her office, bristling with pent-up frustration. Sara wasn't in sight, and she considered that a good thing. The shame of last night's fiasco still rankled, thanks to Superstorm Nina. What really burned was it had all been for nothing. As her grandmother used to say, "she'd rather walk through Hell in gasoline drawers" than get back with Nina.

When more than one person on the elevator looked at her in alarm, Mikaela realized how hard she was breathing. She plastered on a smile as she took a deep breath, held it, then let it out slowly and changed the channel in her brain. She had more important things to worry about than Nina and, though it hurt to acknowledge it, the nonexistent chance she had with Sara. Things like going after that promotion. The first step was doing an outstanding job with Bill's meeting materials. After all, the work had to be good enough to silence any grumblings when she landed the job. Not silence, she decided as she exited the elevator. They had to blow any misgivings about her ability to do the job out of the water.

"Mikaela."

The strident tone burst her bubble of world domination, and with reluctance, she slowed her step as she approached Christine. Obviously someone had been waiting for her. "Morning. How are you today?"

"What's this I hear about you doing work for Bill?" Christine sounded as pissed off as she looked.

"I'm doing fine by the way, thank you," she said, calling on her Southern belle persona instead of the ghetto fabulous Shawniqua. She didn't have the job yet. "As for what you may or may not have heard, why, I can't begin to guess. You know how the rumors fly around here." She smiled sweetly.

"Is it true that Jolene asked you to do some work for one of Bill's meetings? Why would she do that? She didn't ask me and I'm first in line for her job."

Mikaela could only think delusion was an ugly master—especially first thing in the morning. "It's true I have been practicing, but I have to tell you, I haven't quite been able to get mind reading down cold. Come back next week. I might have conquered it by then." She wanted to laugh at the look of bewildered rage on Christine's face. That too was an ugly thing. "But you know, I have a better idea. If you have concerns about what I'm working on, take it up with my boss. Problem solved. You have a wonderful day now." She brushed by Christine, adding an exaggerated sway to her behind.

After putting away her things, she sauntered to the break room, fixed herself a cup of coffee and took some time to gloat. She was allowed because, after all, she'd been chased down, questioned like she was a criminal and had still cut Christine down to size. She laughed, remembering the look on Christine's face. Maybe the old biddy would think twice about huffing and puffing next time. Too bad there hadn't been a bucket of water nearby. Christine might not have been liquefied, but she would have lost that polished look she seemed to love.

"Good times." Mikaela toasted herself and then returned to her desk, her mood greatly improved.

"Morning." Talya walked up to Mikaela's desk thirty minutes later and dropped off a fruit cup. "Healthier than donuts, no?"

"Thanks." Her stomach had already forgotten the yogurt consumed for breakfast. "I should warn you that Christine's on the warpath this morning."

"Don't tell me you bitch-slapped her without me around to see it?"

Mikaela smiled at Talya's playful pout. "Thought about it, but no. She found out I'm working on that stuff for Bill and demanded to know why Jolene hadn't asked her. She *is* first in line for that job."

"I assume you didn't tell her it's because she hasn't had an original thought in fifty years." Talya's eyes narrowed to slits. "If she has the time to come to you and whine, then she must have those reports I asked her to pull together. Set up a meeting in fifteen to discuss her progress. Brannon's old office will do."

"More than happy to." Mikaela smiled. Her day really was looking up.

Talya returned ten minutes later. "Have you checked for postings yet? Bill said any day."

"I guess I know what my next task should be."

"You do. After my little powwow with Christine, I'll head directly to my nine-thirty with Bill." Talya checked her schedule. "God, then on to the next three meetings. It's getting so I don't remember what my office looks like."

"Too bad this is happening when you have one of your people in training and the other out on paternity leave."

"Remind me again. Is Gerri coming back Friday or Monday?"

"Monday. The training's over tomorrow, but she took a couple days' personal leave to hang out with an old college friend."

"Gives me extra time to figure out ways to foist some of these minor meetings off on her. Be sure and check about the job before you go to lunch" was Talya's parting shot.

"Nag, nag, nag," she muttered as the sound of Talya's footsteps faded away. But to be on the safe side, she scrolled through the job openings. And there it was—Executive Assistant. Her excitement built as she read the job description.

The responsibilities had been changed, making it a stepping stone to entry management level. "Whoa." The requirements had been updated as well. There were going to be some very unhappy people. Too bad she wouldn't be around to catch the expression on three particular faces.

She reread the job description, plugged in her personal flash drive and updated the cover letter she'd worked on the night before, highlighting her experience and training that matched the duties.

The rest of the morning passed without further provocations and she was able to make good inroads on the meeting materials. At five till noon, she backed up her work, grabbed the folder with copies of the job description and her cover letter, and then grabbed leftovers from the fridge and headed to Marianna's break room. She passed Ilene by the stairwell. As she geared up for battle, Ilene glared but walked by without a word. Somehow that seemed worse than a snarky remark.

She spotted Marianna waving from a table in the back of the break room. "Crowded today, huh?"

"Practically had to push somebody out of the way to snag the last table," Marianna replied. "Please tell me some of the Brunswick stew made it."

"Saved it just for you."

"Sit. I'll do microwave duty."

When Marianna returned, Mikaela was enjoying a Diet Cherry Coke, her price for sharing her leftovers. "Wish we had these upstairs."

"Then what would I bribe you with? Hey, were you a little sore this morning?" Marianna settled in across from Mikaela and scooped a generous portion of Brunswick stew onto her plate. "I woke up this morning and thought Erin must have beaten me during the night."

"How many times do I have to tell you to keep any talk of your depraved sex life to yourself?" She laughed when Marianna stuck out her tongue. "Surprisingly, I felt fine. Well, my muscles did anyway. Come to think of it, I was too pissed off at Nina's actions to feel anything but anger this morning." It hadn't been enough for Mikaela to vent to Casey. She'd called Marianna and given her an earful as well.

"You still mad about that? I thought I talked you down last night."

"That would be yes for the first, no for the second. But we can trash her more later. First, read this." She handed Marianna a copy of the job description. "Then this." She passed her the cover letter and took another sip of her drink while she waited. "Well, what do you think?"

"I want this job." Marianna looked up. "But seeing as you covered yourself so well in the *cover* letter, why would I bother trying? If they don't hire you, they're crazy."

"So the cover letter works?"

"Big time. How long is it open for?"

"Two weeks. Two long weeks."

"Oh yeah, you're going to be catching hell. This dumps The Three in the junk mail folder."

"I passed Ilene on the way down and she didn't open her mouth. That's some serious fury."

"Probably on her way to put the finishing touches on the voodoo doll that, strangely enough, looks just like you."

"Not funny. I think they'll be more direct than that. In fact, I'd be surprised if she or Christine don't complain to HR."

"Let them. They have nothing to complain about. Maybe in their little fantasy world they get to have a say, but not in the real world the rest of us inhabit."

"Like that will stop either one of them. You watch, somehow they're going to find a way to blame this on me."

"Don't see how they can. Job qualifications are on HR. Once again you're trying to make problems where there are none."

"Easy for you to say."

Marianna smiled. "It really is. Now on to your real crisis. I did some thinking after we hung up last night."

"And we both know how dangerous that can be. But go ahead."

"Okay, now remember I'm just the messenger, but have you considered Nina's acting this way because she thinks she's been replaced by a white woman?"

"What she's doing is being stupid and childish by lashing out at the first handy person because she can't have her way." Mikaela exhaled, fighting off anger at the memory of the night before. "Why should it matter to her who I go out with anyway? Black, brown, white or green. It's none of her business because, hey, we're not together anymore—by her decree."

"I'm just saying."

"Saying what exactly?"

"Okay, maybe she never struck me as the tolerant type, if you know what I mean."

A rock found its way into Mikaela's gut and weighed her down. "What aren't you telling me, Marianna?"

"I overheard her say something about me. It was only one time though."

Mikaela put down her fork. "One time is too many. Why didn't you tell me?"

"She didn't realize I was there. And okay, it was her house, she can say what she wants."

"No, she can't, not and have a girlfriend who's half white. I may not have anything to do with my egg donor and her family, but that's like insulting part of me. And she'd be the first person to get pissed off if you did the same thing to her. Rightfully so."

"My saying anything was only going to cause trouble." Marianna chewed on her lip. "It didn't seem worth it at the time."

"I'm sorry you felt that way. My grandmother raised me to see people for who they are, not make decisions based on their skin color." She took a sip of her soda and decided she needed to take it down a notch. "Sorry. Let me crawl off my soapbox."

"Hey, I agree with you. I may judge women by their yummy butchly exterior, but never by their heritage."

"I know. I mean, why limit yourself? Grab the rainbow."

"I can drink to that." Marianna raised her can and took a sip. "We okay?"

"As long as you promise to speak up next time. You could have saved me from wasting a few months of my life, you know." She picked up her fork, then put it back down again. "God, how did I not know she was a complete asshole?"

"The sex, the hot body, the good looks? Take your pick."

"Yeah, yeah. If I give up shallowness, do you think she'll disappear?"

"No."

"As my friend you could at least pretend."

"As your friend, I want to know what you're going to do about her."

"I'd like to go all Warrior Princess on her ass, but since we both know that's not an option, I'll try reason. Use avoidance as a backup."

"Actually, I meant about Sara."

"Avoidance works there too. What else can I do?" She covered her cheeks, knowing from the heat of them that she was blushing. "Anything else is too embarrassing to contemplate. Think about it, Marianna. She's minding her own business, and the next minute she's getting threatened by some woman she doesn't even know and because of me. If you were her, would you want to have anything to do with me? Be honest."

"When you put it that way." Marianna frowned. "Damn Nina. If you like, you can take Erin when you go talk to her."

She actually considered it for a hot second. Erin was just shy of six feet of solid muscle and had kickboxing trophies. "I'd better not widen the circle of trouble."

"She wouldn't mind. She's got a little non-sexual crush on you anyway."

"Shut up. Now I'll feel funny the next time I see her."

CHAPTER TEN

Sara didn't think she'd ever been so happy for her shift to end. She'd finally lost the fight with the low-level headache that had plagued her since shortly after eight thirty when she discovered her visit to the Police Records Department was a waste of time. Reports took the same amount of time to process whether you showed up in person or mailed in the request.

It hadn't been a total loss actually. She'd had the pleasure of finding out that reports older than seven years could take up to ten days longer. Ten *business* days, she reminded herself and trudged up the stairs to level three of the parking garage. Because she'd been late, her usual space on the first level had not been available.

Now all she wanted was to go home, plop her butt on the sofa and veg out in front of the TV for a couple hours. Then maybe she could clear her head and figure out how to keep her mind occupied until the report arrived, until she could feel like herself again.

She unlocked her car and wondered if she knew what being her old self even felt like. Her old self was six years old. No way she could go back to that. No way she wanted to go back to that.

She climbed into the car, trying to come up with what being her old self really meant and if a piece of paper confirming there had been no accident could change anything. She sighed and realized it couldn't. She had her memory back and it wasn't going away this time. If she was lucky, she might eventually be able to let go of the pain. But even then, dealing with the way her parents had died was going to be hard to get her brain around. Car accidents happened with regularity; but someone she knew getting murdered...

Sara rested her head against the steering wheel, her heart heavy. Being murdered like that—shot down in their own home—brought with it its own set of questions. Questions she wasn't sure she wanted to ask, much less have answered. Questions that brought the decency of her parents to the forefront. She didn't think she could bear it if they turned out to be criminals, killed because of the lifestyle they'd chosen.

"No. No," she said, shaking her head. Her memories of them might be clouded with the veil of childhood, but they had been loving parents and they had loved each other.

The thought that even bad guys could be loving parents lodged in her head and her certainty dropped a notch. Didn't matter. Criminal or not, they'd been her parents, they'd taken good care of her. They'd given her love. That's what she needed to hang on to, to remember. That was what was important.

She was backing out when the obvious smacked her on the back of her head. "Idiot!" She'd forgotten about the old newspapers. Before she'd only been concerned with articles about interstate pileups. She needed to head back now and search for murders. Pulling forward and parking, she grabbed her bag and hurried downstairs, then cut through the building to cross Peachtree Street to the library.

The same librarian was there to help her get set up. She found a tiny article, all but hidden in the back of the local section. The information was no more than she already knew. The article simply stated that a young couple had been found by their young daughter, murdered in their home. Names were withheld until next of kin notification. On the one hand, Sara was pleased to see that the names of the police officers called to the scene meshed with her memory. On the other hand, it meant that it *was* a memory, that it had happened the way she dreamt it.

The article in the afternoon paper wasn't much more forthcoming. The detectives assigned to the case were named, and of course, details were being held back to aid the police investigation. There was no mention of suspects. Sara jotted down the names of the detectives to aid in further searches.

The rest of the week there were more articles with more information about the murder victims and their seven-year-old child, including names. It was surreal for Sara to read the articles, to know they were about her and her family. Later that week, the time of death was reported, along with a statement from a witness who claimed to have seen a black van parked on the street around the same time. The police appealed to the public for help but made no mention of possible motive.

Finally two weeks and one day after the murders, Sara found what she was looking for. There on the front page under the bolded title "Murder Mystery Solved"' was a photo of three men in shackles leaving a police car. After devouring the article, she no longer blamed her aunt for keeping the truth from her. Hell, she wished she had kept the truth from herself.

Pressing her fingers against her eyes didn't stop the tears this time. They poured out like giant drops of rain as the senselessness of her parents' deaths squeezed her heart. Her parents hadn't died because they were involved in any criminal activity. No, they died because some idiot transposed his numbers and ended up at the wrong house. After killing her parents, he and his partners ransacked the house, not looking for her as the police had initially theorized, but for their boss's stolen money and drugs.

An anonymous tip had led the police to one Keyshawn Murphy and one of the guns used in the shooting. Hoping for leniency, Keyshawn rolled on his partners. Sara didn't know whether to be glad or upset when she saw the follow-up story about the death of Keyshawn and one of his partners while they were out on bail and the disappearance of the third suspect. There was speculation they'd been taken out because of their very public failure.

She removed the microfilm from the machine, feeling numb. She had her so-called closure, knew the how, the who and the why. One day it might bring her comfort. But not today. Today she would mourn the loss of her family.

* * *

The streetlights were on when Mikaela trudged up the hill to home. A last-minute request for a report had sent Talya into a tizzy, which led to both of them working late to ensure it would be at headquarters first thing in the morning. So now she was tired and hungry in addition to being mad.

Not surprisingly, she hadn't been able to reach Nina, despite leaving numerous messages. Mikaela figured she was hiding out, hoping the incident would blow over, be forgotten. Well, that crazy bitch had another thing coming. Threatening Sara wasn't going to be forgotten as if it never happened. How could she forget when she'd spent too much time today thinking about that stolen infinitesimal chance?

As usual, her thighs quivered in relief upon reaching the gate as her brain told them the hardest part of the trek was over. But relief quickly vanished as soon as she spotted a big, black SUV parked in front of Casey's condo. A quick check of the vanity tag, 2G2BT, confirmed her suspicion. How the hell had Nina gotten through the security gate? And why? Her step quickened and anger, banked the whole day, flashed over. If Nina wanted some nerve, she'd damn well give her some.

Casey opened the door before Mikaela could get it unlocked. "I guess you know who's here."

"Yeah," she said, her smile tight. "Seems I owe apologies all the way around."

"Don't apologize. I let her in."

"Why? I was hoping to keep you and anyone else out of this mess."

"I thought the sooner you got this over with, the better. For all of us." Casey gave her a half smile. "And here she doesn't have her posse to back her up. It's two to one and I like those odds."

"Smart," she said and relaxed her shoulders. "I like those odds too. And now I don't have to drag my tired ass to her house and lay siege."

"She's parked in the kitchen. I wanted a chance to talk to you first. Make sure I didn't have to hustle her out."

Mikaela propped her bag against the wall, threw her coat over the coat rack and took a deep breath. "Let's do this."

"You go ahead. I'll stay out here on alert." Casey stood ramrod straight, her hands behind her back.

"Okay, GI Jane. I feel so much safer now." When Mikaela entered the kitchen, Nina was standing by the sink, looking out of the window onto the minuscule patio. "Well, don't you have some nerve, showing your face around here."

Nina turned, her smile as arrogant as ever. "You're the one who's been trying to get a hold of me. Last time I checked, it was six calls. Miss me much?"

"God, you're an ass. You know damn well why I've been calling you, and it has nothing to do with missing you. I didn't miss you after you kicked me out, why the hell would I miss you now?"

"Come on, Mike, last night was simply a misunderstanding. No need for upset. If you want, I'll even apologize to that wanna-be security guard."

"Misunderstanding? That's what you're going with?" Laughing more from frustration than humor, she grabbed her head and squeezed, afraid it was going to blow apart. She'd obviously crossed the threshold to an alternate universe. There could be no other explanation.

"Let me see if I got this right. Ordering Sara to leave me alone was a misunderstanding?" Nina nodded. "It's been a long day, so please explain to me how that could possibly have been a misunderstanding. I'm obviously confused. And while you're at it, explain about the part where you threatened to kick her ass and the kind of misunderstanding that was."

Nina held up her hands. "I don't know nothing about that. Not my fault when some white girl thinks I'm threatening her just because I'm black. I was trying to figure out where I knew her from. That's it."

"So this is all black and white, huh?" Mikaela hoped the disgust she felt showed on her face. "You're a liar, Nina. A bad one. And guess what? I don't have to deal with liars in my personal life, so bye-bye."

"Who you calling a liar?"

"That would be *you*," she said, jabbing her finger in Nina's direction. "I don't know what's going on in that tiny little brain of yours and frankly I don't want to know. What I do want is for you to stay away from me, stay away from my friends, stay away from my job. Hope that's simple enough for you."

"What? You think you can tell me what to do?" Nina's lips twisted into a sneer. "You're delusional."

"Why are you still here? I'm done with you."

"Just like that, huh? You ain't gonna give me a chance to say my side."

Mikaela grabbed her head again and screamed. "Enough! I don't know why in your limited wisdom you suddenly decided you have to have me when six months ago you couldn't get rid of me fast enough. But know this. I do not care," she said slowly. "Please get that through your incredibly thick skull. I don't care about you. I don't want to care about you. I never will care about you again. How hard is that to get?" She saw movement out of the corner of her eye and figured Casey had been drawn by her theatrics.

Nina's eyes burned hot. "You always did think you were more than you are. Don't know why I'm wasting my time on your bougie ass when there are plenty of other women out there. Real black women who appreciate a sista."

"Don't you dare make this about race," she said, her voice rough and shaky. "This is about me and you and the fact that I don't like you anymore. Wouldn't like you if you were white."

"Now you're breaking my heart."

Mikaela wanted the feel of Nina's thick neck under her hands. Wanted to squeeze it until her eyes popped out. But she didn't because the bitch might like it. "You don't have one to break." She turned to Casey. "Will you show our *guest* the door, please?"

Casey's smile was anything but friendly. "My pleasure. After you, Nina."

Once they were gone, Mikaela splashed cold water on her face. She couldn't remember the last time she'd been this upset, this frustrated with another person.

"She's gone," Casey announced, leaning against the door jamb. "She says for good this time."

"Good." She patted her face with a paper towel. "Can you believe the bull she was slinging? Misunderstanding? Really? Misunderstanding, my black butt. And yes, despite what you might have heard, I have nothing against black butts." She exhaled. "Forget the last part. I know you know who I am."

"She obviously doesn't." Casey slung an arm over Mikaela's shoulders. "Never has, so you need to let that go. She's not worth another second of your thoughts."

"Part of me knows. The anger part wants to hang on. Prejudiced bitch." She rested her head against Casey's arm. "How did my life get to be such a mess? Crazy, asshat ex-girlfriend, who, for reasons known only to her, decides she wants me back. This despite my apparent lack in the blackness department. Where did this come from?" She pushed back, looked Casey in the eye. "Did you know she was like that?"

"Hell no. You know I would have said something to her, then you. My best friend is part white. No dissin' that on my watch."

"Why were we never girlfriends? You're perfect for me."

"Too busy being friends."

"True. Okay, from now on I pay better attention."

"I say from now on, don't be too busy trying to convince yourself you are in love."

Mikaela pouted. "Ouch. You should be nicer to me. Don't forget about my other problem."

"Sara, who you swore was a one-night stand? That problem?"

"This is not the time for 'I told you so.' It's not my fault she doesn't want to count past one despite the good times outside the bedroom. When you think about it, it's not fair. I mean, would it be so bad to have Nina not want me and Sara panting after me?"

"Depends. Would Sara get the crazy in that exchange?"

"I'm not in the mood for philosophical discussions. What I want is something high in calories and low in nutritional values." She opened the fridge, then closed it quickly to block out the sight of the good for you food. "Why did I let you talk me into going to the Farmers' Market?"

"Your idea. Remember the whole 'needing to lose weight, eat healthy' push?"

"Adding insult to injury, Case. I want pizza. No, I deserve pizza. It's been that kind of day." Thumbing through the menus attached to the fridge, she pulled off the one for Carnus Pizzeria.

"Don't tell me you changed your mind about the job?"

"Pizza first." She speed-dialed Carnus and, as a concession to her diet, ordered a medium veggie pizza. If she added a salad, it would be almost healthy. "Thirty minutes to pizza heaven."

"Now maybe you can tell me what's going on."

"The job got posted today, totally jazzed up and with new requirements. Can I say I so want that job? But anyway, in true Christine fashion, she stormed into HR and pitched a fit about the job being tailored for some people, thus giving them an unfair advantage. Of course, she applied anyway. How do I know this, you ask? I'll tell you. Her crony, Irene, made a point of telling someone when I just so happened to be in hearing distance. Then people started looking at me like I had something to do with it." She opened the fridge and grabbed salad makings. "You're having salad, by the way. Okay, so if that's not bad enough, Christine's waiting for me first thing, all pissy. Somehow she found out about the work I'm doing for Bill. And get this. She demanded to know why *she* wasn't asked to do it. Seriously, though?" Mikaela grabbed a knife and sliced the cucumber with more force than necessary. "As if she could. It wouldn't have been so bad except I was already pissy myself about you know who."

"The court concedes you do deserve pizza."

* * *

At ten o'clock that night, Sara threw back the covers and admitted she wasn't going to fall asleep. This despite being stupidly tired. Between the breakdown at the library and a six-mile run, she'd been sure deep, dreamless sleep was in her future. She'd been wrong again.

Tabitha blinked at her, then found another spot to curl up.

"Sorry," she muttered and stepped into the sweatpants she'd recently discarded. Another night spent watching TV was obviously in her future.

Once settled on the lumpy couch, she flipped through channels and settled on an old episode of *Rizzoli & Isles*. Soon though, her thoughts wandered. Not, as she expected, to her parents, but to Mikaela and last night. She'd managed to get through the day without seeing, let alone speaking to, Mikaela. On the one hand, that was good. It spared Mikaela another apology and another look of embarrassment on her face. On the other hand, she was curious about the situation with the ex. Wanted to make sure the ex wouldn't cause Mikaela problems.

Not that it had anything to do with her—Mikaela or the situation with her ex. Sure, Mikaela had helped her through a bad patch, had lain in her arms after making her feel more alive than she'd ever allowed herself to feel. Not necessarily a good thing for her lifestyle. She didn't want another woman to have the ability to make her feel anything but lust. Maybe a little mental stimulation to fuel the lust. "And how dumb does that sound?"

Sara sighed, flipping the remote from one hand to the next. Emotions never did what you wanted them to, making them a good thing to stay away from. And she'd been successful in doing just that until she picked Atlanta as her next place to live. If not for that, she might have gone her whole life without remembering. Gone without the nightmares filled with blood and tears. Without meeting a woman who wouldn't stay out of her mind. Without a scrap of paper she always carried around, even though she knew the number by heart.

Her phone was in her pocket, right where she left it. Without giving herself time to think it through, she dialed Mikaela's number.

"Please tell me Nina's not threatening you again?"

"No. No. I, uh, I didn't get a chance to see you today, and you know, I wanted you to know I don't blame you for last night. You can't control other people's behavior."

"Thanks, but I still feel guilty."

"Not your fault if she can't accept rejection."

"Funny you should say that. She originally dumped me."

"Then she must be crazier than I thought. What's her deal?"

"You'll know as soon as I do. But since I convinced her there's no going back, we may never know. And, you know, I can live with that."

"I can live with not having to worry about her. That's the first time I've ever been threatened in public. I can skip the repeat."

"Does that mean you've been threatened in private? Do tell."

"Me and my big mouth. Maybe we should move on to something else."

Mikaela laughed. "Did you manage to have any fun volunteering?"

"I'm going to say you were right. But only if you don't crow about it."

"Killjoy. Where's my fun in that?"

"No pouting. Okay. You're allowed a teeny tiny bit."

"So..."

"'A needle pulling thread'?"

"God, no. As in a teeny tiny bit of 'I told you so.' What in the world are you talking about?"

Sara groaned. "Flashback. It's a song from *The Sound of Music*. My aunt loved that movie. Loved as in she watched it over and over and over and sang along so loudly I could never get away from it. Seems it's still stuck in my subconscious."

"Now I remember. That's the song those kids were singing as they ran through the streets wearing clothes made from ugly curtains. The dad, was like, all upset about the singing when he should have been mortified that they were wearing hideous outfits in public."

"That's your take on the movie?"

"Sure, there was the whole stand-your-ground-against-tyranny stuff. When you think about it though, he was a tyrant himself. So he softened up when he married the nun, but come on, I bet a year later he was back to his old controlling self. She would have been better off staying with the nuns. I mean, there was that cute one with the adorable accent."

"Interesting take on the movie. I believe my aunt's head would have exploded by this point."

"Hey, I call them like I see them. It's a skill."

"It's, uh, something. What about you? Any movie overkills in your past?"

"With my grandmother around? Even her favorite movie only got watched once a year. Any more than that and she thought it diluted the impact."

"Was she strict about everything?"

"No. She was great. Stepped right in when the woman who gave birth to me opted out. Sure she was old-fashioned in a lot of ways, but they worked to my advantage. I'm where I am today because she took her responsibility seriously. I'll never forget that."

Sara envied the obvious affection in Mikaela's voice. "How old were you when your mother left?"

"Real young. It was no biggie because I had my grandmother, my play mom and enough relatives to fill a stadium. There are few people who can compete with my stories of crazy relatives, let me tell you. But here we are talking about me again. Not that I mind talking about me, as I'm sure you've figured out.

However, you were supposed to be telling me about the fun time I knew you would have."

"Don't blame me if it's not as entertaining as your stories." Sara decided to share the story of her persistent three-foot-tall helper who, for reasons unknown to her, attached himself to her side for the whole day.

"So after it was done, there wasn't anything I could do but let him sit in my lap and share my food. Not when he was the boss's grandson."

"And yet you somehow survive the ordeal and have a good time. Was he as cute as he sounds?"

"I guess. Yeah," she added grudgingly. "He gives sticky kisses though. And sticky hugs."

"They do tend to be sticky at that age."

"You...You don't have any, do you?"

"God, no! But when you have a big family, they come standard with every event. You have to be quick to dodge a lap plop and I never seem to be quick enough."

"You don't sound like you mind."

"Not really. They cuddle so well, and when they start acting up, you can give them back."

"Which I was eventually able to do with my shadow."

"You know, you don't sound like you minded all that much."

"Okay, you got me. It was kind of neat. But I should let you go."

After ending the call, Sara leaned back and smiled. Mikaela had come through again and taken Sara's mind off her problems. No, she thought, Mikaela had done more than that. She'd cheered her up. Maybe tomorrow Sara would decide if that was a good or a bad superpower.

CHAPTER ELEVEN

Sara pump-faked, waited until her opponent was off balance, then took her shot. Nothing but net, she noted with a satisfied smile. Two points and game over. She slapped hands and accepted congrats from her teammates as they made their way to the bleachers and their belongings.

"You up for a beer, superstar?" Jackie asked, toweling off sweat.

"Not tonight." Sara pulled on sweatpants, ignoring the question in Carmen's eyes. She'd expended enough energy, and now she was ready to go home and chill. Maybe crawl into bed early and actually sleep the whole night.

"You sure?" Carmen trailed a finger down Sara's arm.

"Maybe next time," she replied kindly, not tempted by the heat from Carmen's touch or the invitation in her eyes. How could she be when there was only one woman stubbornly clinging to her thoughts?

"Call if you change your mind later. I'll be available." Carmen's smile was full of promises.

Not going to happen, Sara thought, even as she nodded. Aside from her jumbled feelings for Mikaela, Carmen had been strictly a one-night deal. The sex had been enjoyable, but there was nothing else to draw her back to that path. With a casual wave, she headed out.

Outside, she zipped her jacket as the cold wind chilled her sweaty skin. Maybe she should consider making her next home in the Southwest, she thought, and started her car. Or even southern California, and maybe for longer than a year. But that would require more planning than she usually did. Any job wouldn't do. Not when it had to last. Pulling out of the parking lot, she mulled over what her next job could be.

She'd had plenty over the years. She needed to make a list, pick out the ones she'd liked best and go from there. Once she had a short list, she could research cities, see the type of jobs available. She'd been putting money aside with the idea of eventually going to college, doing something with the brain her high-school math teacher claimed she had. That was something else to throw into the mix.

"This is good." She pulled into the parking space near the door. She was actually planning, thinking ahead for a change. Thinking about a future, her future. She wasn't sure a future would be complete, though, if she never made a connection to another human being.

Unbidden, thoughts of Mikaela surfaced and Sara sighed. As much as she'd tried, Sara couldn't get Mikaela out of her mind. And the more she thought about her, the more she didn't want to think about her. She realized in hindsight that she shouldn't have made that call Tuesday night. She'd been lower than low and instead of going out and picking up a woman for meaningless sex, she'd called Mikaela. And damn if she hadn't ended up feeling better anyway.

She'd been brainwashed somehow that night, she decided. That was the only explanation for her giving serious consideration now to trying something new. Something like getting to know Mikaela outside of the bedroom. Most people would call that dating, but Sara wasn't sure she was ready for that big a step. She'd thought they could start small, be friends, then work toward something else.

Which was a little crazy and explained why, when she'd woken up Wednesday morning besieged by old doubts and old fears, she'd dismissed the notion. And why, for the past two days, she'd kept her distance, treating Mikaela no differently than she did any of the other tenants. Sure, she knew she was being stupid, cowardly even, but so far that hadn't been enough to make her call or try to explain her behavior. Hadn't been enough for her to take a chance, find the off button so she could get out of the loop she was stuck in.

Tabitha greeted her with a rumbling hello and a head-butt against Sara's leg before looking toward the kitchen as if asking for another dinner.

"No more food or you'll get too fat." As she stooped to pet the purring cat, a variety of aches and pains made themselves known. She'd pushed herself hard in the third and decisive game and was now paying the price for no longer being in her twenties. Another reason to start thinking of the future.

"Soak time," she told Tab, stretching out her back.

Ten minutes later, she slid into the tub and exhaled. To her sore muscles the hot water felt like heaven. Resting her head against the back of the tub, she closed her eyes and replayed the last game. She might be on the verge of climbing into the top half of her thirties, but the moves were still there. Not as fast or as slick as they once were and yet enough for where she was now. Enough to score the winning points. She was going to have to look into a monthly membership before her pass ran out, make Thursday night ball a regular thing for as long as she was in Atlanta.

Her lease ran for another seven months, giving her enough time to figure out what she wanted from life. Her parents were gone; that was a given. Nothing she did or didn't do had caused their death. It was one of those "shit happens" things, a tragedy. But wherever her parents were, Sara had enough good memories of them to know they would have been glad she'd stayed hidden, glad she was still alive. They'd be glad, too, to know she was living her life fully. That's what she should focus on, damn it, and not on running away from it like she was doing now. On *living*, not on moving here, moving there, always looking and yet never spending the time to find.

Living fully also meant letting people in past the barriers she'd built around herself. That brought her back to Mikaela and her fears. Since she couldn't seem to evict Mikaela from her thoughts, the fears had to go.

"Tomorrow." She'd start with the new her tomorrow.

* * *

Mikaela stared at the time on her monitor and willed it to change. It was Friday afternoon and she'd been ready to leave hours ago. After staying late three nights in a row, she considered it only fair she be allowed to leave early. Any minute Talya would be back from her last meeting of the day and decide it was time to close shop. Any minute, if the stupid clock would move faster.

As she closed her eyes and rubbed her neck, Mikaela envisioned going home, changing into her rattiest sweats and spending the evening with a good book. Not exactly exciting plans, but someone had shut her down after their last conversation, so she didn't feel like doing anything else.

With a sigh, she opened her eyes and caught the startled expression on Debbie Larson's face. Debbie was looking extra mousy today in a gray suit that seemed to leech what little color she had out of her complexion. Add to that the graying brown hair and a pair of unattractive glasses and you got someone who Mikaela thought must not want to stand out. "Help you?"

Debbie shot a glance over her shoulder. "I wanted to wish you good luck with…you know," she added quietly. "And to tell you to watch out."

Mikaela hid her surprise. Based on past history, this had to be a trick, courtesy of Christine and Ilene. They'd been glaring at her all week, and Debbie rarely did anything on her own. "Uh, thanks. What about you?"

"I've decided not to apply. I don't meet the qualifications and the job does come with some challenges."

"That's what makes it worth having."

"I hope you think so after. You really need to—"

"What's the game here, Debbie? Your good buddies send you over to get friendly, feel me out for info, what?"

Debbie's lips thinned and she pushed at her glasses. "No game. I hear things. Ugly things."

"Ugly things?" She rolled her eyes. "Why me? If they know I've applied, then they know who else has applied."

"Don't be naïve. Everyone knows you're the most qualified." Debbie actually smiled. "They don't like that at all."

Mikaela shook her head, watching Debbie leave as quietly as she'd arrived. The weird kept getting weirder and now she had "ugly things" to worry about as well.

"Finally," Talya said singsong, her arms loaded with folders. "Time to go. I'm dropping this stuff in my office. We'll deal with it and anything else that comes up first thing Monday."

"There is a goddess." Mikaela logged off her computer, cleared her desk and waited for Talya to join her. She didn't have long to wait.

"Take me to Margaritaville."

"And make your man jealous? I think not." Mikaela led the way to the elevator.

"Ha, ha. FYI, expect to get a letter and a certificate from HQ thanking you for helping coordinate the volunteer deal." Talya pushed the down button a couple of times. "They were impressed with the number of volunteers we had and I made sure they know that was your doing. They've promised T-shirts for next year, maybe goody bags."

"I could make that work. Need to start earlier next year. Get even more people. Maybe add a little competition to the mix."

"Does that mean I can put your name down as lead coordinator again?"

"Sure. You know it'll only take a little nudge to get Pat to be the other coordinator if you're ready to give up the title."

"Only if we have the after-party at my place again. That was fun."

"I'll put you down." Mikaela pushed the down button for good measure. "Sorry. I am so ready to get home, slip into something comfortable and let a book take me away."

"That's your plan for the night? You're single. Shouldn't you be out acting wild, doing things you'll regret in the morning?"

Mikaela laughed. "That's on my schedule for Saturday. I do get a night of rest."

"Honey, that's what Sunday is for."

* * *

"Come on. I've met her and she's really nice." Casey nudged Mikaela's bare foot with her hand.

Mikaela moved her feet. "*Nice* is known in blind-date speak as synonymous with *ugly* and/or *socially awkward*."

"Wrong. She's not a blind date and she's cute. I think you'll like her."

Mikaela put her book aside and looked up at Casey. She'd been enjoying pretending to read while stoically wallowing in pity about the state of her love life. Not that she had one of those anyway, judging by the silence of her phone. "She's a doctor. What could I possibly have in common with a doctor?"

"Not a medical doctor. A PhD. If you come to dinner you can find out what you have in common. Come on, Mikaela. You'd be doing me a favor, and it's not a date. Suzette thinks Beth'll be more comfortable if someone else is there."

"You swear Beth doesn't think I'm her date?"

"I swear. Dinner's on me, so no worries about money."

"Yeah?" Money, or lack thereof, was always a spreadsheet consideration when dining out. She swung her legs over the side of the bed, then gave Casey a steely-eyed look. "Okay, I'll do it, but be aware you're going to owe me big if she's boring. And you don't want to know what you'll owe if she thinks I'm her date."

"Then I have nothing to worry about. We should leave in an hour. Keep in mind there's a good chance we'll hit a club after. Suzette's firm scored some complimentary passes to the latest hot spot."

"Club?" Mikaela's lethargy was suddenly gone. "You should have said that first."

Casey rolled her eyes. "Now you tell me. And an hour means *an hour*."

"I'll be ready." Walking to her closet, she threw the door open. Tonight would be a good night to wear the wide-legged designer jeans she'd gotten ridiculously cheap after digging forever through the sale tables at Macy's. And if they did go dancing, she'd want to wear the little red shirt that was all about cleavage under the fitted, long-sleeved purple shirt, which was "this is not a date" casual. Satisfied with her ensemble, she took a shower, put on perfumed lotion and fixed her hair in a stylish French braid. She dithered back and forth, but finally decided on the deep red lipstick. She had to look cute.

With five minutes to spare, she paraded into the living room. Casey of course was already there, wearing a white turtleneck sweater and jeans. With her hair down, she looked like an athletic goddess.

"You look like you've lost weight," Casey commented.

Mikaela felt ridiculously pleased. Maybe slaving to the treadmill master was worth something. "Really?" She smoothed her hands down her jeans. "That new scale of yours says two pounds, but I just thought that might be because I threatened it with death Sunday."

Casey's lips twitched, but she didn't smile. "You do have to watch what you say to machines, sensitive feelings and all. I'm sure watching what you eat and exercising could be a factor as well."

"It better be or I'm dismantling that top of the line treadmill of yours. Do you know how hard it's been to get up an hour earlier?" She frowned at Casey's smile. "Well, it is."

"And that hour looks wonderful on you."

"Suck-up. Where are we going anyway?"

"Blue Moon. A friend of Suzette's is a partner. It's gotten some good reviews."

"As long as they have food, I'll like it." Mikaela slung a tiny pocketbook over her shoulder. "Ready. And, I hope you notice, on time."

Casey fed Mikaela the information she knew about Beth as her luxury SUV ate up the miles to Suzette's home on the north side of the region. "Letting you know now that I *will* say I told you so once you find out you like her."

"As long as it's not a date, I'm prepared to like her. Say what you *will*."

Casey shot her a quick glance. "That's a pretty good attitude for someone who was moping an hour ago."

"How many times do I have to tell you I do not mope? I was wallowing. There's a difference."

"Right. What were you wallowing about? The Three still giving you grief?"

She sighed. "It's stupid."

"Sara?"

"Yeah. I can't seem to stop wishing things were different between us. She was bordering on flirty on the phone, then the next day she was...distant. One minute I don't know what to think, then the next I'm getting mad at myself because I know better. I know I shouldn't have expected anything from her. Except she's the one who called me. That has to mean something. What do you think?"

"Maybe she's bipolar and doesn't take her meds. In which case you'd want to stay away from her."

Mikaela would have hit her if she wasn't driving. "You're no help."

"Okay, so maybe she's confused about her feelings for you. Maybe she's not wanting to take a second look."

"And that helps me how?"

"It tells you that you're different from other women she's hooked up with. That you're better because she thinks about you."

"That sort of makes sense. Doesn't make me feel better, but it fits."

Casey checked the rearview mirror, then eased into the crowded right lane. "I say keep being your charming self and you'll have her worshipping at your feet in no time." She exited the highway, made a quick right and followed the curvy road, which eventually led to Suzette's upscale subdivision.

"Will you look at the size of these houses," Mikaela said once they made it past the gated entrance. "Law school paid off big."

"She comes from money."

"Never would've known from the way she acts."

"That's one of the many reasons I like her," Casey said and swung into Suzette's long driveway.

"Wow!" Mikaela peered up at the brick monstrosity. "One of my aunts had stories about cleaning houses like this."

"I think this is the first time I've ever seen you awestruck." Casey nudged Mikaela with her elbow. "Cut it out before you embarrass her."

"Turning off awe. I promise not to gawk when we get inside. That is the proper way to say I won't stand around looking dumb with my mouth hanging open, isn't it?"

"Jeez, Mikaela, maybe I should have left you at home wallowing."

"Don't even think you're getting rid of me now. You're stuck with me and my hungry, dance-deprived, awestruck self."

"That's what I'm afraid of."

Suzette was waiting at the door. Mikaela had only met her a couple of times before, but she had no trouble remembering her. Suzette was an attractive brunette with light blue eyes and a hard-to-resist smile. And judging by the look on Casey's face after the welcome kiss, Suzette's lips were good for more than smiling.

Mikaela had a hard time not gawking at the inside of Suzette's home. From the intricate woodwork on the arch in the foyer to the high ceilings with fancy-looking chandeliers and the huge grandfather clock anchoring a corner in the living room, it all said money, classy money. To her it was like something out of the magazines she leafed through in the doctor's office—not quite real. As much as she disliked herself for it, she saw Suzette in a different light. A "seriously rich girl" light.

Suzette's friend Beth, with her sharply defined features, was more striking than beautiful. Her skin was creamy brown to go with red hair cut close to the scalp and an arch of freckles over the nose. To Mikaela's relief the smile in Beth's golden-brown eyes was the friendly kind with no trace of first-date jitters.

By the time they made it to the restaurant, Mikaela was ready to admit Casey had been right on both counts. Not only was Beth likeable, but like Mikaela, she'd grown up in a poor neighborhood that was a suburb away from Mikaela's, giving them a lot in common. Further discussion led to the discovery that Beth had gone out with one of Mikaela's second cousins in high school. Best of all for Mikaela, Beth loved to read the same kind of books she did. Dinner was spent with the two of them dissecting recent reads.

After dinner everyone agreed they should use Suzette's VIP pass, go to Buckhead and dance off dinner. On the way, Suzette explained that while it wasn't a gay club, it was gay friendly. Even though it was early by club standards, the line to get into the parking lot was backed up a block on either side. At Suzette's urging, Casey pulled into a nearby parking lot and they walked from there to Revolution. The pass let them bypass the line at the door and gave them entrance to the sleek upstairs lounge overlooking a huge dance floor.

With a glass of Moscato, the one drink she was allotting herself, Mikaela leaned against the railing and let the pounding beat of Rihanna's latest soulful hit flow through her veins. The dance floor below was almost empty, but the three bars were doing brisk business.

"Have you been here before?" Beth asked as she joined Mikaela at the railing.

She shook her head. "Truthfully, it costs too much to get in. I mean, don't get me wrong, it's a nice place. But a dance floor's a dance floor." Her gaze sharpened as the spotlight scanned the crowd and momentarily settled on a familiar figure. She bit back a curse and deliberately looked away from Sara, who had a shoulder cocked against a wall and seemed to be scanning the crowd. Probably looking for a bed partner, she thought with a bitterness she couldn't suppress. Thank God she wasn't at home waiting for a call. "Casey tells me you're here for an interview with Spellman College, which I went to for two years. I couldn't help wondering why you'd leave a blue state to come to a very red Georgia."

"Partly to be closer to my mom. She's getting older and I'd like to be able to visit more frequently. But mainly for the job. It's a tenure track position, and after meeting with some of the department faculty today, on the outside it seems like a good fit." Beth shrugged. "The competition is fierce, so we'll see. If I don't get it, I'll stay where I am and keep looking."

"What do you teach?"

"Creative Writing."

"Cool." Mikaela couldn't keep her gaze from returning to the site where she'd last seen Sara. And she was in the same place, beer in hand. As Mikaela watched, a woman walked up to Sara and said something. She held her breath and only released it when Sara smiled and shook her head.

"What are you looking at?"

"Nothing but trouble," she replied. "See that woman under the neon Budweiser sign?"

"Very nice."

"We had this one-time deal and I foolishly got in over my head."

"I can see why. We should go down, dance in front of her. Give her something to regret."

"I like the way you think."

"Hey, why come to a club if you're not going to dance, right?"

After a quick word with Casey and Suzette, who seemed to be off in their own world, Beth and Mikaela took the winding staircase down to the dance floor. Beth reached for Mikaela's hand and wound through the few swaying bodies until they were positioned in Sara's sight.

Mikaela took some satisfaction at Sara's reaction to the sight of her and Beth dancing close on the floor. "She just spotted us and she doesn't look very happy," Mikaela said, leaning close to Beth's ear to be heard over the loud, pounding beat.

Beth maneuvered until she could see Sara. "You're right. I think I have a hole in my head from the lasers shooting out of her eyes. That's not the kind of look I'm used to getting from hot women."

Mikaela laughed. "I'm sure of that." They danced until thirst called. Instead of returning upstairs, they moved to the closest bar, which happened to be the one they had to walk past Sara to get to.

"Sara," Mikaela said as if she'd just noticed her. "How's it going?"

Sara's gaze slid momentarily to Beth, then their clasped hands. "Okay."

"You haven't had any more trouble, have you?" When Sara shook her head, she said, "Good. Let me know." She managed to walk off without looking back to judge Sara's reaction.

"Very cool and smooth." Beth gave her the thumbs up sign. "What are you drinking? My treat."

"Just water. Watching calories," she said with a grimace.

"You don't look like you need to."

Beth's appreciative glance was more friendly than anything else, so she struck a pose. "Tell that to the scale. Not that you would know anything about that."

"Luck of the draw. I take after my mother's side of the family—thin and bootyless."

After getting their drinks, they lingered at the bar and mocked some of the dancers.

"Heads up," Beth said and reached for Mikaela's hand. "Someone our way comes."

Mikaela put on a bright smile and, since she'd been warned, didn't jump when someone tapped her shoulder.

"You wanna dance?"

"Why not," she replied offhand. Sara's hand closed over hers and her heart started pumping. If she had any sense, she would have turned back around. She really did have to get over this infatuation. But that was better left for tomorrow.

"Friend of yours?" Sara asked once they were on the dance floor.

"Yeah."

"Just a friend?" Sara persisted.

"What does it matter to you?"

"Just asking. Maybe I want to ask her out. She's very attractive."

"No, you did *not* say that." Mikaela stormed off the floor and headed for the bathroom.

"Mikaela, wait!" Sara grabbed her arm. "I don't know why I said that. Stupid. I'm stupid." She exhaled. "Sorry. That was uncalled for and a lie."

"So you didn't mean to throw it in my face that you're looking for another bedmate?"

"No! I was jealous. There, I admitted it." Sara ran her fingers through her hair. "I don't know how to do this."

Though her heart fluttered at the adorable look of frustration on Sara's face, Mikaela knew she needed to proceed with caution. "What do you want me to do here, Sara? I've left you alone like you want. That is, until you don't."

"You think I know? I don't know anything. That's why I'm saying stupid crap. Maybe we could go out and do friend stuff. See how that goes."

"You sure that won't make you go all weird on me? Make you act like you don't know me when you see me at work?"

"I know I've been acting like an idiot. I swear, it was going to be different today, but I didn't see you and I wanted to apologize in person. Then when I do finally see you, you're with another woman and I…I blew it, okay? Give me a chance and if it doesn't work, I'll…I don't know. Wave when I see you at work?"

"Smile. You've got a great smile. I don't necessarily mean right now," Mikaela said. But it was too late. Sara's smile had done its job. "One more chance. If I don't hear from you in a week, don't bother calling."

"I'll call you tomorrow."

"Don't make promises you might not be able to keep."

"You can count on it," Sara said solemnly.

"Maybe I'd take it as good faith if you actually gave me your number." She coded it into her phone as Sara rattled it off. "You want to dance some more?"

Sara shook her head. "I'm heading home. I got more than what I came for. Have fun."

"I can live with that. And yes, Beth's just a friend." With mixed feelings, she watched Sara leave. Was she setting herself up for future heartache? On the other hand, Sara was leaving alone. That had to be good.

* * *

The ringing of her phone jarred Mikaela from a pleasant dream. She squinted at her alarm clock and groaned. It was only nine o'clock and she'd gotten in around four, so she was three hours short on sleep. After fumbling for her phone, she answered without bothering to check caller ID. That would have required her to open her eyes again. "'Lo."

"Sounds like I woke you. Sorry."

"Sara?" Her eyes popped open as sleepiness receded. "Hey, you called."

"I promised, didn't I? I was wondering if you'd like to go to a movie tomorrow? I was thinking we could catch a matinee and see what else happens."

"Sounds like a plan." She rolled over onto her back and tried and failed to remember what was currently showing. "You have one in mind?"

"That futuristic action flick with the cool-looking aliens. But only if you like that kind of thing."

She would have said yes to anything. It was even better to be able to say yes to something she enjoyed. "Yes. Aliens, what's not to like?"

"Does the three-thirty show work for you? It's at Atlantic Station."

"Perfect." A yawn caught her off guard. "Sorry."

"I guess you were out late last night."

"Technically it was early. We left Revolution when it closed and went to a club in North DeKalb that stays open past the time of reason. But you only live once. I think."

"Then I'll let you get back to sleep. Wanted to call because, well, I did promise."

Damn if her heart didn't zing without permission at hearing that. Mikaela decided she would put it down to lack of sleep rather than hope blooming. "I'll have to find my gold stars."

"Yeah?" Sara sounded pleased. "I'll pick you up around two forty-five."

"Looking forward to it." Mikaela sighed and hugged the phone to her chest. "She called." Mikaela laughed at herself, feeling like she'd been transported back to high school. Back then it had been calls from boys she sighed over. More because that was the way it was supposed to be than because of any real longing. But secretly she would have given a lot for Stephanie, the class bad girl, to call.

Yawning, she threw back the covers, shivering as the morning chill hit her bare skin. If she was going to the movies tomorrow, she was going to need popcorn. And movie popcorn screamed for butter and something chocolate to balance the salt. That many future calories screamed for sweaty exercise. If she held on the railing of the treadmill, she could manage without opening her eyes.

An hour and a half later, second cup of coffee in hand, she settled on the sofa and powered up her laptop. In the spirit of doing the right thing, she figured she might as well finish her assignment for the business writing class she was taking online. It was her last course and she intended to go out with an A.

The class wasn't a requirement, but she needed the hours and figured it could only help as she hauled her ass up the ladder at Baker. And now that Talya and Bill had boosted her ego, she easily saw herself five years down the line as something more than an executive assistant. At thirty-two, there was time for her to move up. Then she would use the job as a launch pad, if not at Baker then at some other place.

Assignment momentarily forgotten, she played through the conversation with Debbie. More head games, away to get her talking so she'd say something they could use against her. As if. She was smarter than the three of them put together. One day they would figure that out, but only after it was too late and she had the job.

* * *

"What did you think?" Sara asked as she and Mikaela exited the movie theater.

"I'm a sucker for save-the-world movies. And for once, the aliens weren't the bad guys. Gotta love that."

She held the door open for Mikaela, enjoying seeing the excitement on her face. "The action was incredible. Add in the 3-D and it was right in your face."

Mikaela laughed. "I know. I almost pressed through the back of my seat trying to get away more than once. Good times."

"You hungry? There's several places around here to eat."

"Not after all the popcorn I stuffed down. We won't mention the M&M's." Mikaela pressed a hand to her stomach.

Sara wasn't ready for the date to end. She'd decided to make today a belated birthday celebration. Part of the new her. "Uh... would you be interested in going to Lenox? I've been wanting to check out the Apple store, see what the hype's about."

"You had me at Lenox. Pass up a mall? Never."

Mikaela ended up dragging her into a number of stores in the mall. Sara soon found that she didn't care, that she was having a good time. The day was turning into the best birthday celebration she could remember.

"Here next." Mikaela stopped and peered at the clever display.

"It's a toy store," she felt compelled to point out. "No kids."

Mikaela tapped a palm against her forehead. "Why didn't I see the sign saying 'Kids Required to Enter'?"

"You're kidding, right?"

"Come on." She grabbed Sara's hand. "Toy stores are for big kids too."

Sara's first impression was of noise. Followed quickly by bright lights and hordes of children. If Mikaela's grip hadn't been tight, she would have backpedaled.

"Isn't it great?"

"Great?" She took in Mikaela's joyful expression. "Great," she agreed. "What does one do in a toy store?"

"Play. We're obviously dealing with a deprived childhood."

Mikaela must have decided it was her mission to correct that fault as she dragged Sara up and down every aisle, with frequent stops for demonstrations and sometimes a demand that Sara participate. To Sara it was like being in a foreign country. A far cry from her childhood, where toys had not been a necessity.

"Thanks for dragging me in there." Sara turned to give the display window a last glance. She'd come back and next time, she would buy something. "That was fun. You know your toys."

"Hey, just because I left childhood behind doesn't mean I have to act it. No comments." Mikaela gave her a playful shoulder bump. "I hope I'll want to play with toys the rest of my life. I think it keeps you young."

Sara shrugged. Who was she to argue? "Where to next?"

"We've hit all my highlights. In case you were wondering, those are the places I have no trouble leaving empty-handed."

"Has the popcorn worn off? My stomach's telling me it's dinner time."

"As long as you let me pay. You did pay for the movie, the popcorn and the candy."

Sara shook her head. "I owe you for making this the best birthday celebration I can remember."

"It's your birthday?" Mikaela lightly punched her in the arm. "Why didn't you tell me? I would have baked you a cake or something."

"Technically it was last Monday." She stuck her hands in her pockets, shrugged. "I didn't feel like celebrating until now, I guess."

"It's like that sometimes."

"Been like that for so long I'm not sure how to act. My aunt wasn't big on birthday celebrations. She wasn't big on much when it came to me actually," she added with a trace of bitterness. "Eventually it was like any other day." If she didn't include the dreams.

"That's sad. I guess you went to live with her after your parents died."

"Yeah." Sara swallowed hard as memories pushed to the surface. "So, dinner. Where should we go?"

"It's your birthday. You decide."

"California Pizza Kitchen? I love their barbecue chicken pizza."

"Pizza and birthdays do go together. No matter what age you are."

"Thirty-four. You?"

Mikaela batted her eyelashes. "Sugar, don't you know it's not polite to ask a woman her age?"

Sara threw back her head and laughed. Definitely the best birthday ever.

CHAPTER TWELVE

Sara was the first person Mikaela spotted when she entered the lobby at work the next morning. Her heartbeat sped up at the smile on Sara's face, and she took a moment to say hello, then forced herself not to linger. "Slow and easy," she muttered as she floated to the bank of elevators.

"Hey, you."

Mikaela pressed the elevator button, then smiled a welcome to Marianna. "Hey back. Good weekend?"

"Wonderful." Marianna exhaled loudly. "I did absolutely nothing. Of course, that means I have to take care of errands during the week, but so worth it. What about you?"

"Danced my ass off Friday night. Let's see, anything else?" She lowered her voice. "Oh yeah, on Sunday I went to the movies with Sara Gordon."

"What? That Sara?" Marianna whispered, motioning with her head.

"Yup," Mikaela said with a grin. "She asked *moi* to go to the movies with her."

The elevator door opened and Mikaela joined the throng entering the elevator. "You coming?" she asked an obviously stunned Marianna.

Marianna glanced in Sara's direction before squeezing on. "I could have sworn that was you complaining about being ignored on Friday. What gives?"

"That was then, this is now." She punched the buttons for their respective floors. "You know how it is. Go to a club, somebody sees you dancing with another somebody and bang, the first somebody has a change of heart."

"What?"

"You heard me."

Marianna looked around, then lowered her voice. "So did bang mean something else and was it good?"

"Meet me for lunch and we'll talk. I believe this is your floor." She smiled sweetly into Marianna's glare. "Eleven thirty." She was still smiling as she stowed her things before seeking that needed second cup of coffee. Her good humor took a dive and she almost turned back at the sight of Christine and Ilene whispering near the coffee machine. Holding her head high, she said a friendly "Morning," and filled her cup. As expected they didn't return the greeting, but she could have sworn she felt their eyes boring holes into her back as she took her time doctoring her coffee.

Crabby Patties, she thought once she was back at her desk. That's what they were. And with the mentality of a starfish, so maybe she should rename them after that Sponge Bob character, whatever his name was. Deciding to stick with The Two, she got to work.

At some later point, she jerked in surprise when someone tapped on her desk. Her annoyance quickly faded at the sight of Gerri Xavier. "Welcome back, girl. What did you bring me?"

Gerri smiled. "Knew you would ask." She placed a large binder on Mikaela's desk and dug in the shopping bag she was carrying. "Ta da."

She laughed and accepted the gaudiest-looking replica of the White House she'd ever seen. "You outdid yourself."

"I know." Gerri slipped off her coat, moved the binder aside and took a seat on Mikaela's desk. She was tall and lean, with skin the color of milk chocolate, killer cheekbones and expressive brown eyes. "What's the haps?"

"Brannon's getting forced out and most of the work he should have been doing is getting dumped on Talya. Some of which she dutifully promised to dump on you."

"Bring it on." Gerri rubbed her hands together. "I'm happy to move up on her coattails. Anything else?"

"Jolene's retiring in five weeks and yours truly has a good shot at getting her job. Some are grumbling because HR changed the qualifications. Not me because, hey, I meet all the requirements. And some are complaining about that as well."

"Bet I can guess who *some* are. You leave for a couple of weeks and everything changes. Well, I should see what other changes await."

"Be sure and get me your receipts in the next few days so I can file for reimbursement," she called after Gerri and got a nod of acknowledgment.

By the time Talya arrived at ten thirty, Mikaela had a good handle on the contents and layout of the rest of the handouts for Bill. "How was your meeting?"

"Despite being called at the last minute and on a Monday morning at that, we accomplished a good deal. Apparently I made too many suggestions because I'm now the chair. Unfortunately for you, it'll be your responsibility to type up and distribute the notes to the rest of the group by end of day Wednesday. I'm also going to need you to check schedules and set up a date for the next meeting. A month from now would be good. I'll send you the necessary contacts as soon as I put the rest of this stuff down. Oh, how's the project for Bill going? Probably should have asked that before I started giving you more work."

"Really good. I should have something for you to look at by tomorrow afternoon. Got a brain blast last night and realized I could do a little more to snazz up the layout."

"Keep up the good work." Talya walked toward her office, stopped and returned. "I almost forgot. Block off Friday afternoon on my calendar. I'm thinking of squeezing in a half day. Anything else I need to know right now?"

"Gerri's back."

"Great. Let's see if we can work her into my schedule today."

Mikaela pulled up Talya's calendar. "How about two? Your lunch meeting ends at one and the meeting with Brannon's old section isn't till three."

"Perfect. Put the three o'clock meeting on her calendar as well."

* * *

At five to three, after much internal debate, Mikaela slipped the toy car she'd brought as a belated birthday gift for Sara into her skirt pocket. Last night it had seemed like a good idea to gift the gently used toy to someone who hadn't gotten many. Now, in the light of afternoon, she wasn't so sure and she was way past second-guessing her decision.

Remembering that Marianna had pointed out that Sara would think of Mikaela every time she looked at the toy, she made her way to the first floor. If Sara didn't like it, well, she would live with that. Be embarrassed as hell, but live nonetheless. And if Sara liked it, more points for her. Besides, every child should have a toy. Didn't matter if it was thirty years late.

When Mikaela made it downstairs, Sara was standing by the back door. "Hey, I…uh, well, here." She thrust the car at Sara. "I know it's not much, but you have to start somewhere."

Sara's smile lit up her face. "Thanks. I take it this is from the collection on top of your dresser?"

She nodded. "I would have wrapped it, but I thought you might not want to bring attention to your birthday. His name is Speedy, and he's from the movie *Toy Story*."

Sara slipped the car into her back pocket. "I vaguely remember seeing a trailer for that years ago."

"You haven't seen it? We'll have to rectify that. I owe you a birthday dinner anyway. You could come over for dinner one day this week and check out the movie. I'm a good cook."

"You don't owe me anything, but I won't turn down a home-cooked meal. Does Wednesday work?"

"Perfect. Seven okay?"

"I'll be there." Sara pulled the car out of her pocket. "Thanks again for the gift. I promise to treasure it."

"That's all I can ask for." Mikaela could feel the grin pulling at her face and decided she needed to take things down a notch lest she start to resemble a maniacal clown.

"So, Wednesday?"

"Yeah."

"I look forward to it."

Mikaela might have stood there looking at Sara forever if they hadn't been forced to move aside to let someone exit.

"Okay, I'm going that way, uh, back to work." Mikaela floated across the lobby. Once she hit the up button, she turned around and found Sara watching her. Sara couldn't know how sweet and yet sexy she looked, holding the toy as if it were a treasure, but Mikaela knew.

Give a gift, get a gift, she thought and entered the elevator. While it wasn't a date, Sara had agreed to dinner and a movie. That was a start. A good start that seemed to promise more.

As she took the elevator to the seventh floor, Mikaela relived the pleasure on Sara's face when she saw the car. That made all the internal arguing worthwhile. And maybe she should add to the collection now that she knew Sara liked it. Of course, it wouldn't hurt if a little of the shine rubbed off on her.

Once seated at her desk, she ruthlessly brought her mind back down to earth. After all, she had plans with Sara. If she stayed late today, she could finish designing the layout for the handouts, copy the text in tomorrow, get the results to Talya and leave a little early.

* * *

"My receipts as requested."

Mikaela gave Gerri an absent smile. "Back from the meeting already?"

"Already? It's close to five."

"Can't be." She checked the bottom corner of her monitor to verify. "It is."

"I guess it's a good thing when you lose yourself in work."

"I was planning to stay late anyway. How did the meeting go?"

"I can report that there are now some very disgruntled employees on the eighth floor." Gerri shook her head. "It's a mess. Reports that have mysteriously disappeared, locked drawers that no one has the keys to, and with Brannon on vacation, no one seems to know or care what's going on."

"Bet Talya loved that."

"No bet. If looks could start fires…Don't be surprised if that group puts in extra hours for the foreseeable future."

"Please tell me some of it got shoveled Christine's way and my day will be made."

Gerri grinned. "You should have been there. She opened her mouth and now she's in charge of creating a database of the missing reports and coordinating the efforts to find them. That will certainly keep her busy."

"But not busy enough to stop running Gossip Central, I bet." She caught the frown as it flickered across Gerri's face. "What? Has she said something to you?" When Gerri looked away, Mikaela knew she wasn't going to like what came next.

Gerri picked up Mikaela's stress ball and gave it a couple of squeezes. "Look," she said, then paused, a pensive expression on her face. "I didn't want to tell you this and at the same time I didn't not want to tell you."

"I'm sure I'd rather hear it from you than Christine."

"I overheard Ilene telling Jennifer in IT that you pulled a Lewinsky on Bill to get him to change the requirements for Jolene's job."

"A blow job? Seriously?" She leaned her head back, closed her eyes and counted to ten. If she lived in cartoon land, smoke would be pouring out of her ears. But this was the real world. The ugly, nasty, low-down real world. "I can't…God, I was expecting something, but this? I can't believe it. Even of them. I guess I should feel special they think I have that kind of power." She rubbed her forehead, not sure whether she wanted to scream or cry or maybe both. "Somehow I don't. Have you heard it from anyone else?"

Gerri shook her head. "I told both of them that if I heard that crap repeated, I would make sure Bill knew who was fanning the flames. They jumped a mile high, and Ilene immediately tried to backpedal, saying how she knew it wasn't true."

"Then why repeat it? Because it's part of their plan," she said, answering her own question. "Debbie warned me to expect something nasty, but did I listen? No. I thought she was playing their game, you know? This. This is going too far." Mikaela covered her face with her hands, trying to recall any funny looks thrown her way. She couldn't, so maybe it wasn't that widespread—yet. "God, this makes me so mad." And hurt, she admitted to herself. Feeling the burn of tears, she bit her bottom lip hard. Those bitches were not going to make her cry.

"Hey, no one who knows you is going to pay that any attention. You've worked with enough people around here for them to know that's not you, know that you would never take part in anything like that." Gerri put a hand on Mikaela's shoulder. "Maybe I should have kept my big mouth shut."

She dropped her hands. "You did the right thing. I would've hated to be the last to know." Taking a deep breath, she let it out slowly. "What to do? Part of me wants to confront Ilene, make her tell me where she got her story from. Which would be a waste of time and give her the satisfaction of knowing they scored a direct hit. What do you think?"

"Why don't I check around tomorrow, see who else might have heard. If it's only a few people, I say do nothing, let it die out. Now if it's widespread, I say we go to HR, tell them what I heard and you can file a complaint against Ilene. I'll be happy to tell my side of things. That should be enough for something under that new workplace bullying deal they put in place."

"I guess that's better than my first instinct. And my second." But Mikaela wasn't so sure a rap on the hand from HR would help her fight an invisible enemy.

"If it's any consolation, I thought about dunking Ilene's head in the toilet."

She managed a wan smile. "We could have gone to the same high school. That was my second choice."

"Then I probably don't want to hear your first choice. Hang in there. Pulling a stunt like this stinks of desperation. I guarantee I'm not the only one who sees it that way."

"Thanks. For the pep talk and letting me know." She fisted a hand on her thigh as Gerri walked away. She hoped Gerri was right and most wouldn't take it seriously. Unfortunately, there also would be those who'd say they didn't believe it even as they fueled the fire.

No, she couldn't worry about them, couldn't let them bring her down. The ones who mattered would know it was bullshit, would see the vindictiveness behind the accusation. If they didn't, well, they would be dropped from her list.

Any thoughts she had of working flew south. What she needed was to go home and get the sour taste of this place out of her mouth, then come back tomorrow, mask firmly in place.

Her phone rang before she could get away, and though she knew without an iota of psychic powers it wasn't going to be good, she answered anyway. "Mikaela...Be right there." She replaced the receiver gently when she really wanted to give it a couple of good bangs. Given her recent conversation with Gerri, she could well imagine what this unexpected summons to Bill's office was about. "Damn, damn, damn!"

She stopped by the bathroom to find her cool. There was a small chance this had nothing to do with the Lewinsky rumor. "Bull!" She'd read too many police procedural novels to believe in coincidences. And if Bill knew, the story had gotten further than Gerri suspected.

"Fuck!" Mikaela looked around for something to kick. As she drew back her leg to annihilate a plastic trashcan, she remembered what shoes she was wearing—the Manolo Blahniks—too cute and definitely too expensive to risk possible damage. What she needed was a bat. She'd use it like she had in high school when she'd been on the softball team. Step up to the plate and hit a home run with Ilene's head. Her sorry-ass boyfriend always said she was a good hitter…for a girl.

Damn if she wouldn't show those bitches her girl! She exhaled and blinked away tears. No time to fix makeup, she told herself sternly. And crying was part of what they wanted. But it was hard not to be furious. And embarrassed, she added as she left the bathroom and took the stairs to eight. Embarrassed for herself, for Bill, for anyone else caught up in this horrible game.

Jolene met her in the hallway in front of Bill's office, her expression grave. "You can go right on in. And try not to worry about a thing."

More worried than she'd been before Jolene opened her mouth, Mikaela walked into Bill's large corner office. Her little fantasy of the meeting being about something other than the Lewinsky maneuver poofed when she noticed the head of HR, Dennis George, sitting at the table with Bill and Talya. She could tell by their expressions she'd been right—they knew. "You wanted to see me?"

"Have a seat, Mikaela," Bill said with a strained smile. "What we have here is a delicate situation." He cleared his throat. "It has come to my attention that allegations concerning unbecoming behavior have been made. Talya thought since these allegations involve you, it was best to apprise you of the situation immediately. Dennis and I concurred. However, I see by your expression that perhaps we're too late."

Reeling under the sting of humiliation, she nodded. If life was fair, she'd be transported to anywhere but here, she thought, watching as Dennis smoothed back his thinning hair. He'd come on at the same time as Bill and it was said they were old friends.

"Are you comfortable sharing how you found out?" Dennis asked.

"Gerri. Gerri Xavier. She overheard someone saying… well you know what they were saying." She clasped her hands, looked down at her lap and concentrated on keeping her cool. "I guess you'll have to talk to her now and she's okay with that. She did mention that Ilene—that's Ilene Jacobs—was, uh, the one doing the talking. I can't believe someone would spread something this bad about me. About you, Bill." She looked at him, remembering his pretty wife, his young sons from the holiday party.

"Don't worry about that," Bill was quick to say. "The concern here is how this will affect you."

"It's troubling, but I won't let it interfere with my work."

"We didn't have any doubt about that," Talya said.

"I will need to speak with Gerri," Dennis said.

"Yeah." She looked at him, then quickly looked away. "I really don't want to have to file a complaint."

Dennis closed the folder in front of him. "Hopefully, it won't come to that. But rest assured, any complaints you may need to file in this matter will not reflect badly on you. This accusation will be taken seriously, coming as it did on top of complaints about the Executive Assistant job posting."

The noose around Mikaela's neck loosened enough to allow for a shallow breath. It was comforting to know she wasn't the only one questioning the timing. "What should I do now?"

"Nothing at this point. I plan to speak with Ilene after I get with Gerri." Dennis glanced at his watch. "Given the hour, neither conversation will happen until tomorrow."

"Go home and try to forget about this," Talya urged. "But know that the three of us are taking this seriously. That there will be consequences."

She could only nod. When she closed the door behind her, she took a moment to steady herself.

"You okay?"

She blinked away the tears under Jolene's watchful gaze. "Never expected anything this vicious, I guess." But she should have. Next time she'd pay closer attention to what Debbie had to say.

"Nobody could. I'm sorry."

"Me too. I mean, I…I've never been so humiliated in my life." She blew out a sharp breath. "Okay. Need to get it together. I don't want to give anyone the satisfaction of seeing me upset."

"Whoever is behind this—and we both have our suspicions—made a big mistake. They don't understand the old mind-set is gone. I promise you Bill and Dennis will *not* let this go."

"Good. That's how it should be. I hate to ask how he found out. Bill, I mean."

"Ilene told the wrong person, and that person realized Dennis needed to be involved."

"Finally something good to focus on. I was going to go home, set up on the couch and wallow in my sorrows. Now I can think fondly about the person who took a stand. And not so fondly about Ilene and how she's going to explain why she was spreading something she didn't believe, not once but twice."

"A little wallowing never hurt anyone. I hear wine goes well with that. And chocolate."

Mikaela managed a genuine smile. "I'll take that under advisement."

Once downstairs, she gathered her belongings, then stopped by Gerri's office and gave her a heads up. "I owe you big for the advance notice."

"You don't owe me. I know you'd do the same for me."

On her way to the elevator, Mikaela walked by a small group of women who stopped whispering as soon as they spotted her. She stared them down until one by one they looked away. Only then did she continue, her head held high. "Fuck them," she muttered and punched the down button. "Fuck all of them."

* * *

Mikaela donned her most conservative suit the next morning and then took extra effort to cover up the signs of the crying jag that had hit at dawn and made it impossible to fall back asleep. After a last glance in the bathroom mirror, she was satisfied she'd done the best she could.

As planned, she was the first to arrive in her area. After grabbing coffee, she returned to her desk and saw Sara. Her outlook improved. "Morning."

"You're here early," Sara said with a big smile. "Not that I'm complaining."

The flirtatious tone made her feel even better. "Gotta take care of some things I didn't get to yesterday. The bathrooms safe today?"

"So far so good. We're still on for tomorrow, right?"

"Absolutely. Is there anything you don't eat? I mean food-wise," she quickly clarified when Sara snickered.

"I'm adventurous. I'll try most things once."

"The problem seems to be getting you to try something more than once," she dared to say.

"No fair," Sara said. "I am working on it."

"And it's much appreciated."

"Good. On to the sixth floor. Hopefully I'll get a chance to see you later." She fingered one of the tiny dolls on Mikaela's desk. "Don't tell anybody, but I played with the car last night."

Mikaela laughed at the mischievous expression on Sara's face. "I'm glad. Stick around me and I'll have you playing like a kid in no time. Now go make the bathrooms safe for the world."

"Hey, now. I check stairwells too."

She batted her eyes. "My hero." Mikaela watched until Sara was out of sight, thinking it was funny how a little flirting with the right person could change one's attitude.

Talya arrived an hour later at eight, early for her if she didn't have a meeting, bearing gifts. "Fruit cup and a grande nonfat latte."

"Special thanks for not going with doughnuts. In my current state I could easily down half a dozen before guilt kicked in."

"I weighed the comfort of hot Krispy Kreme doughnuts versus saving the diet with fruit. Let me tell you, it was a tough choice." Talya repositioned her grip on the bag in her left hand.

Mikaela sniffed the air. "What's that smell?"

"I should get to my office. The meeting summary can go out this afternoon if you need the extra time."

She narrowed her eyes. "You bought doughnuts for yourself, didn't you?"

"I'm hurt that you would think that."

"Oh, give it up," she said, shaking a finger at her boss. "I can smell doughnuts from a mile away."

Talya sighed and her shoulders slumped. "I suppose you want one?"

"Thanks for the gracious offer," she said, "but no. And when you check your email, you'll see I sent out the summary already.

I'm waiting for a couple of responses before I can set up the next meeting."

"How early did you get here?"

Mikaela looked away from Talya's concerned gaze. It probably wouldn't be the final one she'd have to face today. "Closer to seven. Figured I might as well be productive." She shrugged. "Better than worrying."

"Let me put my stuff down and we'll talk."

"That's okay." Mikaela squeezed her eyes shut for a moment. "Talking about it will make me all emotional and ruin my makeup. Beauty like mine takes time."

"You know I'm available anytime you feel the need to talk or vent."

She nodded, not trusting herself to speak. Work is the answer, she told herself and returned to adding the finishing touches to handout number two. Touches she meant to finish yesterday before everything fell apart.

"Stop." She was not going down that path again. She already knew it was a winding road, leading to a dead end of "if only." Her time was better spent making her work shine. So she put the anger and the sadness away and locked them down for later processing.

She was mentally patting herself on the back for completing not one but two handouts when someone cleared their throat. Mikaela looked up with a ready smile that quickly wilted. "Hey."

"You got a minute?"

It took almost that long for Mikaela to identify the woman in front of her. Three measly degrees of separation were standing at her desk in the form of Tasha from IT, who worked with Jennifer from IT. No way could this be good. She'd probably come to see if there was any truth to the rumors, Mikaela decided. "How's it going?"

"Good. Thanks again for organizing the volunteer deal."

"I should be thanking you for signing up. What can I help you with?"

Tasha shifted from side to side. "Actually, I wanted you to know that I'm really sorry about what's being said." The expression on Tasha's dark brown face was earnest. "And I guess I wanted you to know that I know it's not true."

Her brain froze, then clumsily shifted gears. Not at all what she'd been bracing for. "Uh, thanks. You can't know how much I appreciate you coming to tell me that."

"I'm not the only one. Other people I've talked to know it's bogus. So I thought, hey, if it was me I'd want someone to, you know, say something."

So not what I'd expected, she thought, blinking rapidly. "I don't know what to say except thank you, thank you, thank you. It's nice to know everybody isn't talking bad about me behind my back."

"Hang tough. Once they see no one's going along, they'll stop."

Mikaela was struck by how young Tasha was, how sweetly naïve. "Thanks, Tasha." Once she was alone, she pulled out her compact and dabbed at her damp eyes. She was presentable. Now to stay that way.

"Send what you have to Bill," Talya said from the doorway of her office as she wrestled with her coat. "I should be back by one thirty. Two if that blowhard Simons gets on a roll. Do I owe you anything?"

"We're good. Enjoy the mystery chicken. Oh, I need to go to the Georgia State library for my class. I'll go on my lunch break, but I may run over."

"Take all the time you need."

The rest of the morning brought a steady stream of fellow employees dropping by to offer support and encouragement. Many of them were ones she'd sweated with at Hands on Atlanta day, but there were a few she hadn't had much contact with. Those she especially treasured. At one point she retreated to the restroom to repair her makeup.

* * *

Mikaela hurried off the elevator. She'd taken longer at the library than planned. Her time had been well spent, and now she had the information necessary to complete her next two class assignments. She could finish them up over the weekend and be more than halfway through the course. All in all, it was a victory, and she needed that.

Baby noises brought her up short. "Pat!" She dropped her bag on her desk and crossed to pull him into a hard hug. "Why didn't you warn me you were coming?"

Pat Manes' green eyes twinkled down at her. "And have you disappear? No way."

She laughed, stepped back and gave him the once-over. He was still thin, despite his protestations to the contrary, and his dark blond hair was longer, brushing his shoulders. "Maternity leave looks good on you, 'Mom.' Now let me at my baby."

Pat gently freed his firstborn from the carrier at his feet. "As you can see she's grown a little since you last saw her."

"Ooh. Looks like she's going to have Laura's red hair." The wispy blond strands Emma had been born with had been replaced by tufts of red. Mikaela held Emma close and breathed in the scents of baby lotion and innocence. "You're a little beauty, aren't you? How's Laura doing?"

"Good. I dropped her off at the spa for a full body massage. She deserves it. Who knew one little baby could be so much work?"

"I hear it only gets worse, Daddy." She rocked from side to side as Emma burrowed against her. "It builds character, I think. Love the 'do man."

He put a hand on top of his head. "It's getting chopped off this weekend. Laura says I'm too pretty to have long hair."

"You are pretty, Manes. Does Gerri know you're here?" She kicked back her chair and sat. "No. She has that meeting until two thirty."

"Talked to her on the phone. She told me about the s—crap flying around here. What's up with that?"

"You know."

"Guess I do." Pat plopped down on Mikaela's desk. "What I can't figure out is who these morons are who are buying you needing to get on your knees to get that job. Do we really have that many stupid people working here?"

"Apparently fewer than they thought." She told him about her string of visitors. "Wait. You wouldn't be one too?"

"There, there." He patted her on the head. "I had to be out. Why not swing by, see how a friend is doing?"

It was exactly something he would do. "Thanks. You know I've probably used that word five hundred times today."

"Last I heard you don't get charged for it. And if so, I'll take up a collection. Charge money to hold Emma."

"My car made me stop by the cookie place. I ate one, so—Pat! And Emma!" Talya gave him a shoulder bump and thrust the bag of cookies at him. "Eat." She put down her briefcase, flung her coat over the desk and held out her hands. "Gimme. Ooh, red hair. She's really grown since I last saw her. Eye color?"

"Jury's still out on that. I think blue, Laura thinks gray."

"Either way, she's a little sweetie pie. Yes, you are." Talya kissed Emma's mostly bald head.

"Before you ask, Laura's at the spa being pampered," Mikaela said.

"What does she think about going back to work?" Talya asked. "I remember her talking about going back part time after a month."

"That was B.E., Before Emma. Now she's going for the full eight weeks, maybe even part-time for a month after that." Pat reached for one of Emma's fingers. "It'll be good for our girl."

"Agreed. When I had Jason, six weeks was the norm. I had to push to get eight and my boss at the time was not very happy with me. Thank God things have changed. What about you? You want to extend your leave beyond the three weeks?"

"I need to build up leave time for emergencies, so I'll be back Monday morning."

Talya gave Emma another kiss, sighed and then passed her to Mikaela. "There's plenty of work waiting for you."

"I hear you've sort of taken over for Brannon. Any talk of a merger?"

"A few days ago I would have said no. Now all I can say is nothing is outside the realm of possibility. Good to see you, Pat."

"If we do merge it'll be because of what she's done," Mikaela said after Talya was in her office. "She's been busting her butt."

"Well, I'm excited. More possibility of cross training and promotions. Not that all of us need it from what I hear."

"Wipe that smirk off your face. How many times do I have to tell you people no decision has been made?" Mikaela gave in to the lure of the cookies, then passed the bag back to Pat. She wanted company with the fat and the sugar. "Yum."

"And still warm." Pat devoured his cookie in two bites, then eyed the bag.

"Have another one," she urged. Lord knows it would save her ass. "Hey, any interest in being co-captain of the MLK Jr. Service Day team next year with yours truly? I've got big ideas."

"Only if I get a say in selecting the project."

"Deal."

CHAPTER THIRTEEN

"You're looking better this morning." Casey removed the cup from the coffee machine and handed it to Mikaela.

"Feel it. Good night's sleep, exercise out of the way and"—Mikaela paused for dramatic effect—"Sara for dinner." She added artificial sweetener and cream to the coffee and took her first sip. "Feel even better now. You know you're welcome to dinner?"

"Already have plans." Casey lifted her cup in a toast. "Suzette wants to go to Pool, then we're meeting some of her friends for dinner. I'll be late, if at all."

"Shameful. And on a school night."

Casey grinned. "I know. I'm sure you kids will have fun too."

"Dinner and movie only." Mikaela rummaged around in the fridge and finally settled on low-fat yogurt. She had two cookies to atone for, thanks to her sadistic boss. "I'm introducing her to the joy of *Toy Story*." She grabbed a spoon, then closed the silverware drawer with a hip. "What's the eye roll for?"

"All the movies we have in this house and you're going for a kiddie movie? That's sad."

"Your opinion. Wrong as it is." She spooned in yogurt, thinking of the great evening she was going to have.

"God, you are in a good mood. You're humming and I know it's not because of the yogurt."

"Am not." She frowned. Okay, maybe she had been humming. It was appropriate. She had plans with a sane, gorgeous woman. "You should be happy I'm happy."

"After dealing with that storm cloud hanging over your head Monday night, I'm positively ecstatic."

"Was I that bad? Don't answer that." She finished her yogurt and rinsed the spoon. "I'm off to divide and conquer. If you hear of butts getting kicked on Peachtree, think of me."

"Don't forget to take names."

"Don't you worry. The Three, or I guess they're down to The Two, are in my sights."

Her good mood followed her downtown and put pep in her step as she fought the headwind from the bus stop to her office. And yes, she hummed.

Sara wasn't in the lobby, and in some ways, not seeing her made the anticipation for the evening sweeter. Mikaela squeezed on the elevator and only stopped humming when she caught on to the sideways glances she was getting. She imagined there was some relief when she got off on seven.

The humming faltered and then stopped when she saw the meeting notice from Dennis. It had been sent after seven the night before, and it was a mood killer. Grumbling about lies and old biddies, she accepted.

"I thought you would be in a better mood." Talya rushed in and placed a muffin on Mikaela's desk. "It's no fat and no sugar, so it's okay."

Mikaela didn't see how anything could be okay with no fat and no sugar, but she thanked Talya all the same. "Care to tell me about this meeting I have with Dennis in forty minutes?"

"That's nothing to worry about." Talya waved her hand dismissively. "An update to let you know what's being done. I thought this morning would be a good time for that."

Her brow furrowed. "Why?"

"Thought you'd feel better after all the visits yesterday."

"I really did. Do. Was that your doing?"

"I think Tasha and Gerri, but don't quote me."

"As long as it wasn't forced."

"Trust me, no one wants to make the situation any worse than it is."

"Tell me Bill's not in trouble with the higher-ups."

"Talk to Dennis. I've already said enough."

Mikaela watched her go and leaned back in her chair. Bill must be okay or Talya would have said something. If he was okay, then perhaps she would be okay too.

"Morning." Gerri walked in, wearing a dark blue suit with the thinnest of stripes and carrying her coat over her arm.

"Don't you look spiffy."

Gerri preened. "Talya's taking me to her morning meeting. Gotta look the part."

"Mission accomplished." She debated mentioning yesterday's visits and decided to let it go unsaid. "You need anything before you go? I'm heading up to meet with Dennis."

"Something else come up?"

She shook her head. "Strictly an update."

"Let me know. I've got my ear to the ground and nothing else has been said as far as I can tell. You've got to know by now you have support out there."

"Yeah, thanks to you."

"You'd do the same for me and anyone else. That's why most know this is bull."

* * *

Sara smoothed back her sweat-soaked hair and unlocked the front door to her apartment. She had to admit the workout with weights and forty minutes on the elliptical machine had taken some of the edge off what she classified as Anticipation Times Two. Now she only had a couple of hours to fill until dinner with Mikaela.

Her cell chimed as she stepped aside to allow Tab to enter. She checked the caller ID and almost dropped the phone. She hadn't heard from her cousin Russell Thomason in almost a year. Obnoxious as he was, he was sort of family. "Sara."

"It's Russell. Bet you're surprised to hear from me."

"How did you get my number?"

His laugh sounded forced. "Long story. Listen, uh, some lawyer type is looking for you. Something about your dad."

"My dad? You got a name, number?"

"Hang on. It's here somewhere. Walter Tibbs. Works with some law firm up north. You know him?"

"He leave a number?"

"I gave him yours. I mean, I guessed you'd want to know since it involved your dad."

"You remember the name of the law firm?" There was more rustling of paper. She figured she should be glad he'd bothered to write anything down.

"Well, seems I don't. I bet you could look him up on that Internet."

"Gotta run, get ready."

"Wait. You think this may be about an inheritance? Mom always said your dad's family was rolling in it."

What Sara remembered was her aunt's bitterness that she'd never gotten her hands on any of that money. "At this late date? Get real. More likely to be a scam."

"Oh. Let me know, will you? We're family, you and me."

"Family? Right." She doubted he'd catch the sarcasm.

"That's right. Family. Got two kids now. Can always use extra money."

"Who couldn't?" She ended the call thinking *like mother, like son*. Her Aunt Liddy had always been chasing a handout—from the government to the jerks she picked up regularly and even from her kids and Sara when they got to working age.

But the moneygrubbers weren't the issue here, she knew. The mysterious Mr. Tibbs was. She was going to be forced to get Internet access and spare herself the trips to the library. Though even the Internet couldn't tell her why he was calling or what his connection to her father was. It could give her a number, though, and then she'd call him. That would be better, more proactive.

As she showered, Sara considered the possible reasons for the lawyer's call. The only information she had on her father was from Aunt Liddy, who'd never met him. And since he'd been estranged from his family at the time of his death, she was suspicious of a call at this late date. Some guy was probably trying to pull a fast one, make her think there was big money if only she'd send him a deposit. If he thought she was as gullible as her cousin, he was in for a big surprise.

A couple of hours later, butterflies dancing on her nerves, Sara picked a cat hair off her nicest jeans. She'd paired them with a colorful sweater she'd been told brought out the blue in her eyes. Not too casual and not too formal. Perfect for a date that wasn't really a date, and yet it wasn't only two friends getting together either. Her insides fluttered. Whatever it was, she was looking forward to spending time with Mikaela, hearing more of her crazy theories about the world. Looking forward to peering into those bright eyes and seeing if they could be more than friends.

She pulled on her heavy coat and grabbed the bouquet of flowers and the bottle of wine she'd picked up on her way home from work. Due to her inexperience with dating and its rules and regulations, it had taken her far longer than it should have to decide on what to take. In the end, impatience with her indecisiveness had forced a choice, and she still wasn't certain she'd made the right one. Telling herself what was done was done did nothing to calm her nerves on the short drive over.

Mikaela buzzed her in right away and was waiting in the doorway when she crossed from the visitors' parking spaces. Her heartbeat sped up. Mikaela had let her hair down and changed into a dress that was casual and at the same time sexy, the way it flowed around her curves. "Hi. Uh, I picked up some things," Sara explained and passed the bouquet and wine to Mikaela.

"You didn't have to, but I love it. Come on in."

As Sara stepped over the threshold, images of what they'd been doing the last time she was here flashed through her mind and were quickly squashed. She wasn't here for that, as enjoyable as it had been. This time they would talk, get to know each other. Maybe share a kiss at the end of the evening. To be on the safe side, she stuck her hands in her pockets.

Mikaela led the way to the living room and pointed to the sofa. "Have a seat. What can I get you to drink? I have water, ice tea, Coke, beer, wine."

"Coke is fine." She lowered herself to the sofa and tried not to remember what they'd done to each other in this room. Getting to know her, she reminded herself, and looked around the room, seeing what she hadn't that other night. The furniture was meant for comfort with the overstuffed couch and matching chairs, the sturdy end tables and the decorative wooden trunk that passed as a coffee table. The big-screen TV hanging on the opposite wall was on, the volume low.

"Here's your soda." Mikaela set the can on a coaster, then slid it over in front of Sara.

"Something smells good," she commented as Mikaela sat down beside her.

"Baked chicken in a balsamic and herb vinaigrette. I saw the recipe in a magazine at the doctor's office. I hope it's as good as it smells."

Sara smiled. "Oh, so *you're* one of those page rippers?"

"Guilty with extenuating circumstances, Officer." Mikaela batted her eyes. "No pen and paper handy, and I knew I wasn't going to remember. What else could I do? And I wasn't the first one to remove a page."

"Oh well, then, that makes it okay."

"Glad you agree. Now if the magazine had been in perfect condition I would've paused a moment or two before ripping out the page."

"Then it's definitely the doctor's fault for tempting you."

"Exactly." She squeezed Sara's leg. "You get it."

"A toast then." Sara touched her can to Mikaela's. "To understanding."

As Mikaela laughed, a buzzer sounded. "Be right back." She was back a moment later. "Let's move this party to the kitchen."

Sara grabbed both of their drinks and followed Mikaela. Good, she thought, as she entered the brightly lit kitchen. A room we haven't had sex in. The small table was already set with the flowers she'd brought as a centerpiece. "Can I do anything to help? I know my way around a kitchen."

"I wouldn't have pegged you for a cook," Mikaela said. She gave her a considering look.

"My work history is long and varied," she explained. "I think last count is three, no, four restaurant jobs over the years. From dishwasher on up."

"Yeah? What else have you done?"

"What haven't I done. A couple of years ago I was a nanny for this rich couple's miniature poodles. Talk about indulgence."

"Get out!"

She laughed. Mikaela's expression was priceless. "Not kidding. I watched the dogs during the day while the couple was at work. We played, took walks, went on doggie playdates, got doggie massages. Blew my mind all the things that were available for dogs to do, all the things my charges did. Plus I made extra money staying overnight when the parents went out of town. I was more than a little sorry to let that job and the doggies go. They were sweet in spite of their parents."

Mikaela transferred the chicken to a platter and began to carve. "What happened?"

"Nothing really. I was ready for a change of scenery." She stuffed her hands in her pockets and rocked back on her heels, unwilling to admit she'd been afraid of missing something if she didn't keep moving. "I don't like to stay in one place too long. Always looking for something new to do, learn."

"Where all have you lived?"

"Most of the big cities, like New York, L.A., Miami, San Francisco, Chicago and the like. I spent a year in Vegas and discovered I had a knack for blackjack. That wasn't so good since I worked for a casino. Never made it to Hawaii. I kind of developed this thing about flying after 9/11. If I can't drive there, I won't get there."

"I've only lived in Boca Raton and Atlanta. But I've lived in six different neighborhoods since I moved here…well, I won't say how many years ago." Mikaela smiled sweetly.

"Don't ask, don't tell, right?"

"You do pay attention. My grandmother always said never reveal your age. That way you can never get caught up in a lie." She placed the platter with the cut-up chicken on the counter between the bowl of colorful tossed salad and the bowl of bowtie pasta. "Dinner's ready. Hope it's okay to eat in here? Since it's the two of us."

"Fine with me. Where's your roommate? Casey, right?"

Mikaela nodded. "She has plans. Meeting the girlfriend's friends for the first time as girlfriends. We'll do this buffet style because there's not enough room for the food and plates on that table."

Over dinner Sara found herself sharing more stories of the jobs she'd had over the past sixteen years and the cities she'd visited.

"When's the last time you made it back home to Oklahoma City?" Mikaela pushed her plate to the side.

"I haven't." Sara once again didn't correct Mikaela about Oklahoma City being home. "No good reason to yet. I keep thinking one day I'll go back, see if the zoo is as good as I remember. Visit the monument and pay my respects."

"Were you there when the bomb went off?"

She shook her head. "April nineteenth, two thousand and five. I wasn't anywhere near there, but I didn't have to be to know someone who was affected by it. One of the girls I used to hang out with sometimes in high school worked in the building. Her two daughters were in the daycare center."

"People suck sometimes."

"But what can you do? Gotta live."

"Amen to living 'cause the alternative sucks."

"Right again."

Mikaela flexed her arms. "Two for two."

"I guess you were one of the smart ones in school."

"At the school I went to that wasn't hard to do. Helped that my grandmother was adamant about education. And my cousin Lisa. We used to compete against each other about everything until she pulled so far ahead I couldn't keep up. We started

Spellman at the same time, only she graduated, then moved to Colorado and got her master's."

"The nerve."

"Exactly. I shouldn't complain. She was a free place to stay the one time I made it out there. I'd like to go back, climb some mountains."

"Some pretty country up there. Got some great day hikes. Skiing too."

"Let me guess. You worked at a lodge?"

"Yup."

Mikaela gathered their dirty plates. "Figures."

Sara jumped up. "Let me help you with that."

"I got it. When you invite me to your place, you can do all the work."

"Okay." She sat back down and thought about what she'd fix for Mikaela. It would have to be something special. "Do you like Italian?"

"Food and I are very…What's the word? Symbiotic maybe. Anyway, food likes to be eaten and I like to eat it—too much." Mikaela put the dishes in the sink. "Can I get you coffee or anything else to drink?"

"Coffee's good."

"Casey, the gadget queen, bought one of those fancy one-cup brewers. It takes less than a minute and makes great coffee. We have quite a selection if you want to choose."

Sara selected hazelnut decaf; Mikaela, the French roast decaf.

"We can take this to the living room. Be more comfortable." Mikaela added sweetener and creamer to her coffee. "I have dessert."

Sara patted her firm stomach. "Too full. You did a great job with the stolen recipe."

"That's 'borrowed,' thank you. I like to cook. Especially when I have someone appreciative to cook for."

Mikaela settled on the couch once back in the living room and patted the space next to her.

"Sometimes it is hard to get motivated to cook for just myself." Sara took a sip of coffee. "You're right, this is very good."

"I know coffee. My boss thinks I'm addicted. She may not be wrong."

"Speaking of work, how's the quest for promotion going?"

"Someone must think it's going well. There's this rumor that yours truly performed a sexual act on the head honcho and now he's under my power. I mean, really? That's the best they could come up with?"

"I take it you know who they are?"

"It's so obvious. Though I heard today that the one caught spreading the rumor claimed she was on mission to find the person responsible. Really?" She rolled her eyes. "The HR manager didn't say it, but I got the impression she'd been reprimanded since not one, but two people told on her. And that's all well and good, but I still want to stomp two somebodies into next week. As long as I'm wearing the right shoes, of course," she added primly.

"Goes without saying. Let me know if you need any help." Sara held up a size nine-and-a-half, boot-clad foot. "I'm pretty good with that."

"Wouldn't mind holding your coat while you did it. Maybe even wipe a sweaty brow."

Mikaela's smile went directly to Sara's head, then settled lower. Time to take a step back. "Hopefully it won't come to that."

"Pity. Okay, enough about me. Not that I don't love the subject matter, but I want to know more about those jobs. Have you ever had one where you used your drawing skills?"

"It wasn't really a job."

"But..." she prodded.

"Senior year I drew a cartoon strip for this underground quarterly anthology. A glimpse into the life of a girl who, unlike me, was Ms. Popular. She was also the leader of what we would now call mean girls. Unfortunately for my heroine, as much as she and her meanies planned, their pranks always backfired on them."

"Bet the real mean girls loved that."

"Their shower of affection was embarrassing. I guess lucky for me, they showed their displeasure with words."

"High school is another layer of hell."

"For you? I figured you to be one of the popular ones."

"I know it's hard considering my refined current self, but I was only popular in my small circle of friends. Most of whom were relatives. Those mean girls didn't like a bit of me. They thought I thought I was all that because of the color of my skin and eyes and I had good hair."

"Is there bad hair?"

"Not by me, but anything other than kinky hair is considered good by some. It was so unfair. Like I have any control over who my sperm and egg provider were. Anyway, freshman year was hell until one of my brothers found out they were beating on me in the bathroom. I don't know what he said, but they kept it to words after that. And God, you did it again. What am I going to do with you?"

"Will it make you feel better if I tell you I've talked more around you than I have in a long time?"

"Maybe. I'll let you know *after* you cook me dinner."

"That seems fair. I'd better go," she said reluctantly. "It's gotten late, and wake-up time comes early in my world."

"I'm glad you made it over. Oh. Almost forgot." Mikaela rushed out of the room and returned shortly with a gift-wrapped box. "Chocolate-chip birthday cookies."

Sara took the box, held it close and searched for words. Two gifts when she'd barely received any growing up. "My sweet tooth appreciates this. Or was I supposed to say 'you shouldn't have'?"

"The way your eyes lit up was thanks enough."

Sara walked to the door, the box safely cradled in her arm.

"So, uh, what day?" Mikaela asked as they stood in the foyer. "For dinner, I mean."

"Wednesday again?"

"Yeah. Seven?"

"Yeah." Sara fixed her gaze on Mikaela's lips, then lowered her head, bringing their lips together. The thought that Mikaela's lips were as soft as she remembered flashed through her brain, and then there were no more thoughts, only feelings. As heat pooled between her thighs, she deepened the kiss and slipped her tongue into Mikaela's mouth. The sweetness was overwhelming. One of them moaned as they pressed their bodies closer together. When the kiss finally ended, Sara wasn't sure her feet were touching the ground.

"That was…wow," Mikaela said, breathing heavily. "I thought I imagined it."

"Imagined what?"

"What a good kisser you are."

"It's not me, it's you." Sara rested her head against the top of Mikaela's head, her heart pounding madly. "I'd better go." She dropped her arms and stepped back. "I'll see you tomorrow."

"Count on it." Mikaela leaned in for a quick kiss. "Maybe next time we'll get around to watching the movie."

"Bring it with you Wednesday." Sara walked to her car, the taste of Mikaela's kiss on her tongue. There wasn't a doubt in her mind she'd just been on a date. And for once, the thought didn't scare her. In fact, she was looking forward to next Wednesday. At the same time, she was wondering if they should move dinner up to the weekend. No, better to try for another movie over the weekend. Save dinners for Wednesdays. It was an outstanding way to break up the week.

CHAPTER FOURTEEN

"Tell me everything," Marianna demanded, waving her buffalo chicken sandwich. She'd made no bones about bribing Mikaela with lunch.

Mikaela took a bite of pickle and chewed slowly. She only laughed when Marianna narrowed her eyes. "Strictly dinner and conversation. There's not that much to tell. Well, except she's wonderful and I had a great time."

"No kissing, no groping, no sofa wrestling? I think I want my money back."

"One kiss and some serious groping as she was leaving. After which I had to reattach my head to my neck." She blew out a breath. "She invited me to dinner at her place Wednesday night. Italian."

"That's too far away. You need to strike while she's still in a weakened state. What about this weekend?"

"Let's not get greedy. It's enough for now that she suggested we get together again. She doesn't want to rush into anything, and despite my natural inclination to throw her down, rip her clothes off and let her have her way with me, I'm going along."

"But Wednesday's too far away. I saw that there's this animated movie coming out Friday. Call and ask her to that. You can say it's to do with that toy theme you've got going."

She snorted. "Toy theme? It's a movie, Marianna."

"All I'm saying is they're both kid stuff. If she didn't have toys, I bet she didn't get to go to kiddie movies either."

"That's not a bad idea. And it is payday, so I'll have extra to treat her. You may be onto something."

"May be? It's as solid as titanium. Now what's that you black people say? Oh, yeah. Give me my props."

Mikaela choked on her drink. "You crazy racist," she rasped between coughs.

Marianna buffed her fingernails on her sweater. "I have my moments. So, when are you going to call her?"

"Might be better to run into her downstairs, bring up the movie idea then. It'll seem more casual, unplanned."

"I can see that." Marianna nodded. "Like an aside, no pressure. That's good."

Mikaela bared her teeth in a fake smile. "What's that you white people say? Oh, yeah. I have my moments."

"Crazy racist." When Marianna laughed, Mikaela joined in. Their snorts and giggles drew looks from a nearby table of college students. It only served to make them laugh harder.

"I'll take a break close to three thirty," Mikaela said as they walked back to work. "Loiter around the lobby and catch her as she's leaving."

"You're dressed for it."

"What?"

"All that cleavage? No way she'll say no."

"Get out!"

"It's true." Marianna held up her right hand as though being sworn in. "I could take a photo, send it to Erin and let her weigh in."

"Shut up." She punched her in the arm. "Please don't tell me I look like Ilene?"

Marianna pulled open the front door. "Maybe in fifty years. Look, there she is." She gave Mikaela a nudge. "Now is as good a time as any."

"Okay, okay." She passed the bank of elevators and joined Sara. "Hey."

"Hey back. Good lunch?"

"Yeah. Wanted to tell you again what a great time. You know, last night."

"Same here." Sara hustled to open the door for a group of women entering the building.

Mikaela couldn't help but notice the flirtatious smile from the petite brunette with the boob job. Since Sara's smile stayed polite, she figured she didn't have to slap the smile off the brunette's face. And really, how could she blame the woman? Sara was magnificent.

"Hey—"

"So—"

"You go first," Sara said.

"There's this new animated film coming out this weekend. I know Casey won't go with me, so—"

"Yes," Sara interjected. "I was going to ask you the same thing. Maybe not the same movie, but it's only fair you get to pick this time."

"That means I get to pay."

"We'll see. Any particular day or time?"

"Saturday? We could catch the matinee, then decide which mall I'm going to drag you through."

"We'll see about the mall."

She settled for a smile instead of pulling Sara down for a mind-blowing kiss. Though it would probably do a lot to dispel any lingering doubts about her and Bill, she controlled herself. "See you…Wait, should I be the one to pick you up?"

"You live closer. I'll pick you up around, say, two thirty like last time."

"I'll be waiting." When she got to the elevator, Mikaela was pleased to find Sara's gaze focused on her. This is good, she thought. Real good. She might owe Marianna lunch.

* * *

That evening Sara unlocked the front door to loud meows. Underneath her coat, she was a solid mass of sweat. She'd run into Nina and her friends on the court. After a couple of cheap shots, which had cost their team in points and goodwill, they'd mostly left her alone. Unfortunately for them, they'd woken Sara's inner warrior, causing her to play better than she should have been able to. She was psyched that she'd played a pivotal role in sending Nina and her crew away in defeat.

After throwing her coat over the back of the sofa, she gave Tab a good scratching under her double chin. "That's enough for now. I need a shower in the worst way. You'll thank me later," she added with a sniff of her underarms.

Her phone chimed as she sang in the shower and she rushed to answer, thinking it could be Mikaela. "Hello," she said, flicking water out of her eyes.

"May I speak with Sara Gordon, please?"

"This is she," she replied, determined to dispatch the unknown caller posthaste.

"This is Walter Tibbs. I apologize for not returning your call earlier."

She'd looked him up and discovered he was one of the partners in Tibbs Truman and Isaacs, LLP, a firm rated as one of Boston's finest. She'd also found his number, but she hadn't expected a return call after leaving a message with his snooty assistant. "What's this about? You should know I haven't had any contact with my father's family or their money."

"I realize that, Ms. Gordon. You're a hard woman to track down."

"Why would you need to? I've already explained that I have no contact with my late father's family."

"I should start by informing you that I am the Gordon family's attorney. I need to send you official notice that all legal challenges against the late Mr. Charles W. Gordon's estate have been dropped. You can expect a check from the executor of the late Mr. Gordon's will, which will include the amounts originally set aside for you to receive upon attaining the ages of twenty-one and thirty."

She didn't know what to say or what to feel. So what if the old man had left her a little money. Too bad he hadn't thought to give her a home when she needed it most. If this lawyer thought she was going to fall to her knees in gratitude, he was doomed for disappointment.

"Ms. Gordon, are you still there?"

"So he could leave me money, but he couldn't be bothered to see his grandson put to rest or see about his great granddaughter?"

"Ms. Gordon, it could be you're not aware Mr. Charles Gordon was bedridden at the time of your father's death. He did, however, send a family representative, your father's cousin, in his stead."

His disapproval was thick enough to cut with a knife and damned if it didn't make her feel defensive. "That was nice of him, but what about me? Oh that's right. He left me money? I would have had to wait fourteen years to get. What a stand-up guy."

"Mistakes were made, Ms. Gordon. Your great grandfather felt you would be better in the hands of your mother's people and Lydia Thomason seemed eager to take responsibility for you. Please remember, he gave your aunt money for your care. It was when she pushed for more that he reconsidered the custodial arrangement. Unfortunately, he died before any decision was finalized."

"She got money for taking me in?"

"Of course. Mr. Gordon would never let a relative of his go without."

Sara closed her eyes, tried not to feel hurt, betrayed. Everything her aunt had told her had been a lie. All the complaining about going out of her way for her cousin's child had been for show. Her aunt's mistreatment had been about greed, about not getting enough money. "How much? How much did he sell me for?"

Tibbs cleared his throat. "You are looking at the situation incorrectly, Ms. Gordon. Even though estranged from his grandson, Mr. Gordon was very concerned about your welfare.

He did not *sell* you. He believed you were in the care of someone who would take good care of you. Had he lived, I am certain he would have made different arrangements as you got older."

"How much, Mr. Tibbs? What was the monetary amount of his concern?"

"Fifty thousand, with more to come when you turned thirteen and your needs changed. Mr. Gordon made the mistake of not adding a codicil before his death, and your father's cousin, Mr. Bernard Gordon, his primary heir, was under no legal obligation to make additional payments."

What about moral ones? she wondered. Family must not mean much in the Gordon clan. Maybe less so when money was involved. "Why am I just hearing about this now? If this is legitimate, shouldn't I have received some kind of notice from you before?"

"I can't be sure. However, the first two letters I sent you did not garner a response. The third was returned, marked 'Addressee Unknown.'"

"I never received any letters from you to ignore."

"They were sent to your aunt's address, which is the only address I have on file. We were recently able to contact your cousin and even he did not have a current address for you."

"That's the way I like it, Mr. Tibbs. But back to this will. Why now?"

"The person contesting the will has passed on and his heirs decided not to pursue the challenge."

If this was a scam, the guy was good and no amount of questioning on her part was going to trip him up. She might as well give him what he wanted and see how things played out. "What do you need from me?"

"A current address, which I will share with Mr. Nathan Baldwin, the executor of the will. Feel free to contact me with any additional questions, Ms. Gordon."

Sara gave him her mailing address, a post office box, and ended the call. He could try to find her from that and fail, she thought with satisfaction. Whatever was sent, she'd read it carefully. She may not have attended college, but she wasn't dumb.

She resumed her shower, not knowing what to think about this new development, her aunt, her great-grandfather or her grandfather's heir. They'd all played a role at a pivotal time in her life. A role she hadn't been fully aware of.

The fifty thousand and the chance for more must have had her Aunty Liddy salivating. She'd probably thought she was set for life. That she had a source she could tap anytime. How furious she must have been when her very first request was denied.

But as Sara worked shampoo through her hair, she wondered where the fifty thousand had gone. They'd never lived lavishly. As best she could recall, they'd lived in apartments barely big enough to fit the five of them. She'd shared a room with Alexia and Allene until Lexie got married at seventeen and moved out. Sara had been fourteen at the time and grossed out by the pimply-faced boy Lexie claimed she couldn't live without. Ally had left a year later to make her mark in Nashville. Sara had vague memories of missing Ally, missing hearing her sing.

Strange, she mused, as she rinsed the shampoo out of her hair. She hadn't thought about those two in forever. Had lumped them with their mother, their brother, the bad times. Because of that, she'd also let go of the happier times when it was just the three girls. Times when her aunt was off with her latest guy and Russell was hanging with his loser friends. That was the story of her life, wasn't it? Burying everything that happened in the past to keep from having anything to bury in the future. Pathetic. More so because it hadn't worked. It had only delayed the return of the memory of her parents' deaths.

Deep in thought, she dried off and pulled on clean sweats. Settling on the sofa, she meant to grab the remote, do some channel surfing. She really did. But she wasn't terribly surprised when instead she grabbed the phone and dialed Mikaela's number. "It's Sara. Hope I, uh, didn't call at a bad time."

"As if you could. I was doing some reading, losing myself in someone else's more glamorous life. What's up?"

She gripped the phone tightly. "Don't think I'm crazy, but not sure why I called. I got…a strange call earlier tonight. Threw me off."

"Are you in trouble?"

"Not the way you mean. It's just that this year's been… different. Not even through January and my past has turned into something I never knew. My parents didn't die in an auto accident and my aunt did get money to take me in. Seems she treated me like crap because the old man wouldn't fork over more. And then there's the old man throwing out money because there wasn't anyone on my dad's side of the family who could be bothered to see about his daughter. Do I have a great family or what? And why do I care?" Sara took a breath. "Sorry. Didn't call to dump all over you."

"Sounds like you took a knock. It says a lot that you thought to call me. Dump away."

"I didn't know I knew how to dump. How pathetic is that? Holding everything inside till I blow."

"We all cope in different ways. Me, I talk and talk and talk. Bet you never noticed that."

Sara exhaled. This was what she needed. "Maybe a little."

"You're probably wondering right now if I ever shut up."

"Wrong. I was thinking that calling you was the right thing to do, smarty pants."

"That's a start. Have you figured out who you're madder at between the old man and your aunt?"

"Her. I never met him, and in his defense, it sounds like he might have been frail at the time my parents died. Aunt Liddy? There was nothing frail about her, wailing all the time about the sacrifices she made to take me in. Fifty thousand's a sacrifice all right. She must have blown through the money sooner than expected, then got her feelings hurt when the old man refused to fork over more. What I can't figure out is what she did with the money. I remember grocery shopping and her separating out the items she could pay for with food stamps. Just about everything else we bought came from one of those charity-type stores. It seems like that woman was always looking for a handout. If not from the government, then from one of the loser men she'd bring around. I never wanted to be like her. Got my first job at fourteen. Gave her a little money when she bitched and moaned, but saved as much as I could."

"She sounds 'positively charming,' as my grandmother would say."

"The most. She had no right to treat me that way. No right at all. And I wasn't a burden, no matter what she said. It was her, never me. I was only a kid." Sara rubbed her cheeks, feeling the anger burning bright. Anger she'd never really dealt with while her aunt was alive.

"Exactly. She's the one who accepted the responsibility and didn't follow through. That's on her. You have every right to be angry. Don't think for one hot second you don't."

"You would have made a great Crusader."

"Doubtful. Honey, those people were crazy. And while I can be a little touched in my own way, I ain't that crazy."

"Only a little touched?"

"Yes. And since this is not about me, I hope you feel better."

"I do. Bet you didn't think you were going to get the long answer, huh? Now you're the one wondering if I'll ever shut up."

"Wrong. I'm thinking you bought the 'strong, silent type' bull. You've buried these feelings so long, it's no wonder they're spewing like a geyser now. That's a good thing, Sara. Get it up, get it out, get it gone. Do you know what happens to the strong, silent types? I'll tell you. They turn into serial killers. Ever hear of one who talked all the time?"

"So you mean spewing all over you saved me from being a killer? Isn't that a stretch?"

"Be skeptical if you will. I only speak the truth."

"Then it sounds like I need to be paying for the movie Saturday. You saved me from a life of killing after all."

"Don't even try it. I am letting you drive, oh butchly one."

Sara laughed. "Got me there. Hope I get the chance to see you tomorrow."

"I'll have to try and make that happen. Sweet dreams."

"They will be now." Sara dumped the phone on the sofa, pulled Tab into her lap and scratched behind her ears. "Life's not so bad. But I don't have to tell you that."

* * *

Mikaela placed the phone on the end table, the book in her lap forgotten. She could have told Sara she knew about women who pretended they were going to do the right thing and didn't. Her mother had done it. Pretended to want her child until it hadn't been convenient, hadn't fit with the life she wanted to return to.

Mikaela had been thirteen when she'd found out why she didn't have a mother. Until then, she'd assumed her mother, who was never spoken of, was dead. She had a friend of Lisa's to thank for bringing her down with the truth.

She could remember how hurt and angry she'd been when her grandmother admitted her mother had abandoned her. How it was the only way for her mother to regain acceptance and support from her conservative parents.

For a couple of months, Mikaela had been mad at the world. It didn't help when her period showed up shortly after the revelation. All she knew was that her temper got stuck on hot and her eyes never seemed to dry. Looking back, those few months were easily the worst time of her life. She didn't doubt her relatives would agree it had been the worst time of their lives as well.

Eventually, she got over herself and realized what she was doing to her beloved grandmother, to the family that loved her. She'd put that woman out of her mind and set about making amends. Probably easier to do when you were surrounded by love, she thought. In that regard she was much luckier than Sara had been.

Hearing Casey's footsteps, she looked up. "Well, well, well. Look who finally found her way back home."

Casey shut the door with her butt. "Jealous much?"

"As if. Though you do have that rosy glow. What have you been up to, young lady?" She laughed as Casey's cheeks turned red. "Never mind. Answer's written all over your face. I should be asking why you're here."

"Early meeting and clean clothes." Casey draped her garment bag across the chair. "Anything new with you?"

"A movie date with Sara on Saturday *and* dinner at her place next Wednesday."

"You wow her with your cooking or did something happen after dinner?" Casey wiggled her eyebrows.

"Hey, I'm good company outside the bed too. She's slowly coming around to my view of world order."

"Good." Casey sat on the arm of the sofa. "I wouldn't want to have to flex my muscles, have the 'don't make me hurt you' talk with her."

"Yeah."

"Hey, Beth's been called back for a second interview. You interested in catching happy hour tomorrow?"

"Perfect. I finished the project for Bill. Barring any major changes, it should be put to bed by tomorrow. Just going by Talya and Jolene's reactions, I aced it and therefore deserve adult beverages."

"Absolutely. I'll give you a call, let you know the time. I figure you can either come to my office, or I'll pick you up and we can ride together."

"That works."

CHAPTER FIFTEEN

By four o'clock Friday, Mikaela was watching the phone, waiting for Casey's call. She'd had a great day so far and was ready to top it off by hitting happy hour and hitting it hard. Maybe she could talk Beth into dinner after, so they could discuss books again. No dancing this time. She wanted to be fresh for her date with Sara.

"Date." God, her life just kept getting better.

Mikaela snatched up the ringing phone when she saw Casey's name on caller ID. "Please tell me we're still on."

"Rockfort Saloon," Casey replied. "Come to my office after you get off and we'll fight our way north from there."

"I can be there in thirty minutes tops. Fair warning, I'll be the one ordering something bubbly."

"What are we celebrating?"

"Kicking asses and taking names. I'll explain later, but you'd better hope the size of my head goes down so I can fit in that big bruiser of yours."

"I have WD-40. We'll squeeze you in somehow."

"You're too kind."

"Yeah, it's a problem. Later, Big Head."

"That's Ms. Big Head to you." Smiling, Mikaela replaced the receiver. Rockfort fit her mood. It would be loud and crowded—the perfect place to celebrate. She grabbed her pocketbook. Time to refresh her makeup.

She pushed open the bathroom door, feeling energized. Her steps faltered as she spotted Ilene and Christine having what looked to be a hushed conversation. They must have heard about this morning, she thought, and she returned their baleful glares with a smile and a wave. She slipped into the stall farthest from them, prepared to wait them out. No way she needed them to attempt to kick the shine off her halo.

After a couple minutes of loitering, she gave up. They were going to outwait her. They were standing in the same spot, eyes trained on her. "You need something from me?"

"Everything is not about you," Ilene said.

"Unlike *you*, I know that." Mikaela placed her pocketbook by the sink and put her hands on her hips. Obviously she was not going to get out of here without a fight. "For some reason I thought since you're standing here, trying to stare me down, that you might have something to say. My bad." With a dismissive flip of her wrist, she turned her back on them.

"We know what you did," Christine said as Mikaela washed her hands. "Walking around here like you own the place. It doesn't matter how Dennis tries to spin this to make you seem innocent. We know you're not."

She took the time to dry her hands. "Funny. I know what I did too. I used my knowledge and experience to do a damn good job. Not only on this last project, but every day. What I haven't been doing is spending my time spreading lies that make me look stupid and desperate. You want to talk about me for doing that, go ahead. Do your worst. Oh wait, you already tried that and failed."

"You should be careful what you wish for," Christine said with a tight smile.

"What I wish for? I'll tell you what I wish for, and that's for the two of you to get a life and stay out of mine." Mikaela held up her hand when Ilene opened her mouth. "You don't want my inner bitch to slip her leash, so shut it. Y'all have a nice weekend." She flashed a smile as fake as plastic flowers and sailed out.

She'd have to find a synonym for "worse than pathetic" because that's what they were. People too pathetic to know they were pathetic. But not now. Now it was time to leave work and its irritating problems behind. She was more than ready to toast her accomplishments, which now included squishing The Two under her heels without getting her shoes dirty.

* * *

The Rockfort Saloon was packed when Mikaela and Casey arrived at five thirty. As usual Friday rush-hour traffic had been horrendous, so to Mikaela it seemed apropos that they had to fight their way through the loud crowd around the bar to join Suzette and Beth.

After exchanging greetings, it was decided that Beth and Suzette, who already had drinks, would grab a table on the sheltered patio while Casey and Mikaela waited in line for their drinks.

"Champagne?" Casey asked. "My treat."

Mikaela's earlier words had been forgotten after a glimpse of the special: a King Kong–sized margarita. "Changed my mind. I'll have one of those." She pointed to a group of women toasting one another. They made the drink look festive and she wanted that. "With salt."

"You got it." Casey leaned over the bar to shout her order to one of the four bartenders.

They found the patio was only marginally quieter.

"Beth, how did it go?" Casey asked once they were squeezed around a table meant for two.

Beth beamed. "Unless I misread the signs, they're going to offer me the position. They promised to let me know either way by Tuesday."

"A toast to Beth," Suzette said and raised her glass of wine. The others followed suit.

"But Beth's not the only one with something to celebrate." Casey looked at Mikaela.

"True." She told them about having an hour to pull together a presentation about the meeting materials, the knocking of her knees as she walked in to find not just Bill, Talya and some bigwig from HQ but all the managers as well. "I tell you, it was nerve-racking to have them all looking at me. Kind of like a pop quiz. But as it turned out, I slayed the beast, and— unofficially— it seems I talked my way into a job."

"You know it was more than talk." Casey nudged her with her elbow. "There was good work to back up the talk."

"Much to the chagrin of some people." Mikaela lifted her glass high. "Here's to kick-ass presentations that impress the ones in power."

"Hear, hear." Beth raised her bottle of beer. "To a successful day and good friends."

Mikaela took a healthy sip of her frothy drink and found it to be exactly what she needed. "Today is a great day. It'll be a better day when Beth moves down here."

"And yet another good thing to drink to," Beth said.

"Most things are," Casey said. "I got assigned to a high-profile case today."

"You could have said so sooner. To Casey." Mikaela raised her glass. "And you, Suzette?"

"My mother's threatening to come for a visit. But that's not something to toast. Drink to, yes." Suzette finished off her wine.

"I'll get you a refill," Casey said. "Anyone else?"

Beth held up her hand.

"So you and your mom don't get along?"

"We get along fine. Especially if she's in another city." Suzette looked over her shoulder, then turned back to Mikaela. "I think she wants to vet Casey. She and Lisa never quite saw eye to eye, so I'd like to delay the meeting with Casey as long as possible."

"Don't worry. Everybody loves Casey. They can't help themselves."

"It's true." Beth reached for Suzette's hand and gave it a squeeze. "I love her already."

Suzette smiled. "You love anyone who buys you a beer."

"You'd think people would move away from the bar once they got their drink," Casey grumbled and placed a beer in front of Beth, then handed Suzette her wine. "Anybody else ready for food? I missed lunch."

"We could leave them here, go to the other side and grab dinner," Suzette said. "This early we shouldn't have any trouble getting a table."

"Works for me," Beth said.

Mikaela raised her drink.

Inside, they fought their way through the bar crowd to the more subdued restaurant section. The restaurant was richly appointed with a combination of wood and leather, a direct contrast to the flashy, modern-looking bar side they'd come from. As Suzette had predicted, they were quickly seated.

Mikaela opened the menu and winced at the prices. She was going to have to rework her credit card payoff spreadsheet after paying for dinner tonight, then tomorrow's movie and possibly dinner after. But spreadsheets were meant to be changed. And if she limited herself to water, the hit wouldn't be nearly as bad. Plus once she got the new job, she'd be making more money and have to change it anyway, thus evening out everything. How she loved, loved, loved rationalizations. That and the tilapia stuffed with a creamy crab sauce that she was going to order.

Their efficient waiter who wore a crisp white shirt and black slacks that matched his bowtie, brought them water, took their order and bowed before gliding away.

"Good service," Mikaela said, squeezing lemon juice into her water. Though it and the food should be, given the prices.

She need not have worried. The food was excellent and consumed amid conversation about what the weekend might hold.

Her stomach pleasantly full, Mikaela regretfully declined the sinful-looking desserts, even as the dark chocolate mousse screamed her name. To her delighted surprise, Suzette picked up the check.

As they once again fought through the crowd in the bar area to get to the back parking lot, Mikaela came face to face with

Nina. When she tried to slide by with a nod, Nina's hand shot out and clamped on her wrist. She decided then and there that Atlanta was too small for the both of them.

"What's the rush?"

She smelled the alcohol and remembering the previous threats to Sara, made an effort to keep her tone pleasant. "Hey, you wanna let me go? We're on our way out."

"But I just got here. Maybe you wanna change your mind."

Casey squeezed past Suzette and Beth to stand next to Mikaela. "Is there a problem?"

"Good old Casey, still playing guard dog." Nina's smile was anything but friendly and she tightened her grip. "But this doesn't concern you. Mikaela and I have some business to finish."

"Well, it concerns me," Mikaela shot back, embarrassed by the attention they were attracting. "Now I asked you nicely to let me go. Don't make this any harder than it has to be."

"It concerns me too," Beth said, hands on hips.

Nina glanced at Beth, then back at Mikaela. "You already moved on to somebody else, I see. What, that white girl couldn't keep up? Had to get back to black?" She laughed.

"Back off, Nina," Casey demanded.

"No, you back off." Nina let Mikaela go and pushed Casey hard enough to send her flailing back into Beth and Suzette. Only the crowd behind them kept them from falling.

"You have lost your mind." Mikaela rocketed into Nina's personal space. "You need to leave me alone. Now, I'm going out that door and I hope I don't see you again. But if I do have the misfortune to cross your path, don't look at me, don't talk to me, don't breathe on me. I have nothing more to say to you. If you persist in harassing me and my friends, I'll slap you with a restraining order so fast your head will fly off. You know Casey knows how to get it done."

When she tried to walk away, Nina grabbed her with both hands, spun her around and shook her. She leaned in to say softly, "You don't get to talk to me that way in front of my friends. And you don't get to walk away from me. Understand?"

Mikaela's breathing hitched as she struggled against Nina's biting grip, struggled against the stirrings of fear. Every stalker movie she'd seen on the Lifetime channel came back full force. It didn't help to note that she was now surrounded by Nina's friends. "Let me go," she begged unashamedly. "You can be the one to walk away, your pride intact. Come on, please?"

"You trying to play me now?" Nina looked to her friends. "I look like a lapdog to you?" When they hooted, she turned her attention back to Mikaela. "I'm in charge. You better recognize."

She looked into Nina's angry brown eyes and wondered who this stranger was. This testosterone-filled bully couldn't be the woman she'd dated, lived with. "You won, okay? You can let me go now."

"Or what, little girl?" Nina yanked Mikaela's arm.

"Or this." Mikaela aimed her knee at Nina's crotch, missed, and then wasn't fast enough to dodge the fist that snapped her head back. Her already precarious balance was lost. She bounced off one of Nina's friends, and it was only the help of a Good Samaritan that eased her fall.

"You okay?" he asked. "That was a serious hit."

She wasn't sure which hurt worse: her head or her pride. "I'm…yeah. Thanks." When he helped her into a sitting position, she saw that Casey was being held by two of Nina's friends. "Let her go!"

"Stop this right now," Suzette said loudly. She held up her cell phone. "I caught the assault on my phone. Charges *will* be filed."

"That's right." The manager, who'd been summoned by Beth, motioned to the two burly guys with her, and they escorted Nina and her friends to the back. "Are you okay, Miss?" She stooped to Mikaela's level.

She nodded, though pain was kicking pride's ass. "I used to be faster."

"Try this." Beth handed her a napkin covering a bag of ice. She held up three fingers. "How many fingers do you see?"

"Only the one in the middle matters. You got any pain-killers?"

"I have a first-aid kit in my office," the manager said. "Why don't we wait there for the police? Can I assume you're going to press charges?"

Stronger words were on the back of her tongue. She settled for a simple but heartfelt "Yes."

* * *

Mikaela woke up the next morning with a stiff neck, a raging headache and the inability to fully open her left eye. She grunted, brought her hand up to her face and gingerly explored the area made puffy by Nina's well-placed fist. As she expected, it was tender to the touch. And most likely dark enough to stand out. Damn! She had a date in a few hours and there wasn't enough makeup in the world to completely cover the damage.

A light knock drew her attention to the open door. "Might as well come in." Though she'd tried to convince Casey to go to Suzette's last night, she was grateful her friend had chosen to come home with her.

Casey eased the door open, caught sight of Mikaela and winced. "Heard noise, so I thought I'd check to make sure you're okay. See if you need anything."

"It's bad, isn't it?"

"Truthfully, it looks worse than it did last night." She sat on the bed and reached for Mikaela's hand. "I think we need to go to one of those after-hours clinics, have them check you out. Just to make sure nothing's broken."

She shook her head and immediately regretted it. "I'm mostly okay. But you know what really blows is that now I have to call Sara and cancel. I can't have her see me like this." She pointed at her face. "I can't believe that bitch hit me. I mean, I can't even pretend it was some kind of accidental punch."

"I'm surprised myself. I would have thought she took that macho act too seriously to hit you."

"God, what am I going to tell people at work? I can't go in looking like this."

"Take Monday off and wear gobs and gobs of makeup on Tuesday. If they notice, so what? You were assaulted. That's not your fault. And as for Sara, if she's all you think she is, she won't care if you look like you went a few rounds."

"Yeah, right. I need to get up."

"Okay, but let's take it slow. See how your balance is today."

She had vague memories of tripping over her own feet last night. "Please tell me no one I know saw me almost take a dive in the parking lot?"

Casey chuckled. "That should be the least of your worries, but knowing you, it's not. Rest assured you only stumbled around drunkenly in front of strangers and three friends. Now, up."

Mikaela sat up gingerly, feeling the pull of abused muscles to go with the throbbing in her head. "Note to self: learn to bob and weave." When her vision didn't swim, she eased off the bed and, under Casey's watchful eye, slowly made her way to the bathroom. She found out on the way that more than her neck was stiff.

Her shriek had Casey coming in at a dead run. "Look at me," she demanded, pointing a finger at her reflection. A dark bruise fanned down from her swollen eye to her jaw. "I'm a wreck. No way I want Sara to see this. Hell, *I* don't want to see this." She turned from the mirror and used her hands to cover her face.

Casey tugged at Mikaela's hands. "Bet you five Sara'll be upset you were hurt, not that you look…less than perfect."

"Good catch, but I'm far, far away from less than perfect. Some of my family would feel it necessary to point out that I'm 'tore up from the floor up,'" she grumbled. "And I'm not paying you no five dollars. I'll call, let Sara decide. Coffee first though, and something for this headache." She opened the right-side drawer and came up empty. "You have any?"

"Sure. You should grab a shower. No—make that a bath. Then I'll make you an omelet and toast."

She kissed Casey's cheek. "I'll say it again. You're the best friend evah."

Mikaela did feel better after the aspirin, a long soak and breakfast. Still, she delayed an hour before calling Sara. "It's Mikaela."

"Hi. I was thinking about you."

"Really? Good stuff, I hope."

"Of course. How's it going?"

"I've…been better. A lot better. Actually that's mainly why I called. I was in a little altercation yesterday and my face is…let's say, Frankenstein's monsterish. So—"

"You okay? It wasn't The Three, was it?"

Mikaela laughed. "I'll have to point them out to you one day, so you'll understand why that's funny. It was Nina. She took exception to a lot of things last night, and I had the poor sense not to get out of the way of her fist."

"She hit you? She actually hit you?"

"Yeah. Did a good job."

"I can't believe it. Are you hurt anywhere else? Do you need me to come over and take you somewhere or bring you something? Go beat the hell out of Nina?"

"That's sweet, but she's not worth the trouble. It's not so bad. Mostly the left side of my face is affected, with a few twinges here and there thrown in. But I wasn't kidding about the monster deal and I thought it would be best if you, you know, weren't seen in public with me."

"You're worried about me? No need. If you feel like going out, I feel like going out. But since you probably don't, what if I come to your place and keep you company? We could watch *Toy Story*."

Her heart fluttered. Score one for Casey. "That works for me. That really works for me."

"I'll bring Speedy so he can watch himself on the small screen."

"I have popcorn."

"I'll stop by the drugstore, pick up M&M's. Plain, right?"

"Right on the money." Mikaela ended the call, placed her phone on the sofa beside her and spared Casey a glance. "I'm not paying you a penny."

CHAPTER SIXTEEN

Sara arrived at Mikaela's place early. Even with a stop at the drugstore, the trip only took her a little over ten minutes. She'd allotted twenty. She debated waiting in her car, but decided that was dumb. She didn't care if Mikaela knew she was eager to see her. And she wanted to make sure for herself Mikaela was okay. After keying in the code, she pulled into a visitor's spot and grabbed the bag of goodies and get-well balloons she hadn't been able to resist.

When Mikaela opened the door, her hair was loose around her face. It still didn't do enough to cover the vivid bruise that circled her eye and trailed down to her jaw. Sara smiled around the sudden knot in her throat. A knot that made her want to hunt Nina down and do some damage in return. But right now she was needed here, and doing that wouldn't do much for Mikaela's pain and suffering or her peace of mind. "I hope you like balloons. If not, I can go get flowers."

"Love them."

Sara gladly accepted the warm hug, extended it. "How are you really doing?"

"Okay as long as I get up and move around every so often. I didn't realize how many muscles are affected by a punch to the face."

"I'm so sorry it happened." She drew back so she could look Mikaela in the eye. "Is she going to be a problem? And if so, what can I do to help?"

Mikaela exhaled. "Before last night I would have said no way, but now, I honestly don't know what she's capable of. I pressed charges, so maybe that will give her the jolt she needs to stay away. And since you haven't run away screaming, you should come on in. Can I get you something to drink?"

"I'm good right now. And before I forget," She produced a colorful gift bag with flourish. "M&M's, plain, and an emergency chocolate bar. Not that I'm trying to sabotage your diet. Thought you might be feeling down and I know how much you enjoy chocolate. You'll also find a replacement toy car. They didn't have Speedy."

"Just what I need after last night." Mikaela placed the bag on the coffee table and lowered herself onto the couch. "How about you? You feeling any better about that situation with your aunt, your great grandfather, the money?"

"Working on letting the anger go. It's hard going because I'm still pissed that she got money for taking me, a lot of money, and then turned around and treated me the way she did. I tell myself there's nothing that can be done about it now, but..." She shrugged. "Then this morning I started wondering about who this heir was. The one who decided I didn't warrant the extra money or seeing about. It's a good thing I don't plan to have kids because they'd be getting the greed gene from both sides."

"There are worse things to pass on. Look at me. Not that I plan to have kids either, because hey, my family is doing a good job of making sure there won't be a shortage of children. But say I did plan to have them. I wouldn't let having irresponsible parents stop me. And calling them irresponsible is probably letting them off lightly, mind you." Mikaela frowned, pursing her lips. "I had a point in there somewhere. Really I did. Oh, you can't let fear stop you from doing what you want to do. There are no guarantees when it comes to kids, to human beings. And there shouldn't be. Living is all about taking chances. If you're not doing that, then to my way of thinking, you aren't living. And as usual, that's the long answer when you probably wanted the abridged one. Added to that, I'm not sure you even asked me a question."

"Doesn't matter, because I like hearing your views. Skewed as they are." Sara gave Mikaela's hand a squeeze. "And I know somewhere in there was a point about me needing to let go. Very clever."

"I wasn't an A student for nothing. Now I'm going to go pop the popcorn, get the drinks and we can start the show. I'm starting your education with the story of a jealous action figure who ends up having to find his way back home with the action figure he's jealous of. Take notes. There may be a pop quiz afterwards."

Sara pulled a face. "You're strict."

Soon the smell of popcorn wafted into the living room. Sara retrieved Speedy from her coat pocket and placed him on the coffee table facing the TV.

"Here we go."

"Hey, you shouldn't be carrying that." Sara jumped up and hurried to relieve Mikaela of the tray that held a bowl of popcorn and their drinks. "You're on injured reserve."

"It's mainly my face."

"Can't be too careful. Sit." Sara handed Mikaela the popcorn and positioned the drinks on coasters. "What should I do with this?" She held up the tray.

"Put it under the table for now. Oh, you remembered to bring Speedy." Mikaela exhaled and blinked her eyes. "After last night…well, that makes my day."

"I wasn't a B student for nothing." She was pleased when Mikaela laughed.

Mikaela powered on the TV and the DVD player. "Prepare to be awed."

Sara enjoyed Mikaela's reactions as much as she enjoyed having Mikaela snuggled under her arm. The physical pull, though strong, was outweighed by the sense of contentment. This was better than going to the movie theater, she realized, and she could have stayed in the same position for many more hours than the movie lasted.

Mikaela placed the empty bowl on the table as the credits rolled. "What did you think?"

"Pretty good. Who knew toys had feelings?"

"Please, don't tell me you don't know about the Island of Misfit Toys."

"Uhm...okay?"

Mikaela sighed. "Your education is sorely lacking. You're lucky to have *moi* to school you."

"Lucky," she parroted, eliciting a smile from Mikaela.

"You're a nut."

Sara pulled Mikaela closer, dropped a quick kiss on her lips and said, "You're nuttier. I like it."

"I like you." Mikaela pulled Sara in for another kiss.

Sara tightened her arms around Mikaela, deepening the kiss. When she licked her lips, they opened and she slid her tongue into the salty, chocolate sweetness of Mikaela's mouth.

Mikaela twisted to get closer and bumped the side of her face against Sara's arm. She broke off the kiss with a pain-filled yelp.

"I'm sorry. Are you okay?"

She nodded, covering the knot with her hand. "Not your fault. I'd forgotten all about it, thanks to your wonderful company." She grimaced. "It's still tender."

"What can I do? You need ice, aspirin?" Sara could have kicked herself for forgetting Mikaela was injured. "I can run to the drugstore and get anything you need."

"It's okay. I'll pop some more pain-killers and try to remember next time that I'm, as you put it, on injured reserve." She eased off the sofa.

Sara stood and put her hand against the small of Mikaela's back in case she needed extra support. A smile touched her lips when Mikaela leaned into her hand. She followed her to the kitchen. "You probably should lie down after this. I should leave so you can rest."

Mikaela paused in the act of dumping pills in her hands. "There is a part two we could watch if you don't have to be anywhere."

"Here. I want to be here. I think Speedy would get a kick out of watching himself again."

Mikaela leaned into Sara. "I really like you."

"Back at you." Sara's kiss was light as a feather. "Take your meds so we can get on with the show."

Mikaela fell asleep halfway through the second movie. Sara adjusted her to make sure her neck wouldn't get stiff. It was an unfamiliar emotion to want to protect someone else, to want to give comfort. She was used to worrying only about herself, thought she didn't want to have anyone to worry about. To her, worry led to care, care led to love, and love always led to hurt.

She'd obviously let worrying and caring slip past her, she acknowledged, as she studied the bruises. Maybe it wasn't a bad thing that she didn't want Mikaela to be hurt or afraid of what Nina might do. Friends thought that way. They wanted to protect their friends, wanted them to be okay, to feel better. But she hadn't felt like this about her friends in high school.

Only partly paying attention to the movie, Sara tried to pinpoint the moment she'd lost control. The park. That morning in the park when she'd reached out, asked Mikaela to spend the day with her. That was the first time she'd ever sought another's company for something other than sex. She'd been off balance and yet some part of her had known Mikaela was the answer, the road to level ground.

That part of her had been right, she admitted with a rueful smile. And sneaky enough to keep chipping away on the inside, in concert with Mikaela chipping away on the outside, until Sara opened herself up. Until being with Mikaela was so much more than sexual release. So here she was worrying and taking care of the woman cradled against her side. A woman who was making her feel things she'd never meant to feel.

She gave a nervous laugh, felt the tension in her stomach, but didn't move an inch.

Mikaela stirred as the credits ran across the screen. She covered a yawn as she sat up. "Well, now you know what a good hostess I am. Sorry about that."

"Don't be. You obviously needed the rest. I'm glad it was me you rested on."

"For someone who claims to have no experience with relationships, you do a good job of knowing what to say." Mikaela rotated her neck and grimaced. "I'd better stand up, work out the kinks."

Sara watched as Mikaela stretched gingerly. "Want me to give you a back rub? One of my jobs was as a masseuse." She wiggled her fingers. "I promise to be gentle."

"My back's okay, but if you could work on my neck and shoulders I'd be in heaven."

With Mikaela sitting on the floor in front of her, Sara worked out the knots and kinks in her neck and shoulders. If the sounds coming out of Mikaela's mouth made her squirm, Sara wasn't talking. "I think that should do it."

"Yes. And when my bones stiffen back up, I'll be able to stand." She sighed. "You have wonderful, no, magical fingers."

"It's only fitting since I always seem to have a magical time when I'm with you." Sara dropped a kiss on top of her head. "What if I use these magical fingers to order pizza? The popcorn's definitely worn off."

CHAPTER SEVENTEEN

Sara stepped aside to let Roger enter the office first. She had no desire to be run over as he raced to clock out.

"Another Monday done," he said, reaching for his time card.

She imagined he had a calendar where he crossed off each day on the way to retirement. "How many Mondays you got left?"

He punched out. "More than one." He looked at Jackson, who was on the phone, and lowered his voice. "May have fewer if I were to get sick."

She didn't doubt he had his personal hours planned out to the minute. "What're you going to do with your days afterward?"

Roger smiled. "Fishing and hunting come to mind. I reckon I can do anything I want to."

"I'm going to need one of you to check out a situation on ten," Jackson said before Sara could clock out. "Just got off the phone with a client, but she didn't know what exactly was happening."

"I'll take it." Sara returned her card to its slot.

"Thanks. Radio me when you know what the situation is."

She took the elevator, hoping there wasn't another dead body in the bathroom. With that in mind, her first stop was the women's bathroom. It was clear, so she proceeded to the men's and found it clear as well. Whatever the situation, it did not involve dead homeless people in the bathroom, and she liked that.

Sara exited the bathroom, took a right. There was a big law firm that took up the north side of the floor, heavy on staff but usually light on clients. Maybe not so light today.

Silence. That's what met her when she opened the door to the suite. No receptionist, no murmurs of conversation from the offices beyond the receptionist's desk, no nothing.

"Building security." There was no response to her call and unease morphed into concern. Something had happened here. Something that cleared out the normally busy office.

Her instinct was to turn around and walk away. Her duty was to assess the situation. Could be someone was injured and waiting for help. My help, she thought. She tightened her grip on the two-way radio. With her heart hammering in her chest, she moved farther into the suite and found more nothingness. Time to call it in.

She fumbled her radio at the sound of Jackson's voice but managed to hold on. Whatever he'd said was lost. "North suite looks empty. What—"

"Get out. Guy's got a gun on the south end. Cops on the way."

"Roger that!" She took a few seconds to decide it was faster to exit the suite to get to the north stairwell than to find her way through the maze of offices. Legs pumping, she tore down the hall, rounded the corner by the elevator and almost fell as she came to an abrupt stop.

Sara imagined it would have been hard to tell which of them was more surprised: her, the crazed-looking white male or the very pregnant, clearly terrified African-American female with a gun to her head. Sara raised her hands, then held her breath as she waited for the gunman to make the first move. Her breath came out with a whoosh when his response was to level the gun at her. She had a moment to think of Mikaela and wonder why this was happening to her now, when she was finally getting her life together.

"Show me your weapon."

"I…I'm building security, sir. Don't have one."

"Take off your jacket and turn around. Slowly," he cautioned.

She struggled against panic. Instructions on dealing with situations such as the one she found herself in had *not* been in the training manual. She would see that got rectified, but only if she made it. Sweat beaded under her arms as she complied with his demands, this despite promises of dryness from the maker of her deodorant.

"You're going to want to get on your radio and tell your boss I have a hostage and I'm not afraid to use this gun." As if to emphasize his point, he fired a couple of shots overhead.

Once she got her breathing under control, Sara's mind became a little less foggy. "Uh, okay. Yeah, okay. What…uh, what do you want, sir? He's going to ask what you want."

"What I want?" he shouted, waving the gun around. "I tell you what I fucking want. I want my cheating whore of a wife and that motherfucker she's fucking to look me in the eye and explain to me why they decided to fuck up my life. Why they decided to fuck up my kids' lives."

Shit, she thought, why couldn't it be something easy like a plane and money? Something they had a chance of getting. "I need to put down my hands to call, sir."

"Don't try anything, or else." He jammed the gun under the other woman's chin.

Sara's heartbeat ratcheted up a couple of notches. Something she wouldn't have thought possible. "Take it easy, sir. No funny stuff. I promise." She hit the talk button on the two-way radio. "Jackson, we have a situation. He's got a hostage and a gun."

"You okay?"

"Uh, yeah. He wants to see his wife and his wife's, uh, friend."

"You tell him I'm not afraid to use this gun if I don't get what I want."

"He can hear you, sir." Sara rubbed a sweaty palm against her pants and waited for Jackson's response. She hoped the police would get here soon. She would be happy to let the professionals deal with this.

"Sara, do you have your phone?" Jackson asked.

"Yeah."

"Expect a call."

The radio went dead. Moments later, her cell phone buzzed. She looked at the gunman for permission before answering. "Sara Gordon."

"This is Officer Brandies," a smooth, decidedly female voice announced. "How many people are with you now?"

"Two. That includes him. He, uh, he has some demands." Sara kept her eyes trained on the gun, not wanting to see the terror in the other woman's eyes or the tears running down her face.

"You put that on speaker phone!" he demanded. "I want to hear what they're saying."

"Can I get his name and the name of the hostage?"

"You don't worry about that. The names you need to know are Ashley Pate and David Hays. You get them down here and I'll let these people go." He rattled off a number. "My cheating whore of a wife takes that damn phone everywhere. Now I know why."

"Mr...." Officer Brandies' voice trailed off. She was obviously expecting an answer.

"You get them here, we'll talk. Turn that off," he told Sara. "I'm done talking for now."

Check, she thought, as she put the phone in her pocket. There was no way the cops were going to hand over two civilians to an armed guy who was raving mad.

"I...I still need to go to the bathroom." It was said so quietly, Sara had to strain to hear the words.

The look he leveled at the pregnant woman conveyed his disgust. "You lead the way," he said, motioning with the gun in Sara's direction. "Don't try to escape. I'll shoot you right in the back."

She nodded, turned around very slowly and walked to the bathroom, praying the whole way.

The gunman positioned himself in the doorway of the bathroom. "You try anything and this one dies," he told the hostage. "Then you."

The woman scurried into the handicap stall without a word or a look back.

Sara leaned against the wall, her mind racing a mile a minute as she tried to figure out if and when to make a move. She didn't know much about guns except that she didn't want to get shot with one. Didn't want the pregnant woman to get shot with one either. That meant she had to stay alert, stay ready to take action when it became obvious the adulterous couple wasn't going to be produced.

She didn't want to think he would shoot the other woman, harm the baby. He'd been concerned about how the affair affected his kids, she remembered. A man like that surely wouldn't kill an innocent soon-to-be-born child, would surely empathize with another parent.

Her certainty faded five minutes later when they walked into the reception area of B & M Associates. Two bodies were sprawled on the floor. The pregnant woman drew in a sharp breath and covered her mouth. Sara thought it might be to suppress a scream. She couldn't blame her. She was feeling pretty shaky herself, fighting hard not to let the sight of two bodies, of the blood, get to her. It wasn't easy as memories flashed through her mind. She had to remind herself she wasn't a helpless child now. That she hadn't lost her parents again.

It's not them, she thought, making herself look closely at the bodies on the floor. One was facedown. From the looks of things, he had been shot trying to escape. The other one, a young-looking man, was face up. A bright red spot told the story of a shot to the stomach. Sara swallowed hard. This guy was more out of control than she'd figured. More willing to show his anger with his gun and more dangerous. She looked away and wondered how the hell she was supposed to get them out of this alive.

Her cell buzzed, and she gave a start. Her nerves stretched thin, she only answered after getting a nod from the gunman. "Sara Gordon."

"Officer Brandies here. Is Mr. Pate available?"

"Hold on." She held out the phone, her hand shaking. "Uh, the cops want to talk to you."

"Put it on speaker," he demanded, not budging from his position next to the other hostage.

"He...he's here. On...on speaker phone."

"Mr. Pate, this is Officer Brandies with the Atlanta Police Department."

"Have you got them? Have you got those cheating motherfuckers?"

"We have a problem, Mr. Pate. Your wife is not at your house and she's not answering her cell phone. Do you know another way for us to locate her?"

"If I knew where the whore was do you think I'd be here looking for her? She's supposed to be at work. Some big project that was taking all her damn time. Fucking lie! Why didn't I see it was a fucking lie?" He was screaming as he advanced on the phone in Sara's hand, dragging the pregnant woman with him.

"It's not your fault, Mr. Pate," Officer Brandies said, her tone conciliatory. "We will find her."

"And him. Probably with him now. Up in some hotel fucking when they're supposed to be working. Got my kids in aftercare when they should be home 'cause she's working extra hours, 'cause she's so damn busy at work. Lies. All lies."

Sara exchanged a quick glance with the other woman and saw the same concern she felt reflected on her face. Pate was clearly escalating toward a meltdown.

"Mr. Pate, please know we are doing everything we can to locate your wife and David Hays. Meanwhile, I need to ask about the people you have with you."

"You asked your last question, lady. The next time you call it'd better be to say you found the lying, whoring bitch!" He snatched the phone from Sara and disconnected the call.

When he fisted the cell and drew back his arm, Sara was afraid he was going to fling it against the wall. Who knew what could happen after that. Instead, to her relief, he took a deep breath and slipped it into his pocket.

"You two, sit on the sofa. Nice and easy now." He kicked one of the bodies. "You already know what I do to those who don't listen."

Feeling the other woman tremble, Sara put an arm around her shoulders and drew her close. She left off the usual platitudes about everything being all right because she wasn't sure it would be. Wasn't sure he wouldn't shoot a pregnant woman as easily as he'd shot the two men.

As she stroked the other woman's back, a memory of her mom and dad surfaced. Her dad had been rubbing her mother's back, telling her how good she was doing, how they were almost to the last trimester. How everything was going to be okay and how happy they would be when they held their baby boy.

Tears sprang to Sara's eyes. Her dad hadn't known that would never happen. Neither one of them had known, and so her mother had accepted the words at face value. Had felt some relief that her back wouldn't always give her trouble, that having the baby would make it all worthwhile. Even Sara, who had been watching TV, had been happy to know her mom and baby brother were okay.

"I'll do my best to keep you safe," she said softly. "You and the baby. Do you know if it's a boy or a girl?" she asked loudly enough for Pate to hear. She wanted him to see a mother and a baby, not just a hostage.

"Girl." She stroked her stomach. "We haven't picked out a name yet. I like Keisha, after my favorite aunt who passed from breast cancer."

"Keisha's nice. What does your husband say?"

"He likes Jaelynn. Says it's not as popular and our girl will stand out. I told him she could stand out in other ways. I want her to be the first girl in my family to go to college, get a degree."

Sara stole a look at Pate, wanting to know if they had his attention. They had. "When is she due?"

"She's due two weeks from tomorrow. Today was supposed to be my last day at work." She teared up, quickly wiped away tears. "They threw me a shower. We were supposed to have it a couple of weeks ago, but"—she shot a furtive glance at Pate—"there was so much work and Mr. Barns, Nate, didn't get back until today and he wanted to be here for it." The tears flowed freely, and this time, she did nothing to stop them. "He was so sweet, always making sure I felt okay. He has two kids, so he's been through this." She looked at the bodies and said quietly, "Had two kids."

"What's your name?"

"Shawanna. Shawanna Brown."

"I'm Sara Gordon. But you already know that. Pleased to meet you."

"I see you all the time downstairs. I always thought you looked like a nice person."

"I try."

Shawanna yawned. "Sorry. I get sleepy in the afternoon, and what with the shower and all..."

"You're sleeping for two now, I guess."

"Keisha likes to kick at night. Art's sure she's going to play soccer. I had to stop him from buying her a soccer ball. Told him he had to wait till she could walk."

"Art sounds like he's eager to be a father." Sara casually stretched her neck from side to side and discovered they still had Pate's attention. She hoped it was a good sign. Hoped Pate would think about how Art would feel before he hurt Keisha and her baby.

"Oh, he is. He calls me all the time, checking to make sure we're okay. He doesn't work that far from here." Shawanna lowered her voice. "He's got to be worried. I was supposed to get off early, but that man wouldn't let me answer my phone."

Sara didn't have a comeback for that. Art had probably been told of the situation by now. He was probably outside, worried out of his mind and wishing he could trade places with his wife. "Then he'll be happy to see you when this is over."

The office phone rang, making them jump.

"Let her answer it," Pate said, pointing the gun at Shawanna.

Sara helped her stand, supported her past the bodies and to the desk.

"Hello. This is Shawanna Brown." Her voice trembled. She listened, then gripped the receiver tightly and looked at the two dead men. "They're not available…Yes…Yes…Mr. Pate, they want to speak to you."

Sara took the receiver from Shawanna's trembling hand as she moved to shield her from Pate and the gun.

"Who is it?" he demanded.

"It's Officer Brandies," Shawanna said. "She…she has someone you want to talk to."

He snatched the receiver from Sara's hand. "Where is she? Put her on! You put her on right now!"

The moment of silence that followed was louder than his shouting. Sara hoped his wife really was there.

Pate's body stiffened. "Why? Why would you do this to us? To my kids?" Gone was the belligerent man. In his place was one who was obviously hurting. He turned his back to Sara and Shawanna. "I need to understand how you could do this to me."

While Pate was getting his explanation, Sara studied the door, the distance between it and them. She estimated the time Shawanna would need to get there and get out and judged it doable. Pate, distracted by his wife, had obviously forgotten about them. She could probably get to him before he had time to shoot her. But not with Shawanna anywhere near.

"I'll distract him while you run," she whispered. "Elevators are probably turned off. Take the stairs up to eleven because he'll expect you to go down." She slid her security pass out of her pocket, then checked on Pate. She needn't have bothered. He still had his back to them. "This will unlock any door. Call the police and find a place to hide. I'll see you downstairs."

Shawanna squeezed Sara's hand. "Downstairs."

Sara had to admit Shawanna was quick for her size. Her footsteps faded away with no reaction from Pate. She'd wait ten minutes, then slip off.

"No," Pate suddenly said, and he began to sob. "You can't leave me. Love you. Always loved you."

Sara stood perfectly still, unsure of what to do. Obviously the wife had dropped a bomb. A bomb that could get her killed.

Collateral damage, they would probably call it. Dead was dead to her way of thinking.

But as she watched, Pate bent over, racked with sobs. The gun hung limply from his left hand like he had forgotten it was there. Broken apart by love, she thought. But the dead bodies on the floor wouldn't allow her to feel any sorrow for him. The loss of love was what you made of it, after all.

Another strangled cry of "No!" had her backing away slowly. Her heart was in her throat as she prayed he wouldn't remember he wasn't alone. She wasn't so lucky. Panic crushed against her chest, held her motionless as his head turned and his eyes focused in on her.

"Stop!"

He waved the gun and released her paralysis. She took off down the hall, expecting to feel the sting of a bullet at any moment. At the first intersection, she turned left. Thank God she walked these floors regularly, knew the turns, the cut-throughs. She made a right, ran through the copy room, then into the executive office with the back entrance to the elevators.

Once in the hallway, figuring he'd go north, she went south. All she had to do was work her way to the south stairwell, find herself another floor to get lost on. Shawanna would have talked to the police by now, so surely they would realize she was in trouble. If she found a good place to hide, she could wait them out, wait for them to take care of him.

Sara hit the stairwell on a run to find the landing full of cops in riot gear. A gloved hand covered her mouth, smothered a scream. Sucking in air, she gradually gained control, gradually sloughed off the fear. She was safe now, she realized. Safe. The hand dropped away.

"Officer Katz. You hurt?"

His voice sounded strange through the helmet shield. She shook her head. "Is Shawanna Brown with you? Is she okay?"

"She's downstairs, out of harm's way. What can you tell me about Pate's location?"

"He might be in Suite 800A or the north stairwell, looking for me. He has a gun and he's already killed two people. They're in the reception area, just lying there on the floor. You have to get them. Please, you can't leave them there."

"We'll take care of it." Katz patted her arm. "Do you know how many weapons he has?"

"I only saw the one gun."

"Okay. Let's see about getting you to safety."

Sara leaned against the wall, relief coursing through her body, and listened to him bark out instructions. She wasn't in charge anymore. No one's life or death was in her hands. She took a deep breath, let it out slowly and waited for her escort to arrive.

Shawanna was the first person Sara saw as she walked off the elevator and into the safety of the lobby. They met halfway, hugging as best they could around Shawanna's bulk.

"Thank you," Shawanna said, sobbing. "You saved me. You saved little Sara Keisha Jaelynn."

Sara opened her mouth, then closed it and settled for holding Shawanna close. She'd done it. They'd done it. "I…" She gave in to tears of release. It was over and she'd been able to keep her promise. She wasn't sure how long they stood there, hanging on to each other, crying, living.

"Oh my God, feel." Shawanna grabbed Sara's hand and placed it on her belly. "She's kicking."

Sara couldn't have said a word as she felt the baby's strong kick against her hand. Her brother hadn't made it, but this baby girl had, in part thanks to her. Full circle. She'd come full circle.

"Sorry to interrupt," one of the numerous officers occupying the lobby said. "We need to get your statements. It would be better for all if we did it at the station."

"Uh, yeah." Sara released Shawanna and used her sleeve to wipe her face. "Maybe Shawanna could do this tomorrow. It's been a stressful day, especially for someone in her condition."

Shawanna put a hand to Sara's cheek. "Always the protector." She exhaled. "I want to get this over with. I have a nest to finish building before my baby girl makes her entrance."

"We can give you a ride, ma'am."

"My wife is coming with me." A thin blond with a dimple in his chin stepped up and put his arm around Shawanna. "We'll be happy to come down to the station," he told the officer, and then took Sara's hand and pumped it vigorously. "Art Brown. Sure is an honor to meet you. There's nothing I can say to express the depth of my gratitude. Anything you need. Anything."

Sara respected the tremble in his voice, taking it as an indication of the depth of his love. He would do his best by Shawanna, by their baby, if the fierceness in his blue eyes was anything to go by. "Seeing Shawanna alive and well is gratitude enough. More than enough."

CHAPTER EIGHTEEN

It was late by the time Sara told her side of the events for the last time and made it back to the office. Most of the lights were off with the notable exception of the tenth floor. It was lit up like Christmas. She thanked the police escort and trudged to the front door. One of the night crew opened the door for her.

"Good job." He thrust out his hand.

"Thanks, Bernie. Been quiet?"

"Except for the cops crawling all over ten. Jackson says he doesn't want to see you tomorrow."

"Jackson doesn't always get what he wants." Sara knew the events of the day—the fear on Shawanna's face, the dead bodies and her fear of failure—would make sleep hard to come by. What she didn't want was for that fear to control her, to keep her from being able to do her job. The sooner she came back to the scene of the crime, the sooner she could conquer that fear, get back the everyday.

She took the stairs to the basement and was surprised to find Jackson sitting at his desk, looking worse for wear. "Hey."

"You done?"

"They may need to follow up. Depending on what he does, I'll have to testify at the trial." She pushed her hands into her pockets, spread her feet. "I'm coming in tomorrow." She shifted her weight to her right leg when he remained silent. "I need to get back to it and soon. Need to assure myself this isn't the norm. That I can do the job without fear riding my shoulders."

He nodded. "Clock out and try to get some rest. Morning comes early. If you're lucky, the press isn't camped out on your doorstep with dumbass questions."

"Already gave my comment."

He smiled. "Wasn't much of a comment. You know those vultures still want to feed."

"They have to have something to fill all those hours."

"You be careful out there. Oh, and Gordon?" He waited until she turned around. "Damn good job today."

She nodded. "Maybe someone else should clock out and try to get some rest."

"I will now."

But when she walked out the door, he was still sitting at his desk, seemingly staring into nothingness. She wasn't going to be the only one having a hard time sleeping tonight.

It wasn't until she was safely locked in her car that the shakes took over. She couldn't say later how long she sat in the dark as "what if" scenarios raced through her mind. But eventually she reached the conclusion that today's outcome—Shawanna and the baby still alive—was the best she could have hoped for. It didn't stop her from feeling the weight on her heart at the lives ruined by the acts of one man, however. She would need to deal with that, get over it at some point.

Three families would be forever changed by today's senseless actions. One set of kids would be without a father. Two, if she included Pate's boys. Their dad wasn't dead, but they would probably be adults before he regained his freedom.

She took a shuddering breath and tried not to draw parallels to her life. It was hard when she knew all too well about disruption, about life changed by violence. Years later and yet the refrain played on. Innocents had once again been shot down for no reason in a place where they should have been safe, and children would suffer. And in this case, three wives as well.

Tears coursed down her face and she felt like the child she'd been—all alone and afraid of tomorrow. "But I'm not that child any more." Saying it aloud helped her see she wasn't alone either.

They'd taken her phone from Pate and placed it into evidence. If she'd been thinking right, she'd have called from the office, let Mikaela know she was all right. She was ashamed to admit she hadn't thought of doing that, though she'd thought of Mikaela. Too much time spent depending only on herself couldn't be reversed quickly. But maybe there was still time. She left the parking lot and headed east.

At the gate to the condo she hesitated, then hit the intercom instead of keying in the code. "It's Sara," she said in response to Casey's hail. The gate opened right away.

Mikaela was standing in the doorway. Sara took in the bruising, now black and blue, the eye swollen half shut, and thought she'd never seen anyone more beautiful. When Mikaela opened her arms, she stepped into them and held on.

"Let's get you inside." Mikaela pulled back, then cupped Sara's face. "You don't know how glad I am to see you."

"Almost as glad as I am to see you."

"Says you." Mikaela smiled. "Have you eaten?"

"I couldn't." She put a hand against her stomach. "It's…I can't."

"Sit. I'll make you some tea."

Mikaela hurried off before Sara could object. She sank into the softness of the couch, closed her eyes and exhaled. She'd done the right thing, come to the right place. Maybe there was hope for her.

At the sound of footsteps, she opened her eyes. "I hope it was okay to come like this."

"More than okay." Mikaela placed the cup and saucer on the coffee table in front of Sara. "You want to talk about it?"

"I was so scared. So scared I wouldn't be able to get Shawanna out alive. This was her last day of work before the baby. They gave her a late baby shower. Not because they didn't care, but because there was a lot of work. And him…" She drew in a shuddering breath. "He was so upset that his wife was cheating on him, lying to him. At first I thought he was as upset for their kids as he was for himself." She shook her head. "He only cared about himself, his feelings. But I didn't know that at first when I got Shawanna to talk about the baby, her husband and how excited he was to be a dad. Had this idea that if he saw her as more than a hostage we might be okay." She blinked through tears. "He shot two people, left them lying in their own blood like they were nothing. All because his wife was doing a coworker." Sara wrapped her arms around her body, feeling the cold as numbness receded. She'd forgotten to grab her coat, and her jacket was still on ten.

"Drink your tea. It'll help you warm up." Mikaela took the throw off the back of the sofa and placed it over Sara's shoulders. "This should help too."

Sara dutifully picked up the cup and took a sip. "I…I can't get over how senseless the whole situation was. Makes it hard to let it go. My parents were shot to death too, you know. Some assholes thought they'd stolen their boss's drugs, money. Wrong house. Can you believe it? They went to the wrong house and my parents died for nothing."

"Oh, Sara." Mikaela placed a hand on Sara's thigh. "And you had to see the bodies today."

"I froze for a second. Thought I was back in our old kitchen. That's where I found them. My first thought was that my mom was going to be mad because the kitchen was a mess. She didn't like messes." She smiled through the tears. "She was always getting on Dad and me about cleaning up our mess. And Dad, he'd wink at me, then sweet-talk her out of being mad. She was eight months pregnant. I was supposed to get a baby brother. I wanted a bike, but I wanted a baby brother more." Sara set the cup down, pressed her fingers against her eyes. "I didn't mean to come here and cry all over you."

"Don't you dare apologize for that," Mikaela said fiercely. She pulled Sara into her arms. "That's what I'm here for. You can say whatever needs to be said. I bet you've never grieved for your parents, your baby brother. It's time." She stroked Sara's back, letting her cry.

"They were going to name him Jonah," Sara said, after the tears dried up. "Because of me. My mom looked really big, so I asked if the baby was going to be as big as a whale. My dad laughed so hard he cried. God, I'd forgotten about that. Mom tried to look mad, but then she laughed too and said 'Jonah, it is.'"

"Sounds like you had great parents."

"They were. And they loved each other. They were always kissing and hugging and dancing." She sighed. "I can't help but wonder what's going to happen to the kids now. The ones of the guy who got shot and the ones of the guy who did it. They'll all be without fathers."

"How sad. I hadn't thought about them, how this affects them too. They showed the guy's wife. She looked distraught as she apologized over and over again. Guess she'll carry some guilt for a long time."

"Forever, I think."

"They also showed the husband of the woman you saved. Said you were a hero and how they were going to name the baby after you."

"He cried when he hugged me goodbye." She smiled as she wiped at her eyes. "Couldn't say thank you enough. I should think of that more than the other. Think about Shawanna getting to go home and get everything ready for the baby. Sara Jaelynn Keisha Brown was the last I heard. The name will be bigger than her. I want to get her something special."

"That's a great idea. We could go this weekend. I know just the place."

Sara whimpered. "Not the mall."

Mikaela slapped her arm. "You. And don't think I've forgotten you owe me a trip, but lucky for you, this place is in downtown Decatur. Found the cutest thing there for my nephew's kid."

"Wait. Your nephew has a kid? How old is he?"

"Fifteen. Good student and star athlete, but not smart enough to put a cover on it. Following in the footsteps of his father, but that's a discussion for another time."

"On that note, I should go," Sara said, though the thought of moving from Mikaela's embrace was the last thing she wanted to do. "Poor Casey's been stuck in her room long enough."

"Poor Casey is in her office working. You should stay here tonight. I promise I won't molest you. Please? I'd feel better."

"Not the sad puppy eyes. You do know I have to get up early, right?"

* * *

A microphone was thrust in front of Sara's face before she could slip into the building the next morning. She murmured, "No comment," and kept moving. They weren't going to use her to sensationalize a tragedy.

Jackson was at his desk and she wondered if he'd spent the night there.

"Get any rest?"

She nodded. Surprisingly she'd slept undisturbed until the alarm sounded. She knew that had a lot to do with her cuddly bed partner.

"You'll see I've got you starting on fifteen. Any problem with that?"

"No." It was exactly what she needed. "They release the tenth floor yet?"

"Most of it. Tape's got part blocked off. B & M is closed till further notice. Suite should be locked down tight. Need to check back periodically, make sure the damn press hasn't found a way to get in there."

"Do we need to keep them from other clients?"

"Some will want to talk to reporters. Most we can do is hold back the aggressive ones. I'll put Roger on morning shift. If it gets bad, we'll pull in some temps to help out."

The thought of Roger having to be on his feet all morning made her smile. He would complain loud and clear, but she figured Jackson already knew that.

"You see anything, and I mean anything, you call it in and get out," Jackson cautioned. "Haven't had a day like yesterday. Don't want another one if it's all the same to you."

"That makes two of us."

The events from yesterday were fresh on her mind as she took the elevator to the fifteenth floor. She eased off the elevator, checking left, then right, then left again. The normal early-morning quiet unnerved her, no matter that her brain knew that was how it was supposed to be. She took one step, then another until she found her rhythm. No area was left unchecked.

Feeling more confident, she worked her way through floors fourteen to eleven. She hesitated before opening the door on ten and called herself all kinds of idiot. Pate was locked up. He couldn't hurt her now. Couldn't hurt anyone now.

"Just do it." She eased the door open and couldn't drop her guard, even when nothing happened. Her heart beat faster and faster and her breathing hitched as she walked down the hallway toward the elevators—the initial point of contact. She rounded the corner and everything was as it should be. No madman with a gun, no hostage needing to be saved. Just normal nothingness.

"I'm the only one here. It's over." Gradually her heart rate decreased and she moved on to the rest of the floor.

In front of the offices of B & M Associates she took a deep breath, then another. The door was secured, the crime scene tape a stark reminder of fear, of death. Sara closed her eyes, bowed her head and gave a moment of silence for the two men who hadn't made it. Wherever they were, she wished them peace. Then she walked away, taking comfort in the fact that she had made it out, that Shawanna had made it out. And on top of that, she was going to have a baby named after her.

Checking the rest of the floors was easy. Since she'd checked every floor, it was later than usual when Sara made it back downstairs. Walking through the lobby, she noted foot traffic seemed lighter than normal. Not surprising really. She caught a few curious glances sent her way, but no one asked any questions.

Kara Alexander, medium build with a mile of dark curly hair, had desk duty. She was on the phone when Sara crossed over to her. Sara could tell from Kara's side of the conversation that someone was worried about returning to the building. She figured they'd get a lot of these types of calls this morning.

"That's the fourth one," Kara said, after ending the call. "Bet there's a lot of sickness going on today. Speaking of which, didn't expect to see you here today. You earned a day off with pay."

"Nothing better to do."

Kara's sky-blue eyes widened. "You need a life, my friend. I can think of a million better things to do. The top of which is taking an uninterrupted nap." Kara had two young, active boys and an ex-husband more enamored with his girlfriend than his sons. "But maybe being here is like getting back on the horse that threw you. Done that plenty of times."

"In a way. I should take my station at the back door."

"Hey, you get any calls to be on TV yet?"

"What are you talking about?"

"You're a hero. Bet those national shows are going to be all over you."

Sara had seen it happen too many times to take that bet. Forgetting about her phone was turning out to be a good thing. "You think they'll call here?"

"Oh, yeah."

"Then I'd better go warn Jackson." Sara took the steps two at a time. She waited for him to hang up the phone. "If the news people call for me, could you please tell them I don't have a comment and I don't want to be on any show."

"Could be you miss a free trip to New York City, fleeting fame and glory."

"Could be I don't want fame and glory, fleeting or otherwise." She thought she saw approval on his face as he nodded.

"Yeah. You can catch those pesky reporters who get by Roger."

Once positioned at the back door, she took some satisfaction in watching a miserable-looking Roger deal with the small group of reporters, who were undoubtedly salivating for sound bites.

"Good morning."

Sara turned to see Mikaela had snuck up on her. "Morning again. You're here early."

"When you look like I do, it's better to get here before everyone else," Mikaela said, lowering the oversized sunglasses she was wearing. "I'd like to have as few people as possible pretending my face isn't a wreck."

Sara noted the great job Mikaela had done to camouflage the bruising. "Hey, if it wasn't for the eye no one would know a thing. You look good," she added, pleased to see Mikaela's smile brighten in response.

"The wonders of makeup."

"How's the neck? Still stiff?"

"Actually, it's been okay since some wonderful woman gave me two massages. Better than it was before the hit, actually."

"I do what I can," Sara said with a good deal of satisfaction. But there was still a part of her that wanted the opportunity to use her hands to pound on Nina.

"That you do. How about you? You okay being here?"

"I am. Already did the tour of the tenth floor. Between us, I was a little jumpy, gun-shy I guess you could say. But I did it. And you know what? Despite everything bad that happened, there's going to be a baby girl with my name. How cool is that?"

"Way cool. And I'm thinking you won't be alone with the jumpy. God forbid, but I might have to thank Nina for punching me. Hearing how the drama played out is not at all the same as having been here, so there's some gratitude there."

"I can be grateful you weren't here without thanking Nina for anything. Not when she hurt you." She couldn't stop herself from gently stroking Mikaela's face. "She won't get another chance. Not when I'm around. She's not only dealing with you now."

"I'm going to hold you to that. Better go before someone I know shows up. But you know, what other people say isn't so important anymore. I have someone special in my corner."

"Call if you need me to deal with anyone." As Sara hustled to open the door for someone carrying a large package, she regretted not telling Mikaela that *she* was the special one. She'd make up for that at dinner tomorrow.

CHAPTER NINETEEN

Mikaela was on her third cup of coffee when Talya arrived and came to an abrupt stop to stare at her. "The eye feels better than it looks. I promise."

"Not exactly what I expected. From your description I was expecting, I don't know, a misshapen head at least."

"If you knew how long it took me to get my makeup just right, you'd understand."

Talya peered at her more closely. "You did a great job is all I can say. So, how's the rest of you feeling?"

"Worried my looks could spark more talk. I almost stayed home again today, but that struck me as cowardly."

"Considering how little leave you've taken since working for me, it wouldn't have been unreasonable to take another day. Especially today, given what happened yesterday."

"I heard. Channel Two had a reporter outside at four thirty this morning, rehashing what they reported last night."

"She and others are still down there. I noticed a couple of people stopped to chat."

"People cope in different ways."

"It was nerve-wracking to be hustled out of a meeting only to see an ocean full of cops who looked like they were ready to go to war in the lobby. All we knew was there was some situation on ten. Of course, the rumors floating around verged on the outrageous. Then, get this, they tell us we should go home. That's great, I think, and then I realize my purse with my keys and driver's license are in my office. Of course, later I knew why they wouldn't let anyone up. All in all, a good day to be gone."

"Don't I know it. Patrick make it back?"

Talya nodded. "Told him he could come in late or not at all. He knew one of the guys who got shot."

"Oh no."

"They went to high school together, lost track until they ran into each other here. People say it all the time and you think, yeah, yeah, but you never know when the end's coming."

"Sounds like you should have come in late as well."

"Thought about it. Thought about having Jason stay home from school. But life goes on and as I'm sure you've seen by now my schedule has gone to hell. I rescheduled some of the critical meetings while I was waiting to get back up here. Make a note that Gerri will be running the meeting for Brannon's old section. I couldn't fit it in."

"Any idea what the specially called meeting is about?"

"None whatsoever. I do know it could not have come at a worse time. For me at least."

"Anything I can do? I've already done the notes from Friday's meeting, sent them out. Sent out the notices for next Thursday's meeting and sent you the draft you requested outlining the tasks and skills my job entails. I guess I should say my old job now."

"What time did you get here?"

"Early. Figured I'd put in some time before the staring and chatter started. My plan is to hide out near my desk, get some filing done and finish the cleanup I started in December."

"How would you feel about reviewing one of the reports Christine miraculously found? There's no rush, but it would be nice to get something off my desk."

"I'll take it." Anything was better than filing.

Mikaela revised her opinion after reading the first few pages of the report. Given how poorly it was written, she understood why it had gotten "lost." She began the painstaking task of turning it into something readable and wondered if she could get extra credit in her business writing course for the rewrite.

At nine thirty, with a headache making threats, Mikaela switched to filing. A person could only take so much. Patrick arrived soon thereafter, his eyes filled with sadness. "Sorry," she said and gave him a hug.

"Thanks, but I should be consoling you." He took a long look at her face. "You okay? I mean, this isn't going to turn into a problem, is it?"

"No," she said firmly. "Apparently riding in the back of the police car can be a big wake-up call." She'd also found out through Suzette that Nina's seeming obsession with her had been brought on by getting dropped publicly by the college student and then seeing Mikaela on the date from hell. When Mikaela wouldn't take her back, Nina's ego had gotten involved.

"Still, you never know."

"I can't live my life worrying about what might happen. That's not really living, you know? And what are you doing here already anyway? Talya said you could come in late."

"It is late." He shrugged. "Okay, I got the boot for hovering. And it's not as if Nate and I were that close anymore. He was somebody to have lunch with now and then, maybe a beer after work."

"Doesn't matter. You knew him, so accept the condolences and concern."

"Good. The gang's all here." Gerri walked in, dressed in yet another nice suit. "You two okay?"

"I'm better," Mikaela said. "What about you?"

"Missed most of the excitement. I'd gone on a Starbucks' run, so I had my bag with me. When I got back and found out they weren't letting anyone in the building, I went home and worked from there."

"There weren't many of us left by the time they brought the guy down," Patrick said. "He looked like an ordinary guy, not some crazed lunatic who would shoot up an office. Shows you never know. They're saying he thought his wife was having an affair. Damn shame he didn't confront her at home."

"No," Gerri said. "The damn shame is that he felt the need to solve the problem with a gun. They showed photos of his kids. Think of what could have happened if he'd confronted her at home."

"I knew one of the guys who got shot," Patrick said quietly. "Saw photos of him and his kids, showed him some of mine."

Gerri looked stricken. "Oh, Pat, I'm so sorry. I didn't know."

"It's okay. You couldn't."

"It's tragic any way you look at it," Mikaela said to diffuse the situation.

Patrick nodded. "I'm gonna go do…something."

"Me and my big mouth," Gerri said, once he was gone.

"You're both right. Let it go for now. He'll deal."

Gerri sighed. "She in? She sent me a text about covering an afternoon meeting."

"Dennis called an emergency meeting of all managers. She'll be stuck in there for a couple of hours. Then she has a meeting with Bill. Should be back by twelve or so. Maybe you could meet over lunch?"

"That works." Gerri slung her coat over her arm. "In my office keeping my mouth shut if needed."

Patrick was back moments later with a brightly wrapped package. "Almost forgot. This ought to take care of any run-ins with Thing One and Thing Two."

"Consider 'you shouldn't have' said." Mikaela ripped off the wrapping paper, then opened the box to find a colorful pen.

"It's a two-for. A pen and a recorder. You run into them again, hit this button and everything said is on record."

"I love it!" She jumped up and gave him a hug. "Functional and pretty."

"Knew the pretty would get you."

"Good thing Laura appreciates your worth or I'd be tempted to steal you. You, Mr. Manes, are Guy Numero Uno."

"Praise indeed coming from a Sapphic sister. If you were truly grateful…" He wiggled his eyebrows.

"No, no, no, no, no," she said firmly. "Not going to happen."

"A guy's gotta have a dream."

"But it doesn't have to include me *and* your wife. Next time I'm telling her."

"She knows."

Mikaela threw back her head and laughed. "I've missed having you around. Welcome back."

Talya returned at ten to noon, crackling with energy. "Two things. One, have a pizza from Rosa's delivered. Two, tell Gerri and Patrick meeting in my office in twenty about reorganization and other things." She walked toward her office, stopped and turned back around. "Where's my head? Third thing. They need you in HR at three."

Mikaela groaned. *This can't be good.* "What now?"

"Bullshit is what it is." Talya exhaled. "I'll explain more in the meeting."

"Can't be good" had gone to DEFCON 4 in Mikaela's mind. Talya wasn't one to throw around expletives at work. The Two strike again, she thought, as she dialed.

She stuck her head into Talya's office a minute later. "They can't guarantee delivery until one. I can go pick it up faster than that."

"If you don't mind." Talya reached into her purse and pulled out her wallet. "Take this. I'll get us something to drink while you're gone. Diet Coke okay?"

She nodded. "It should be ready by the time I walk there. I ordered the Greek one you like so much. Tell me the truth. What have they done now?"

"Shut the door." Talya waited until Mikaela was seated across from her desk before she began. "Someone, or I should make that plural as the implication was that it came from a group, sent a letter to HQ."

"Letter?"

"Complaining about management ignoring allegations of inappropriate sexual conduct in this office." Talya rubbed her eyes. "That's what the meeting was for. We wasted a couple of hours arguing about how these new charges should be addressed. I say wasted because HQ had already made the decision that certain staff members will be interviewed by outside consultants, in addition to there being a mandatory training session for everyone on harassment in the workplace. You're being interviewed because your name came up in the letter."

"Figures. Has anyone thought about waterboarding Ilene to get at the truth? I know it's not popular, but I don't think it's been formally declared illegal, at least not yet."

Talya snorted. "And here I was going to suggest a death match. You, Ilene, steel cage. Winner gets the job."

"That could work." She tried to smile and found she couldn't. A simple lie was getting too much play and she was damned tired of being on the wrong end of things. "Isn't this calling a meeting, scheduling workshops over the top? Why hasn't Dennis explained the whole jealousy situation?"

"He has and would be the first to agree with you. His hands are tied."

"Well, it stinks!" She really wanted to kick something. If this kept up, she might as well invest in steel-toed boots. Some enterprising company probably made fashionable ones for the femme ass kickers. "I'll go to the thing at three, but I want it noted I might be a hostile witness."

"So noted."

"It's not funny," she said, catching the little twitch in Talya's lips.

"Absolutely not."

Mikaela frowned when Talya's tone said the opposite. "*Very* hostile."

* * *

Mikaela came out of the small conference room on eight feeling as if she'd been through the longest thirty-minute period of her life. She hadn't been accused of anything, but the constant questions, thrown at lightning speed, had left her with a raging headache. Closing her eyes, she leaned back against the wall and took a few breaths to get back on center. A hand to her shoulder brought her eyes open. Seeing Debbie, she braced herself.

"This isn't right," Debbie said quietly. "I'm sorry they're doing this to you."

"Doing what?" she pressed and activated the pen in her pocket.

"I heard you were going to get fired. You should sue. They can't let you go for nothing."

It took her a moment for it to sink in that, strangely enough, Debbie was once again being supportive. "Actually, they can. But it's kind of funny because no one told me I was being fired. How come you know and I don't?"

Debbie looked away. "I'd rather not say."

Her lips tightened and she fought back the urge to strangle the messenger. "Why am I not surprised? Well, you can scurry back and tell the other rats I still have a job. Oh, and FYI, their latest ploy has upper management in an uproar, so if I was you, I'd find new friends." She pushed away from the wall and took the stairs at a reckless pace, wishing she could outrun the shit storm hanging over her head. Now she was being branded a fired cocksucker.

The door opened as she reached for the knob and she forced a smile when she saw it was Sara. "What are you still doing here? Shouldn't you be on your way home?"

"After yesterday, we're checking the floors more thoroughly." Sara peered at Mikaela. "Hey, you okay?"

"Not really. It's been a hell of an afternoon." Mikaela rubbed her temples. "On the plus side, only an hour before I can get out of the damn place."

"What's wrong?"

"What isn't?" she replied with a half sob. "Sorry. Trying not to lose it here."

Sara reached for her hand. "You want me to wait, give you a ride?"

"I'll be fine. I just had a rough interview with HR, followed by hearing the latest gossip involving yours truly." Mikaela blew out a sharp breath. "Need to shake it off, let it go."

"You found out you didn't get the job?"

"At this point, I would consider that good news. Listen, I can't talk about it now or I'll go to pieces. Maybe I could call you later?"

"Come over for dinner tonight?"

"I wouldn't be good company. Tomorrow's better."

"And I was good company last night? Come on, it's your turn. I want to help."

"You sure? I desperately need to vent. Okay, more spew than vent. I warn you it won't be pretty."

"I'll wear protective gear." Sara gave her a quick kiss on the cheek. "Come over whenever. I'll be waiting."

"Thanks." She framed Sara's face between her hands. "You're a lifesaver. Now I'd better go before you get caught in the damn rumor." She waited until Sara's footsteps faded away before she opened the door and returned to her area.

Talya was at her desk in a second. "Don't need to ask how it went," she said. "Your demeanor says it all."

"I get they had to do that, but I feel dirty. Like I did something wrong. And get this, the newest rumor is that I'm getting fired. Is there something you forgot to tell me? Because if you're going to fire me I can go now. Be done with this stupid stuff."

"Who told you that?"

"Debbie. And no, she didn't say how she knew." Frustration leaked into her voice. "I'm seriously rethinking this promotion business." She held up a hand when Talya opened her mouth. "I know they win if I do, but if winning means I have to put up with this shit, then losing's not so bad. In fact, it's starting to sound good."

"Here's what I think you need to do, go home, relax, lose yourself in a book."

"What does that have to do with all this crap?"

"Absolutely nothing. But after a relaxing evening and a good night's sleep, I'm betting you'll be back up to fighting form."

* * *

Sara rushed home and did a spot check. The place passed because she cleaned every Saturday morning like clockwork. A habit ingrained from her time with her aunt, one of the few constructive ones.

"Italian," she said, peering through the fridge. Sunday she'd been set on spaghetti with meat sauce. Now that seemed too common. Baked shells were as easy and looked fancier. Substituting spinach for the ground beef would cut down on calories and Mikaela would appreciate that. Leaving the sauce to simmer, she changed out of her work clothes and gave the house one last going over. This was the first time she'd done something like this, and feelings of satisfaction mixed with nervousness.

By the time Mikaela arrived, the house smelled of garlic and tomato sauce. "Hope you like stuffed shells." Sara's voice was breathy after an extended hello kiss. She opened the door to the small hall closet and hung up Mikaela's coat. Like her, Mikaela was wearing a sweater and jeans. But Sara would never be able to claim her clothes fit her as well as Mikaela's did.

"Remember, food junkie." Mikaela sniffed the air. "Smells great."

"Come on into the kitchen. The shells are almost ready. You can watch the chef at work."

"It would be better if you had one of those big hats. Maybe only the big hat."

"Funny girl. What can I get you to drink?"

"Diet Coke. No, make that water. Consumed way too much caffeine already."

"I also have wine." Sara held up a bottle of red wine.

"I'm avoiding alcohol at the moment."

"Here you go then." After handing her a bottle of water, Sara drained the shells, then sprayed them with water. "Any particular reason you're avoiding alcohol?"

"When I'm feeling depressed, alcohol tends to make me feel more depressed. And after the day I had, I'm feeling depressed."

Mikaela leaned a hip against the counter and took a healthy swallow of water. “I did warn you I wouldn’t be good company.”

“Fair enough. Fill me in on what went wrong today.” Sara stood on her tiptoes, pulled down a little-used glass casserole dish from the top shelf. “You didn’t get any trouble about your eye, did you?”

“Surprisingly no.” Mikaela was silent for a while as she watched Sara stuff the shells with a spinach-ricotta cheese mixture. “Do you know how humiliating it is to have to tell some strange woman that no, you did *not* have sexual relations with the boss? Have them look at you like you’re crazy when you tell them that you have a good idea who started the rumor and maybe they should be talking to them instead of wasting your time? That if they didn’t want to talk to them, they could look at my résumé and my application and see I don’t need to give blow jobs to get the damn job. It makes me sick. Sick that they can pull the strings without getting hung up in them. Sick of feeling sick whenever I see them. Sick of wondering what’s coming next. I want it all to go away and I know it won’t.” She pressed her fingers against her temples.

“Oh, Mikaela.” Sara gathered her into her arms. “You’re tired. And who can blame you? Between the two biddies and Nina, you’ve had a rough couple of weeks. Why don’t you go stretch out on the couch while I finish up?”

“I should go home and take my foul mood with me. I really should.” Mikaela sighed, but she didn’t let go of Sara. “Problem is, I don’t think I have it in me right now to be that selfless.”

“You don’t have to be. Compromise. How about a glass of wine and you sit and watch a master at work.” She pointed to the table in the corner.

“I guess one glass wouldn’t hurt.” Mikaela gave Sara a squeeze. “Thanks for putting up with my whiny self.”

“Returning the favor, remember?” She dropped a kiss on Mikaela’s forehead and decided this caring role wasn’t so scary. “Let’s get you that wine.” Once Mikaela was seated at the table, she delivered the glass of wine, then returned to stuffing the shells. After dusting them with cheese, she slid the dish into the oven and set the timer. “You okay over there?”

"I am. A small part of it's the wine. A far greater part is watching you work. There's nothing like a butch who knows her way around the kitchen."

Sara flexed her arms. "For my next feat, I'll be making salad."

"Hear, hear." Mikaela raised her glass and took a sip. "Hey, I've been so focused on me I forgot about your problems. You hear anything more from the lawyer?"

"To tell you the truth, with everything that happened this weekend, yesterday and dodging the press today, I forgot all about that. I'll check tomorrow, get that taken care of as soon as possible." Get it off my brain, she thought as she grabbed a tomato. "On a makes-me-happy note, Art, Shawanna's husband, dropped off a thank you card while I was at lunch. Jackson gave him my email so he can let me know when the baby comes."

"That reminds me. Shopping. I was thinking late Saturday afternoon if you're available. After that we could stroll around downtown Decatur, grab dinner. There's lots of good places to eat."

"Now that I can handle. Any chance of finding an art supply store? I'm running low on the paper I like."

"I can find out. I know there's a good one on Piedmont across from the Lindbergh train station. Artlife. Been around for a long time. There used to be one on Piedmont near Cheshire Bridge, but it might be closed. Haven't been that way in a while."

"One's enough. I might swing that way after work, see what they have."

"What kind of things do you like to draw? Other than mean girls and zoo animals."

"Other animals, plants, mostly things that can't talk back."

"I don't remember seeing any on my whirlwind tour of your living room. But, then, I don't remember seeing much of anything on your walls. Not that I can talk. My bedroom was mostly decorated when I moved in. I confess I have this weird rule about never owning more than I can fit in my car. That is, until I can afford to buy a house."

Sara looked up from chopping a cucumber. "Is it considered cheating if you buy a bigger vehicle?"

"Never thought of that. I guess because I have high hopes I'll get that little house with a yard and a dog sooner rather than later."

Sara could easily picture Mikaela in that house, but as hard as she tried, she couldn't say the same about herself. She had strong feelings for Mikaela, no doubt about that. She'd have to figure out if they were enough to make her want to stay in place, put down roots. She thought that would be tough to do after all her years of wandering. "I sort of have a cat. Well, she sort of has me. Moved in when I did and she comes and goes, though lately it seems more coming than going. I call her Tabitha because I think she's a witch."

"A witch or a familiar? Cats are usually familiars."

"Witch. She always seems to know when I'm going to eat. Even when she's not in the house."

"Good witch or bad witch?"

Sara laughed. She should have known Mikaela would play along with the fanciful. "Greedy. She's a greedy witch."

The oven buzzed and Sara removed the dish. "Be right back." She returned to the kitchen with Tabitha at her heels. "Look who was at the door waiting to be let in."

"Witch," Mikaela announced and poured herself another glass of wine.

With practiced ease, Sara had their meal on the table in minutes. She deliberately led the conversation to casual matters while they ate. Mikaela followed her lead, sharing tales from her childhood that left Sara holding her aching stomach.

"You made some of that up," Sara said, wiping her eyes.

"Truth. That woman really thought she could make my great aunt open the door so she could escape the police. She had the wrong house is all I can say." Mikaela patted her stomach. "That was delicious. You can cook for me anytime."

"Thanks. I enjoy cooking, tinkering with recipes, trying to improve them. Trying to come up with something a little different."

"Then why aren't you doing it for a living?"

"After high school, I got this idea that I would change jobs every year or so, keep things fresh. And since I've already done the cooking thing a couple of different ways..." She shrugged, then frowned. "Saying it out loud makes it seem kind of...rigid." She groaned, grabbed at her head. "Ironic, huh? How my pursuit to be flexible has led me to being the opposite?"

"Maybe you needed that at one time in your life and it became a habit more than anything."

"It did. Why didn't I see this before? I feel like one of those cartoon characters when the lightbulb goes on over their head." She shook her head and chuckled. "I can see."

"I have to admit I tend to have an enlightening effect on people."

"You could start a side business. Mikaela's House of Enlightenment. It has a ring, doesn't it?"

"Could be my fallback solution if things get too crazy at work. Scratch that. Thanks to you, I'm in too good a mood to think about work. I have to say, with all that's been going on, you're kind of like my beacon in the storm."

Sara's heartbeat sped up with something like panic. She wasn't sure she was ready for this, or that she even knew what this was. She swallowed past the lump in her throat. "I, uh, I... don't know what to say."

"You don't have to say anything." Mikaela finished off her wine. "I just wanted you to know that I know that you've done a lot to help me these past few days and I appreciate it. That's all."

There was an edge to Mikaela's voice that sparked an alarm. "I...I didn't mean it that way. I mean, I—"

"It's okay, Sara. Maybe you should put your head between your legs before you pass out or something."

She could see the hurt underneath Mikaela's smile and still couldn't think of anything to say that didn't sound like she was backpedaling. And maybe, just maybe, that's what she was doing—pulling back instead of stepping forward.

"I'm gonna go, you know. Thanks for dinner and letting me vent."

"You don't have to go."

"I actually think I do."

"But…Okay." With mixed feelings, Sara walked her to the door and helped her with her coat. "I'll see you at work tomorrow, okay?"

"I'll be there." Mikaela kissed Sara's cheek. "Take care of yourself."

Sara stood on the tiny porch long after Mikaela was out of sight. If only she hadn't overthought the notion of the little house and living in it year after year. But how could it be her fault when she couldn't see herself there forever and ever? Surely she, who looked at the map for the next stop and not the end of the journey, couldn't be expected to change in a day, a week, a month?

The cold broke through her musings and she stepped back inside to warmth. It was surprising to realize she'd only known Mikaela two weeks. Two measly weeks and yet in a way, it seemed like longer. Some of the feelings of closeness and intimacy she was experiencing were probably wrapped up in recovering her memories of her parents' deaths. Mikaela had been there for her when no one had ever been. That was powerful stuff.

As soon as Sara settled on the sofa, Tab claimed her lap and demanded attention. She stroked the cat absently, bent on pinpointing what about Mikaela was so different, so likeable, so…no, she couldn't say lovable. If it was love, the far-away years would be crystal clear. Love should mean everything was perfect. At least that's what she'd told herself over the years. What she'd held as the standard, what she remembered her parents had.

"And almost seven-year-olds know all about romantic love, right?" she asked Tab. "Dumb is what it is." But that wasn't surprising, considering her emotional maturity seemed to be stuck in the past.

CHAPTER TWENTY

Mikaela was sitting in her darkened room when Casey tapped on her open door. She cleared her tear-clogged throat. "Enter at your own risk."

"Want to talk about it?"

"Maybe tomorrow after I've downed my Wheaties. Isn't that the cereal that makes you a champion?"

"Maybe. Should I run to the store and buy some?"

"No. Not having any is in keeping with the rest of my day."

"Okay. Well, Suzette's spending the night, so feel free to walk around naked."

Mikaela gave her a wan smile. "Will do."

Once Casey left, she looked at her overnight bag. The one she'd packed with toiletries and tomorrow's work clothes, with the idea of spending the night at Sara's. Thank God she'd left it in her car, thinking she could run out and get it later if things went the right way.

Won't need it now, she thought, and leaned her head back and looked up at the white ceiling. She wouldn't need it for a very long time if she had any sense. Wouldn't need it if she could remember she and lasting love didn't mix.

It galled. More so because the blame lay at her feet. Open mouth, insert foot. That's what she'd done, despite knowing Sara needed the slow, the patient. Remembering that Suzette was around, she didn't scream. She wanted to. Oh, how she wanted to.

Not that screaming would take her back, let her think before she opened her big mouth. If not that, at the very least let her have said something simple like, "Thanks for being here," or better yet, "Thanks for being a friend." Everybody knew that one and it wasn't the least bit threatening. Didn't even whisper that she was looking for anything more.

Mikaela glared at the alarm clock and sighed. Only a little after ten, but still maybe too late to call someone who had to be at work early. Just as well, because there was no point in calling Sara. If she said anything about what she'd said earlier, tried to backtrack, that would only give it more weight, dig the hole deeper.

What she had to do was pull back to being strictly friends. She could smile, say hello. She could not linger and she could under no circumstances touch. Then and only then, could she eventually make Sara see she wasn't trying to pull a U-Haul on her, wasn't trying to pin her down, to make her share a little house and a little dog.

* * *

Mikaela arrived at her office building thirty minutes early the next morning. She wasn't sure how to feel when Sara was nowhere to be seen. Maybe more upset than glad, she decided as she stepped into the elevator. She had spent her time on the treadmill practicing how *not* to flirt and only in Sara's presence could she determine how well her time had been spent.

So perhaps that meant a little loitering might be needed. She would go down around lunch time, walk around the building and…

"Look like a total idiot," she muttered. It was obviously time for another cup of coffee. Perhaps the caffeine would jolt some kind of sense into her.

She downed half a cup and came to the conclusion that doing nothing was her best course of action. If she saw Sara, she did, and if she didn't, she didn't. Sara had her number. She'd call when she was ready and if she didn't, well, Mikaela would have to drown her sorrows in chocolate and completely screw up her diet. Rules were rules.

After finishing her coffee, she fixed another cup and returned to her desk. The request from Dennis for a meeting at nine fifteen shone like a beacon from hell. "Damn! Didn't get enough blood yesterday?" If a new claim concerning her sexual activities had surfaced, she was going to hunt someone down and share a thing or two. Maybe even three. Enough was enough.

Taking a deep breath, she put her anger on simmer and tackled the mess that was Talya's calendar. Now that the merger with Brannon's old section was a certainty, schedules had to be rearranged. She took a great deal of pleasure in sending one of the first meeting notices to Christine. What she wouldn't give to be there when Christine learned about Mikaela's new role and responsibilities. If there was a higher being, she would be Christine's new supervisor at least for a little while.

Thirty minutes later, with Talya's calendar in some semblance of order, she grabbed another cup of coffee, looked longingly at her now-depleted filing stash, then pulled up the Marco report. She deserved a medal for her dedication, she decided as she corrected sentence after sentence, page after page. Maybe even knighthood.

She was questioning the author's lineage when the sound of rapidly approaching heels attracted her attention. Before she had time to register who the footsteps belonged to, Christine was at her desk, her hands on her hips, her chest heaving. As usual, she was impeccably dressed, not a hair out of place.

"You think you can order me around now?"

"I didn't order anything. That would be your new boss." Mikaela pulled up Talya's calendar, even though she knew what was on it. "It seems Talya's not due until nine thirty this morning. No, wait, then she has another meeting after that. Looks like I could schedule you with her at eleven ten. Will you need more than five minutes to bitch? I believe I can get you ten at the outset."

"I will *not* accept this sort of attitude from you. I'll schedule my own meeting with Talya and I *will* be discussing your behavior."

"Your choice, of course." Her smile was sickly sweet. "Is there anything else I can help you with?" She didn't have time to determine the strength of Christine's glare before the other woman tossed her head and strode off. Someone needed to inform Christine she'd lost her crown with Brannon's demise. Mikaela wished, wished, wished that duty would fall to her.

To ensure the confrontation wasn't a total waste, she emailed Talya to let her know Christine wanted to set up a meeting about their upcoming meeting. Miraculously, her mood began its rise from the ashes.

At ten after nine, she trudged upstairs to her meeting with Dennis. Whatever was asked, her job was to answer truthfully. She'd done nothing wrong and no matter how they phrased their little questions, she wasn't going to get tripped up. She was going to keep her cool.

Dennis' admin was nowhere to be found, so she knocked on his closed door and was invited to enter. He was alone. Maybe today was really about the results, she thought.

"Have a seat." Dennis motioned to the chair beside his desk. "Normally Bill or Talya would talk to you about this, but since they're at a rather important meeting, it's been left up to me to fill you in."

"I see." Mikaela stiffened her shoulders and lifted her chin. Of all things, this was the least expected, but damn if she was going to go out with her tail tucked between her legs.

Dennis slid on his reading classes and peered at the open folder on his desk. "As you may have noticed, there have been a lot of rapid changes around here. Some of them are from Bill, and some of them are from the head office." He smiled at her. "Not that it matters either way. Our job is to make sure these changes are implemented. So that being said, you're scheduled to meet with Angela Buford and Jonathan Giles at nine forty-five in the small conference room. They've both been assigned to the communication materials update project, which, if you remember, was mentioned during your presentation Friday."

"I remember there was some talk about using my material."

"Exactly. They saw your presentation and they'd like your input."

It took a moment for the facts to break through her preconceived notions. Still she had to make sure. "I'm not getting fired?"

He took off his glasses, frowning. "Fired? Why would you think you're being fired?"

She shrugged, because she couldn't say that getting fired would be in keeping with her fucked-up life.

Dennis picked up his glasses, then put them down again. "I apologize if I or anyone else in this organization has given you the impression that firing you was under consideration. Strictly between me and you, the opposite is true. I, along with others, feel you can only be an asset to the firm as we change and grow. That is a major reason for you to be in the meeting with Angela and Jonathan."

Mikaela exhaled. "Okay. Wow. Nine forty-five. I'll be there."

"Good. I should warn you that 'whirlwind' is probably the best term to describe Angela. But as long as you're prepared to give your best that won't be a problem."

"I'll keep that in mind. Thanks for putting my fears to rest. You can be assured of my confidence."

"*Your* integrity has never been in question."

Mikaela's head was the size of a big, juicy watermelon as she made her way back to her desk. The possibility of being assigned another special project was huge. Wait until she told Sara. No, she couldn't do that now when they were in limbo. Or could she? Friends shared stuff like this. Could be the perfect way to start up a conversation and get them back to first base. But she should probably wait until after the meeting to start spouting off. First things first, she reminded herself, deciding to spend the scant half hour before the meeting preparing for it.

By nine forty, she was pumped and ready, confident she could answer any question that came up. Even ones not pertaining to the project materials. She was going to dazzle the other two with her knowledge and perhaps move further away from the rumormongers trying to pull her down.

She arrived at the conference room five minutes early to find it already occupied.

"Their flights got in early," Dennis explained. "Angela, Jonathan, this is Mikaela Small. Mikaela, I'd like you to meet Angela Buford and Jonathan Giles. Angela comes from the Florida office and has recently been assigned to lead the update."

Mikaela had already figured out from the air of authority that the woman, whose thin face was set off by a stylish short haircut, was the one in charge. Angela wore a dark blue suit that was top of the line. Mikaela had priced it once and gotten her hand singed.

"I'm looking forward to collaborating with you." Angela's handshake was firm.

"Same here," Mikaela said.

"Jonathan Giles is from the Chicago office."

Jonathan was young-looking with blond hair, brown eyes and a dimple in his left cheek. When he smiled at her, Mikaela's gaydar pinged. She imagined he was quite the catch and knew it.

"I absolutely adored the work you did on the brochure," Jonathan said, pumping her hand.

"Thank you." She took back her hand. This was going to be interesting no matter how small a role she was to play.

"I'll leave you to it," Dennis said. "If you need anything, Mikaela knows how to reach me."

"How much do you know about this project?" Angela asked once they were seated around the table.

"I know you're developing standard templates for presentations and communications," Mikaela replied.

"That's it in a nutshell." Angela gave her a smile. "After seeing examples of your work, I knew I wanted you on my team. There are three other team members, so we have a cross-section of all regions. Most of the work will be done over the Internet through emails and online meetings. However, I think it's best we meet in Virginia quarterly. Sometimes things get lost in translation and can only be sorted out face to face."

Mikaela wished Dennis was still present to clarify if this was going to be part of her new responsibilities as Bill's admin. Angela certainly seemed to think so.

"You are absolutely right about meeting in person. I can't tell you how many times that's made the difference between right and fabulous." Jonathan tapped his phone. "Any idea when the first meeting is?"

"Two weeks from next Monday," Angela replied. "Chuck's admin is responsible for making the travel arrangements. She has everyone's contact info, so please pay attention to emails from Roxanne Lewis. At that meeting, we will hammer out a schedule we all can live with. But…" She smiled. "There's always a *but* isn't there? The schedule will need to be tight given our drop-dead deadline of December 15th. For now I'd like us to go through what you have, we'll all make comments, suggestions, clarifications and take whatever comes out of that into the first meeting. Any questions? No. Good."

Over the next two hours, Mikaela's brain was pushed to the limit as Angela lived up to her nickname. By the time Angela called it quits, Mikaela was reeling from an energy deficit.

"Good work. I'd like both of you to write up your notes and get them to me as soon as possible. I'll mesh them with mine and send them back for review." Angela gathered the marked-up pages. "Looking forward to seeing you in two weeks."

Only after Angela left for the airport in hopes of catching an earlier flight could Mikaela relax. "Is she always like this?"

Jonathan smiled. "That would be yes. Love her to death, but she does wear me down. You kept pace. In her book, that's a big plus."

"She should come with a warning label. Didn't expect that much energy from someone so tiny."

"Angela loves to play on that. Gets a kick out of leaving bodies in her wake."

"What are your plans for the rest of the day? I'd be happy to take you to lunch."

"My flight doesn't leave until later this afternoon, so I made plans to catch up with an old friend, but thanks for the offer."

"No problem." She gathered together the discarded copies, strewn over the table. "Despite the energy drain, that was surprisingly fun, I think."

"That's the magic of Angela. Wears you out while bringing out the best." He grabbed the handle of his carry-on bag. "So nice to meet you. Looking forward to working with you again in Alexandria. Be sure to rest up."

Mikaela shook his hand, thinking she would probably get to go to the first meeting, assuming Talya didn't need her. She did not, however, imagine Talya and Bill approving her attendance at quarterly meetings for the rest of the year, let alone putting in hours in between. The position as Bill's executive admin didn't have enough wiggle room for that, not as currently structured. She hoped they could come up with a way for her to stay on the project. She figured working with Angela could only help her career.

After escorting Jonathan to the elevator, she went to update Dennis. She found him with Bill at Jolene's desk.

"How'd it go this morning?" Bill asked.

"Really well. We firmed up the schedule and have something to take to the first meeting. I'm to mock up several different versions of the brochure for our next meeting. Uh, it's supposed to be out of town."

"Yes, yes. Talya and I need to discuss that with you." He looked to Jolene. "Has she gotten back with you about setting up a meeting?

"Lunch time is the only window you had available. I suggested lunch in your office in twenty and she's okay with that. Talya's probably waiting for you to get back to your desk to let you know about it, Mikaela."

"I'll check in with her." The possibilities played through her mind. Being assigned to this team could mean she was out of the running for the job as Bill's assistant. That wasn't necessarily bad if in return she got to work on a high-profile project, got some travel out of it and got her name bandied about at HQ.

She was feeling optimistic when she stuck her head into Talya's office. "You were looking for me?"

"Lunch with Bill and myself, his office. I don't know all the particulars, so don't ask me. But I do know you'll like it." Talya grinned. "Looks like you survived Storm Angela."

"Come on, you've got to tell me something. I mean, I get introduced, told I'm part of a team and that we're going to be working together for the next twelve months. Oh, and by the way, this is going to consume a lot of your time."

"Sit. Was it only two weeks ago I found out Jolene was retiring? Feels like years." Talya massaged her neck. "I swear I can barely turn around without something changing around here. I'm not saying that to stall, but I'd really like it if you could wait for an explanation until Bill can give you facts. And let's face it, I'm still reeling from being promoted to a department head and having to take on a group that needs a *lot* of work. Feel sorry for me."

"After struggling through only part of the Marco report, I feel your coming pain. I guess it won't kill me to wait. It's just...I don't see how I can do a good job for Bill and do a good job on the project."

"I can promise no one is expecting you to do both."

"Fair enough. Now I'd better see if Patrick's sent me the presentation for your afternoon meeting. Fingers crossed the color copier's free."

"Already taken care of. Oh, I reviewed your job duty write-up and it's good to go. FYI, be careful who you discuss this with. Dennis thinks this would be a good exercise for all admins."

"Lips are sealed. I'm already in enough hot water around here."

Back at her desk, Mikaela pulled up her budget spreadsheet. There had to be a way for her to finagle a new suit without bankrupting herself. If she had to go to headquarters, she was going in style. Her head was spinning from the hard-fought battle with her budget when it was time for her and Talya to join Bill.

CHAPTER TWENTY-ONE

Later that afternoon, Sara finished out the last rep, replaced the weight bar and sat up. Her arm muscles trembled nicely as she chugged water. Her workout had been good, but she'd stayed longer than normal, needing to occupy herself until it was time to go see Mikaela. She had it in the back of her mind they could catch a drink or coffee while they talked. Or rather, while she tried to explain why she'd frozen like a deer caught in headlights the night before. It would be "tried" because Sara wasn't sure she could articulate how she felt without doing more damage.

She jumped when a warm hand landed on her leg. She looked up and found herself up close and personal with Carmen. The expression on Carmen's face had her wishing there was room to back up. "Oh, hey."

"Haven't seen you here on a non-Thursday before. Pity."

"Switching over from my old gym. Figured if I play basketball here, might as well work out too. Excuse me." She pushed away from the bench, grabbed her towel and wiped her face. "Well, I'm done, so I'll catch you tomorrow."

"Wait." Carmen's fingers fastened around her wrist. "We could be done together."

"Can't. Errands and then I have a thing after."

"Thing?" Carmen's eyebrows crawled up her forehead. "You mean a woman, don't you? Afraid you won't want her after being with me?"

"Truthfully, Carmen, it's the other way around."

"What? She your girlfriend or something?"

Sara wasn't sure what she and Mikaela were. Friends sure, but more. Or they would be once she untangled the knots she'd made yesterday. "Or something," she finally said. Something that made the thought of having sex with another woman unthinkable. And why hadn't she thought about that last night?

"Does the poor woman know how you are?"

The way it was said, almost threatening, made Sara sigh. "You and I, that's not going to happen again, so nothing else matters. Have a little pride, okay?"

"You ain't about nothing," Carmen shot back, her lip twisted in a sneer.

"And you knew that from the start. Face it, you recognized me as being like you. You know that's what you wanted."

"People change."

"They certainly do, but not always in the same direction." Sara grabbed her water bottle and walked away, her conscience clear. She hadn't made any promises here, didn't owe any explanations. At least not to Carmen.

Mikaela was another matter because, as she'd just admitted to Carmen, they were "something." Sara laughed and wondered why she thought the word *girlfriend* was any different, any worse. "Hopeless. That's what I am."

In her car, she removed her phone from her bag and called Mikaela. "Okay for me to come over, in say, an hour? I have dessert from last night."

"Come on. I might have stopped floating near the ceiling by then." Mikaela giggled. "And there might be some wine left."

"You got the job? That's great."

"Job, yeah. Not the one you're thinking of."

"Congrats either way. You can fill me in when I get there."

"Oh, I will. Fair warning. You might not be able to shut me up. I'm so psyched!"

"I'm willing to risk it."

"I'm glad. Listen," Mikaela began, then paused. "I'm really sorry for shooting off my mouth yesterday. I didn't—"

"No! It wasn't you. That was on me and I'm sorry I didn't say something sooner."

"Maybe we should talk that out when you get here. I'd hate for there to be a misunderstanding."

"Me too." Guilt gnawed at Sara as she ended the call. Flowers, she thought as she put the key in the ignition. She could pick some up after she swung by the post office and picked up her mail. The first stop, though, was home and a shower.

Thirty-five minutes later, Sara sat in front of the tiny post office on Decatur Street, the unopened envelope from the lawyer on her lap. It looked official and the return address matched the one she'd found online. She wanted to open it and yet she didn't. For her it represented the last link to a blood relative on her father's side. One who had thought enough of her to put the great-granddaughter he never knew in his will. If only he had reached out in a more personal way—a call, a letter to let her know there was someone who thought about her. She couldn't say for sure, but she thought that might have made a difference to the child she'd been.

Didn't matter now, she reminded herself. The past had to stay there. Hadn't she learned that the past few weeks? It was okay to remember, to reminisce. It wasn't okay to use the past as a reason for not living or holding on to something she could never have again, which she'd been doing for too long.

"No time like the present." Sara ripped open the envelope, read the short paragraph on the enclosed letter, then quickly read it again. She squeezed her eyes shut, opened them and read it a third time. There was no request for money, no request for her checking account information or a credit card number. If the letter was legit, she was going to be rich. Rich-beyond-her imagination rich.

Her hands trembled as she lowered the letter. Staring out the windshield, she wondered if lottery winners felt like she did right now—stunned disbelief. Wondered if they also thought "this could not be happening to me." Lottery players had the advantage of knowing they were in the game. She, not so much, and yet, she'd hit the big jackpot.

Sara looked at the letter again, counted out the zeros. It still added up to ten million dollars. And that was just for her. There had to be a lot of money floating around if her share was ten million.

She couldn't imagine how her dad's family had amassed that kind of money. Maybe once she was a woman of leisure, she could research her ancestors and learn more about where her father—and her mother, for that matter—had come from.

She looked at the letter one more time. "Ten million." There were a lot of things she could afford to do with that kind of money.

Of course she didn't have it yet. All she had was a letter from a lawyer telling her the will had been probated and that she should expect a check from Bates, the executor of the will. Maybe when she checked her bank account, saw that amount on the balance side, she would make some plans, but now it was more like a fantasy.

Mikaela's greeting over the intercom suggested she had not slowed down on the celebratory drinking. Could be to her advantage, Sara thought as she pulled through the gate. Once again, Mikaela was waiting for her and she couldn't help but think about the last time she'd been here. It was hard to believe it had only been two days ago she'd arrived seeking comfort, sure in the knowledge that Mikaela would provide it. Trust. She had trusted Mikaela at a time when she'd been off balance, wounded. Had known she could share her fears, her vulnerability, without judgment. Somehow she'd forgotten that.

Grabbing the flowers, she crossed to a grinning Mikaela.

"You're here! And you brought flowers. My day just keeps getting better and better."

"Can I ask how much you've had to drink now?"

"I'm holding it. Not only in my head," she added and laughed.

Sara smiled. Mikaela was such a pretty sight, her hair loose, layered T-shirts and jeans that showed off her curves. "All right to come in?"

"Oops." Mikaela stepped back and waved her hand wildly for Sara to enter. "It's been a day. An unbelievably great day!"

"Unbelievable, yes," Sara agreed as they moved to the living room.

"I got a new job," Mikaela blurted out and sank into the recliner. "I get to do a little traveling and I get to be on a special team. The team leader, who seems to have a lot of clout, insists *I* be on her team. How great is that? It's mega great is what it is. I worked with her today and is she ever demanding. But I tell you, she can really pull the good out, you know? It's going to be challenging, but I think I'm going to love it." She wrapped her arms around her middle and exhaled. "It's so crazy. So unbelievable. This morning I was all down and then this. A great job. For me. And you're sitting over there wondering when is she going to shut up. Oh, wait. Better yet, you're thinking she could at least offer me some wine and take the flowers."

"Coffee. I was thinking coffee." Sara's mind was bouncing all over the place trying to follow Mikaela's ramblings. She didn't need to add alcohol to that. "So how was your day?"

Mikaela threw back her head and howled with laughter. "Great," she was finally able to say, clutching her stomach. "My day was great, as you somehow guessed. Sorry about the spew. I blame it on Casey for not being here. You can too. Okay. Coffee. And I will take those flowers from you before they wilt. I should switch to coffee myself. Fewer calories and no headache in the morning."

"Goes better with brownies too."

"I wish. If you want sweets, you'll have to find Casey's cookie stash. I told her to hide them and then she did."

"Actually I was talking about the brownies I brought." Sara held up a gift bag. "Dessert, remember?"

"How did I forget that? Gimme." Mikaela took the bag. "This day just keeps getting better. You'd better come with and pick your poison. I'm going to have something full strength to go with these babies."

"Won't that keep you awake?" Sara asked, though on second thought, it might balance out the wine and exuberance.

"I probably won't sleep much anyway because," she paused, did a quick, yet stylish turn. "I got a new job! And oh, oh, oh! While I was in the meeting with Angela, Christine had to make copies for Pat's meeting. She was so pissed. A beautiful thing. But not as beautiful as when she and Ilene find out about my new gig. One that wasn't even posted. Wonder if HQ will get a new letter of complaint. Well, let them try to throw dirt. I don't care. Because…" She looked to Sara.

"You have a new job," she filled in and laughed. "Why do I get the feeling you're still circling just below the ceiling?"

"I am. I really am." She all but danced her way to the kitchen. "You can do your coffee first, I'll put these on a plate. Promise you won't let me eat more than two."

"Promise." Sara turned the carousel with the individual coffees and picked the first decaffeinated one she came across.

"Done," Mikaela declared. "Now that I've talked you to death, it's your turn. How was your day?"

Sara thought about the letter in her pocket. "I have to go with unbelievable as well."

"Not another incident. No. I would have heard about that. More family shockers?"

"You could say that. Got the official letter from the lawyer about the will and the check from the executor."

"Let me guess. The fifty thousand you were supposed to get?"

"Times twenty thousand."

Mikaela blinked. "Please don't make me do math in my head. Wine head at that."

"Ten million." She nodded when Mikaela pantomimed jaw-on-the-floor. "Exactly how I felt. I read the letter at least three times and it has yet to sink in."

"I know this is catty, but it's no wonder your Aunt Liddy thought she'd hit it big. Did you have any idea your family had that kind of stash?"

"One, I have a hard time thinking of them as my family. And two, I know nothing about them. I don't remember my dad ever talking about them, and of course Aunt Liddy didn't, so I grew up not knowing they existed." She removed the cup of coffee and took a sip. Maybe she'd add a new coffee maker to her want list.

"Let me grab my laptop. We can do an Internet search. With that kind of money, there'll be lots of hits."

"Before you do that, I'd like to, I mean, I want to talk about last night. If that's okay?" she added as the smile left Mikaela's face.

"Okay."

"I'll go first." Sara took a deep breath. "I really like you. And I really like who I am with you. It's…when you mentioned the house, I…this is going to sound terrible. I couldn't see myself in that house year after year and that seemed wrong somehow. I'm not trying to hurt you. I'm not. You know I've been on the move for my adult life, so I don't want to say I could settle down in one place and then not be able to. I feel terrible about it, but you deserve the truth and last night I was too scared of what might happen to say it. At the same time, having said that, I realized today I trust you and have no interest in seeing other women. I just wish I knew what all this meant."

"What I said last night was not meant to tie strings around you or bind you to me in any kind of way," Mikaela said. "I wouldn't do that to you. That's not the kind of person I am. I was feeling grateful for all the help you've given me with Nina, with the crap at work, so I opened my mouth and inserted my feet. I don't expect you to want the house, the dog…" Mikaela reached out, then let her hand drop. "I am sorry. I realized later how that might have sounded to someone who's a little bit jumpy, relationship-wise."

"So where does that leave us?"

"Really liking each other and how we are with each other. I'd like to continue dating, continue getting to know each other, maybe kick it up and go back to the bedroom. Let me tell you, I really liked having sex with you. Knowing more about you can only make the experience more enjoyable."

"And if I never see that house?" Sara pressed. She couldn't bear it if that came back to haunt her or Mikaela.

"Never's too far away to worry about. I'm more worried you'll run off with some skinny super model now that you're rich. Let's face it, I'll always be watching my weight, and even then, I'll never be skinny."

"Super model? Really? All the things to worry about and you pick that?"

"It lightened the mood, didn't it? I'm not trying to dismiss your concerns, Sara. I just happen to think I have plenty of time to talk you into that house. Although…" Her smile was sly. "The house and the dog have gotten bigger. Ten mil can buy a lot of house."

"Already spending my money, I see," Sara said, but she was smiling.

"Yup." Mikaela moved to stand in front of Sara. "Should I be worried you haven't said anything about the sex part? It is kind of important." She nipped at Sara's bottom lip. "Okay. Very important."

Sara smiled and wondered why she'd ever been worried. Before her was someone she could grow with, learn with. She pulled Mikaela into her arms. "I thought you'd never ask."

EPILOGUE

Mikaela undid her seat belt as the plane taxied to a stop. Back home victorious, she thought, with more than a little bit of pride. The trip to Virginia had been a total success, the pinnacle of almost a year of hard work. But so worth every minute, she knew. Over the year she'd gained Angela's respect and gotten her name bandied about by the muckety-mucks at headquarters. That there was no more talk of her having serviced Bill for advancement was a decided bonus.

Not that she had to worry about vicious gossip from The Two anymore. When they brought in an outsider to replace Jolene, Christine had decided it was time to retire. Mikaela wasn't sure if it was Christine's absence or the reprimand in her file, but Ilene no longer made the rounds to collect and disseminate gossip.

Once her seatmates were clear, she muscled her bag from the overhead bin. Because her rich girlfriend had upgraded her ticket to first class, Mikaela was one of the first to escape the stale air of the plane. Her plan was to enjoy her long weekend, then return to work, clear up the couple of small projects and sink her teeth into developing an implementation plan.

Although she'd told Sara to pick her up out front, she wasn't surprised to see her big lug standing in the hallway leading to the baggage claim area. The large colorful sign Sara was holding brought a laugh. It was good to be back.

"Welcome to Atlanta, Ms. Ivanna Humpalot," Sara said once Mikaela was standing in front of her. "I hope to make your stay pleasant."

"Do you now?" Taking in Sara's mischievous grin, she felt an overwhelming urge to kiss her and wondered if there'd ever be a day she could do that at Hartsfield-Jackson Atlanta International Airport and not make a scene. Given the changes that had taken place these past few years, she might live to see that day. Today she would settle for a hug.

"You can count on it."

The air of self-assurance was intoxicating. "I should have never encouraged you to go to that arts college. Hanging with those Millennials has turned you."

"No, that would make me a zombie." Sara tucked the sign under her arm and reached for Mikaela's bag. "Which, given my great looks and smooth gait, I clearly am not. So, tell me."

"Nothing but net!" Mikaela did a quick spin. "To say they were pleased is an understatement. And guess what? You can't, so I'll tell you. I get a bonus! Can you believe it? It's not like working on the project wasn't a big bonus by itself. Could have just knocked me over when Angela told us after."

"Considering all the work you put in, I'd say it was well deserved."

"You get plenty of credit too. Sticking with me through my most manic of moods." She could say that now without fear it would scare Sara away.

"All part of the service."

They made their way past baggage claim, out the door and into the parking garage.

"You're probably tired after going all out for three days," Sara said, once they were settled in the sports car Mikaela had helped her pick out.

"Should be, but I'm still wired from the adulation. You know me. I'll probably fall from the ceiling around midnight, then sleep like the dead for ten hours. You up for something? I'm all yours until Monday morning."

"There's something I want to show you if you're up for it."

"Let's do it. But first." She leaned in and gave Sara a thorough glad-to-be-home kiss. "Missed you."

"Missed you back." Sara ran a hand down Mikaela's face. "My life's been too quiet."

"Good." During the twenty-minute ride, Mikaela regaled Sara with more details of her trip. "Nice," she said when Sara pulled into a driveway. The house was an old Victorian sparkling with Christmas cheer in the Inman Park neighborhood and looked vaguely familiar. "A holiday party?" She pulled down the visor without waiting for a response and checked her reflection in the mirror. *Should have refreshed my makeup at the airport*, she thought. She reached for her pocketbook to rectify the oversight.

"You look fine."

Mikaela rolled her eyes. "That's what you always say."

"And I'm always right." Sara hopped out and walked around to open Mikaela's door. "No party, but I do want you to check something out for me."

"Haven't we been here before? That tour of homes during the Inman Park Festival maybe?"

"Yeah. You really liked it, remember?"

"Oh God, yes. It's the one with the beautiful library you practically had to drag me out of. I terrorized everybody at work with the pictures."

"Not just at work," Sara said dryly as they climbed the steps to the porch. "You liked the kitchen too."

"Lusted after it," she corrected. "But a lot of that was for the high-end appliances. Don't tell me you've arranged for me to have my own private tour. I may never shut up about it now. Especially if the Christmas decorations inside are as nice as the ones out here."

Sara rang the bell. "I'll take my chances."

Mikaela put her hands on her hips. "Is that your sly way of saying I talk too much?"

An attractive older woman opened the door before Sara could respond. "Come on in," she said with a welcoming smile. "So glad you could make it. Denise Zimmer." She held out a hand.

"Mikaela Small. I have to tell you, I *love* your home."

"Thank you. Feel free to explore at your leisure. I'll be in my office down the hallway should you have any questions." Denise's heels clicked against the shiny hardwood floor as she walked away.

"Okay, what gives?" Mikaela asked softly.

"Surprise!" Sara took her hand. "Remember when you told me about that little house and the little dog?"

She didn't dare hope. "The one you were worried about because you couldn't see yourself living in it with me?"

"That's the one. Do you also remember how you said you could talk me into it?"

"I hope you know by now that I would never force—"

Sara put a finger to Mikaela's lips. "I do. But the funny thing is that being with you this past year has shown me that staying in one place with one person is not a prison. Thanks to you, I no longer feel the need to run around the next corner alone, searching for the next big thing. Why would I want to experience the next big thing without you by my side?"

"That is so incredibly romantic." Mikaela put a hand to her heart and sighed. "It's no wonder I'm crazy in love with you."

"Crazy enough to consider living here with me year after year?"

"I'd live with you in a shack. But what about the Zimmers? They may have something to say about us just moving in."

"Turns out they're relocating to Boston. Jackie remembered how much you raved about the house, so when she found out it was going on the market she knew we'd be interested." Sara gave a sheepish shrug. "I may have mentioned, after a couple of beers after basketball one week, that I wouldn't mind starting the process of looking for a place for us. That is, us looking for a place for us."

"Oh God." Tears sprang to Mikaela's eyes. "Are you positive? Because I'm to the point where I need you to have what you want. Let's face it, just having you in my life beats the hell out of that little house."

"Positive that I want you." She folded Mikaela into her arms and held on tight. "Positive that I will always want you in my life. That this is a place where we can continue to be happy together."

"Then you've got to marry me. Because I'm positive that I want forever and ever."

"What is this? No knee, no ring?"

Mikaela laughed. "We'll talk about that *after* you show me *my* new house." She pulled Sara down for a quick kiss. "And don't *even* think we're not going to get a bigger dog to go with it."

Bella Books, Inc.

Women. Books. Even Better Together.

P.O. Box 10543
Tallahassee, FL 32302

Phone: 800-729-4992
www.bellabooks.com